I0600037

The Line is Dead

Book ONE

By M.J. Garcia

ALSO BY M.J. GARCIA

Vivipary

—— **BOOK I** ——

DEAD RECKONING

THE
LINE
IS
DEAD

M. J. Garcia

Whalesborough
was a ghost town…

The Line is Dead

For Ms. Courtney

You once wrote back "You've got the magic."
I won't let go of that.

Prologue

Whalesborough was a ghost town.

Not in the sense that it had few inhabitants. Many people tend to visit the quaint island off the East Coast for the salty air or the whale watching. The locals were like any other townsfolk. They kept busy with their work and their rumors; such a small town was always full of gossip. In a tight-knit community, it was a custom that everyone knew everyone else's business.

Which is why everyone knew that 'ghost town' was not a term to imply the island was deserted. 'Ghost town' was the best way to describe the oddity and abnormality of the island.

The eerie fog that would build up, shielding the island off from the mainland. The empty houses littering throughout the wooded areas that, despite their cheap listings, never seemed to sell. The way the winds whispered, creeping under doorways and through cracked windows.

Whalesborough was a ghost town in the sense that spirits were not uncommon.

At least, that's what Michael McKenzie was told.

A skeptic at heart, however, he scoffed when the boy at the counter told him that.

Michael McKenzie did not believe in ghosts.

Not when he was six, when a boy from a foster home tried to scare him away with monsters under the bed. Not when he was nine, when his fellow scouts told gruesome tales at the campfire. Especially not when he was twelve, when the nightmares first began.

He preferred not to talk about them. When his parents asked him how he slept the night before, he avoided mentioning the hours he would spend paralyzed in bed, watching shadows move out of the corner of his eye. He had been told they were something he could eventually grow out of. He hadn't yet.

Despite this, when Michael moved from San Francisco to the East Coast, he was not worried. He felt no traces of fear as he sailed towards the island with his parents and luggage, only the discomfort of seasickness. When they had arrived at the old house, a two-story Cape Cod that seemed to give him splinters just by looking at it, Michael gave his parents the smile they were expecting from him.

And when he awoke during his first night in his new home, he recognized the familiar paralysis. He couldn't move. He couldn't pull the sheets off his body. He couldn't twitch a finger. Even the attempt to strain his neck or blink was futile.

Yet he had a perfect view of her. Hanging there right above him.

Her greasy hair, clumping over her shoulders and sticking to her forehead. Her mouth, agape with rotted teeth. Her eyes, completely glossed over, the color of spoiled milk.

The single tear that trickled down, down, down her cheek before hanging on the tip of her nose.

It froze there for a second before falling and landing right onto Michael's mouth.

He sprang awake.

She was gone, and he could finally move.

Michael wiped his eyes and licked his lips.

He tasted salt.

No, Michael McKenzie did not believe in ghosts.

He knew that the girl above his head was not real.

When he looked out his window, though, he wasn't so certain about the boy in the yard staring back at him.

Ch. One

He was tired of feeling like he was losing his mind.

At least the nightmares were explainable. Rational, something that could be logically defined.

Nightmares, he told himself. *They're just nightmares.*

Michael did not remember the first time he awoke to find his body stiff in his bed, his heart thumping rapidly against his chest, and his breath heaving. He didn't even remember the first time he saw a figure standing above him, drenching him in fear like a bucket of ice-cold water.

He did, however, remember wetting the bed at twelve years old.

The nightmare had been too much, and the paralyzing aftermath had done nothing to ease his distress. When the figure with long nails and no face dragged its finger across his cheek, Michael felt skin against skin, and suddenly it was too real.

"Parasomnia," the doctor told his mother, who had taken Michael to a psychologist after she caught him sheepishly trying to clean his sheets at two in the morning. "Sleep paralysis paired with the incubus phenomenon."

Diagnosis. Inferential.

Michael was not crazy.

That being said, if Michael had any say in the matter, he would much rather spend his time looking for a boy whom he wasn't quite sure was real.

Someone had been watching him, or rather his house, every night for the past week. A boy, Michael was pretty sure, who wasn't much younger than him. Standing there in a clearing of the woods, able to look upon the McKenzie household but concealed enough to be mistaken for a shadow.

He thought about flinging open his window, confronting the stranger from his room atop the second floor. In reality, he would get up out of bed and approach the glass, but the second he took his eyes off the figure, it would vanish.

Gone, as if it were never there in the first place.

Michael was used to this feeling, but it didn't make it any less unsettling.

Unfortunately, he had other things to worry about. He had promised his mother he would try to *mingle* with the local community of Whalesborough before the school year started. After rejecting many suggestions from his mother, including going door to door and introducing himself to all of his neighbors, Michael took up his father's recommendation and decided to get a job in town.

At first, he thought it would be difficult to find a place to apply to, but it didn't take much effort before landing an interview with Robinson's Groceries. It was a Mom and Pop shop, right smack in the middle of the island, family-owned since the '20s.

Michael was charmed by Mr. Robinson, even more so when he was informed that the shop paid 50 cents above the minimum wage. The pocket money would come in handy, he'd have something to keep himself occupied, and his parents would be satisfied. It was a win-win situation. He took the job.

In the back of his mind, a small voice wondered why it was so easy to get the position, but he ignored it.

Now he understood that he should've listened more closely to the sense of doubt.

He tapped his foot anxiously on the floor as he manned the register and tried to ignore the screaming baby from the back room. The Robinsons' youngest had switched between babbling and crying for the past three hours. Two of the other children ran between the aisles of the store, stacking cans of tomato soup into towers or lining up boxes of cereal as dominoes before knocking everything over. Michael had had to stock the shelves ten times already. One of the daughters, a girl a couple of years younger than him, was supposed to be helping him, but she had miraculously vanished the second he clocked in.

Mrs. Robinson was somewhere above the shop, maybe tidying up their living space, maybe hiding from her children. Michael didn't blame her. Mr. Robinson was in the back, going over expenses and stock. Apparently, two other children were lingering around, but Michael had yet to see them. He thought, perhaps, that they were hiding in the vents overhead.

He did not sign up for babysitting.

At least he had permission to listen to his Walkman whenever no one was shopping. To be fair, though, Michael would've been using it even if Mr. Robinson had disapproved.

He leaned against the counter and softly shut his eyes, letting the lulling voice of the narrator drag him down into the unsettling stories of W. Flick. Michael much preferred these teenage horror stories over Stine or Cusick, which seemed to lean towards a more childish audience than Michael felt he belonged to. Flick's writing of trepidation provided comfort to Michael in a curious way, just as *The Twilight Zone* or *The X-Files* would.

As inconvenient as books on tape were, the habit had stuck with him even now. He blamed it on all the road trips his father took him on when writing articles. While his father did his job, Michael made the life-changing discovery of Crackle Barrel and its gift shop, which not only included a wide variety of candy cane flavors but a selection of tapes. It was an easy way to stay entertained on the long car rides, especially when he'd always been so susceptible to motion sickness.

He knew well enough to keep it on the down low. Even his parents made fun of his collection, claiming that it *aged* him. Which was just a nicer way of saying that books on tape were a grandmother's passion. But it was an easy way to indulge in his horror stories, so he didn't let it get to him.

The truth was, even though Michael was smart enough to discount ghosts and psychics and any other supernatural entities, he couldn't stop his fascination with the paranormal. No, not fascination. Interrelation was a better word.

There was a quote his journalist father would say whenever his mother found something distasteful being shown on television. Something about comforting the afflicted and afflicting the comfortable.

That's exactly what it was like.

His own terrors were not so different from those portrayed in scary stories, aside from the underlying reality of the respective circumstances.

Michael's fear was a chemical reaction in his brain. The fear in his books-on-tape and shows was purposely crafted fiction. The intersection between the two was a familiar comfort.

Which was why Michael had already grown a sort of disdain for his new home. Whalesborough was complicating the relationship Michael had with ghost stories.

It seemed as if every time he turned the corner of Whalesborough, there was something there waiting for him and his infatuation. Something to garner his attention, something to draw him a little closer to the concept of the paranormal.

But the townsfolk in Whalesborough were not like Michael. They did not rationalize or disregard the strange phenomena that were rumored to occur. Instead, they reveled in it. They lived off the scary stories that would travel through the town between neighborly chit-chats. The supernatural was not a notion held at arm's length, but rather a way of life for the community.

Michael preferred his audiobooks.

"Hey, Mike." Mr. Robinson popped his head out from the back. Michael tore off his headphones, bringing his story to a halt.

"It's just Michael." He corrected.

"Right, sorry. I'll try to remember that." Mr. Robinson brought out a cardboard box that smelled strongly of frankincense and sage. "Since you're not really doing anything, could you run this over to the shop across the street? The delivery guys always mix up our packages."

Michael eyed the package and then eyed the misbehaving children Mr. Robinson made a point to ignore.

Michael quickly took the package from him, eager to take any opportunity to flee the store. The downtown of Whalesborough was not too different from where Michael lived in San Francisco. It was on a bit of a hill with stone sidewalks and buildings lined closely together. Robinson's sat at the edge of the main square, so there weren't too many people walking by.

Michael hadn't done much exploring the town on his own, so he had yet to look inside the shop across the street. It was smaller than Robinson's, constrained by the other building in a way that made it look stretched and thin. As Michael crossed the road, shifting the box in his hands and mindfully stepping over the cracks that ran through the avenue, he was finally able to read the sign above the door.

Selene's Psychic Readings and Magic Shop

The apostrophe in *Selene's* was drawn like a blue evil eye that peered down at him.

Michael sighed as he pushed through the door of the shop.

He was immediately hit with the strong scent of incense, the thick, smoky air filling his lungs. A wind chime sang above his head as he stepped inside, startling him slightly. The shop was dimly lit with flames and dull lamps.

It was shockingly barren. There were a few shelves with cheap magic tricks kids could use, like mystic playing cards or the classic ball and cups. There were collections of different dyed candles, and some displays of tarot decks that people could purchase. Aside from the velvet curtains and intricate tapestries, the walls were stark.

And there was also nobody there. Literally no one.

Until a boy his age stepped out from behind some curtains.

He regarded Michael for a second, clearly surprised to see him. "Yeah?" The boy said. Even in the dim lighting, Michael felt the cold gaze of his gray eyes from across the room.

"I'm looking for Selene," said Michael. The boy raised an eyebrow. Michael held the box a little higher. "I have a package for her."

"She's out."

"Oh."

"But I can take it."

"Oh," Michael said again. "Okay," he quickly added. As the boy walked over to the counter, Michael scanned him up and down. When he was hired at Robinson's, they gave him a green apron with a matching name tag. The boy was wearing nothing to signify that he worked in the shop, just some faded gray jeans and a t-shirt that said My Bloody Valentine. His hair was a blond mop of loose curls that fell past his ears and down the back of his neck.

Michael had recently started paying close attention to other boys' hair subconsciously. Not in, like, a weird way. For the past nine years, he let his mother give him the same bowl cut every other month, but he finally convinced her to let him see a professional barber. Since then, Michael had been experimenting with new styles, trying to reinvent himself, but it mostly just included stealing his father's hair gel to brush his hair back like Fox Mulder.

The boy gestured for Michael to come join him. After carefully placing the box on the counter, he slid out a switchblade and sliced at the box before tearing it open. Michael watched as he tossed out the bundle of sage leaves and essential oils.

This was the first person Michael had met in the town who was his age, and even though Michael had a decent amount of height on him, he still felt slightly intimidated. The boy's eyes kept flickering between the contents of the package and Michael, clearly sizing him up as well. Michael shifted awkwardly, leaning his weight from one foot to the other.

It was as the boy was folding the box down flat that Michael noticed his left hand and the fact that he was missing the tip of his middle finger.

In his horror novels, this is the part where the boy across the street tells him the chilling backstory of a monster (no, spirit. Spirits were more on par). He would tell the story of a spirit that took his finger and continued to haunt him, waiting for the chance to finish what had been started and claim the boy's entire hand. Then he would go over the implicit rules of the tale, like always keeping your hands in your pockets when walking alone during the night or perhaps not letting your arm fall out of your bed to hang by the floor when asleep. In his horror novels, this is the beginning of all the terror that would come.

Michael wanted to ask what happened to his hand.

He didn't.

The boy caught him staring and slid his arm away under the desk. "So, what's up, *Michael*?" He said it in a bored tone.

"I— Sorry?"

The boy pointed at Michael's chest with his right hand, the one with all fingers intact. He followed the gaze to his name tag. "Is that wrong?" The boy asked. Michael shook his head. "Well then, who are you? I mean, you're new. Obviously."

"Obviously?"

"This town is small as hell, and I've never seen you before," the guy said. "Also, you'd have to be new to this place to take the job at Robinson's."

"What's wrong with Robinson's?"

The boy gave a questioning smile, which eased Michael's nerves. "Seriously? How long have you been working there?"

"About three hours."

"And you haven't noticed how much of a shithole it is?"

Michael leaned slightly to the side, trying to suppress an agreeing smile.

"Exactly. The kids are literal monsters. Not only that, but if you stick around for more than a couple of days, Mrs. Robinson just starts dumping the baby in your arms." The guy nodded to Michael. "Half the people who come in here are just new employees trying to get away from their shift."

"Guilty." Michael rubbed the back of his neck.

"To be fair, it's probably the best job you're gonna get for now." The guy grabbed the items from the counter and began to stock the shelves. "This town is kind of weird with newcomers. Don't really like outsiders too much. You know, all that superstitious bull they spread around." He paused and considered the bundle of sage in his hand. "Actually, I should probably cleanse you of any bad energy you may have carried from the mainland. It's my societal duty as a resident of this town, and all that."

Michael glanced between the boy and the sage he was waving around. He let his arm fall after he realized Michael thought he was serious.

"Kidding. I'm kidding." He dumped it on the shelf and continued. "Maybe I should take back what I said about Robinson's. This entire place is a shithole, not just that shop."

"Yeah?" Michael leaned against the counter to watch him move over to the next aisle. "Why do you say that?"

"Besides the fact that there's literally nothing to do here? There's also the part where it's so small that you can't do anything without the whole town knowing about it. No such thing as privacy in Whalesborough."

"Noted."

"And then there's also the whole bullshit supernatural stuff."

Michael perked up. The boy noticed and smirked at his reaction.

"Key word, *bullshit*. The only reason there are rumors of ghosts and other stuff is that the mayor wanted an excuse for why nobody ever comes down here. Also, it makes this boring place a bit more interesting. Nothing like a sinister backstory to bring up that summer tourism, right?"

"You don't believe in it?"

"What's there to believe in?" He rolled his eyes.

"I don't know. I mean, my mom said that some townsfolk told her about, like, fog spirits or something."

The boy's jaw fell open superficially. "Oh my God, not the fog spirits."

"Or just other strange things." Michael defended.

"Wow, super specific." He nodded. "Look, dude. People get colds or they get chills; they blame ghosts. A kid shatters their dad's favorite coffee mug; they blame the ghost. You hear a creak in the hallway? See a shadow? Lose your car keys? Just blame a ghost. Besides, they only told your mom that because they thought she was a tourist or something. When they find out you guys are staying here, they'll drop the act."

"You really think it's all made up?"

"Yep."

"You work in a *magic* shop," Michael argued.

"So?" He shrugged. "I don't believe in that psychic stuff either. The only reason I'm here is because my aunt runs this place."

"Wait, so your aunt is—"

"Selene Cassidy. I help her run the shop whenever she's out or giving readings." He reluctantly stuck out his right hand for Michael to shake. "I'm Bo."

Michael took it. "Michael."

"Yeah, I know. Name tag, remember?" Bo let his hand fall back before lounging on the stool behind the counter. "Glad to finally put a face to the name. Well, not a name specifically. Selene was talking about the new people who moved into the old Beckham place."

"Beckham place?"

Bo grimaced slightly, for real this time, not just sarcastically to emphasize a point. "Yeah... The house you moved into is kind of notoriously haunted. It's been on the market for like, a hundred years or something. Kids used to go up there on Halloween and play Chicken. You know, just your classic haunted house activities."

Michael rubbed his eyes. He thought of the implications of a random kid hanging around his house on a dare by his friends. He thought of the boy, whom he wasn't quite sure was real.

"I thought you didn't believe in ghosts," Michael said.

"I don't!" He raised his hands in surrender. "But everyone else does. Anyway, you don't really have anything to worry about. People won't mess with it anymore now that you guys moved in."

"That's super reassuring."

Bo shrugged.

Michael gave another glance around the shop, his eyes landing on a clock hanging beside some garland. "I should probably be getting back to the store." Michael sighed.

"Hey, if you ever need a place to camp out, the door's open," Bo suggested.

"Yeah?"

"Well, mostly. Sometimes it gets jammed, so you need to really push it to open. But metaphorically, yeah."

"I'll keep that in mind." Michael found a smile fighting its way out before heading back to where he came in. Stepping out of the shop was no different from stepping in; it felt a bit like narrowly missing being hit by a train.

Which was to say, Michael was almost hit by the town's trolley on his way out.

The strong wind was enough to make him stumble as he fell backwards. The trolley wasn't even moving that fast, embarrassingly enough. He felt the back of his shoes hit the sidewalk edge as he tried to regain his balance.

Then Michael saw him.

In the corner of his eyes, Michael watched a boy leap off the trolley, smacking onto the ground with a thud. Just as quickly as he landed, he was pushing off the ground and racing into the magic shop behind Michael.

He barely got a glance, but it was enough.

It was enough to recognize the boy who had just crossed him.

"Mike! There you are!" Michael's head snapped up to see Mr. Robinson wave at him from across the street. "Come on back. I need some help with some boxes."

His feet stood planted where he was. It was like he was lying paralyzed in his bed. He watched as Mr. Robinson crossed the street over to him.

"The trolley gave you quite the shock, huh?" Mr. Robinson laughed and lightly hit Michael's shoulder before leading him back to the grocery store.

Michael nodded numbly.

From across the street, he peered through Selene's stained windows.

But the boy who had been watching Michael's house was already looking back.

His eyes lingered.

Real, Michael thought. *He was real.*

Ch. Two

Selene Cassidy was a curious woman in the sense that she was completely contradictory.

For example, she had a strict policy on facts and reasoning. If Bo was to make a statement, he had to have evidence for it because Selene would always follow up with her motto, "Show me the stats." It was an ironic habit of hers, given her occupation as a self-proclaimed psychic. Her ability to see the distant past and the near future, retrocognition and precognition, had made her infamous in their town. Despite her policy, when she told Bo what to expect for the day each morning over breakfast, she'd always shrug her shoulders when he'd ask, "How do you know?"

She did not spare time for Whalesborough's ghost stories. When a client came in asking Selene to perform an exorcism on their supposedly haunted house, she made Bo kick them out. "I'm a psychic," she'd explain. "Not a medium," Bo remembered being amused by the exchange for the sole reason that his aunt very much *did* believe in ghosts. When he first arrived at the island, she had told him outright that spirits were as common as whales. They existed, but he'd probably never see one. It was a poor metaphor for the fact that Whalesborough was known for, well, phantoms along with whales.

She also claimed to love her shop more than anything else in the entire world (besides Bo, that is), even though she was never there.

Bo did not believe in psychics. He did not believe in ghosts, either.

Yet he was always lingering around Whalesborough's one and only psychic shop.

He took after his aunt, he supposed. Bo Cassidy was completely contradictory.

The windchime above the shop's door rang, and Bo lifted his head from his hands.

"Hey, hey, hey," Andy said, launching himself across the counter to greet Bo.

"Hey, yourself." Bo squinted at Andy.

For as long as there had been Whalesborough, there had been Alejandro Romero-Almada. And for as long as there had been Andy Romero-Almada, there had been Bo Cassidy's sanity.

Andy turned to sit on top of the counter.

For the past couple of years, this is how it has been. Bo worked on the register, and Andy took the trolley to meet him there. Bo would take his spot on the stool, Andy his spot on the desk, so they both had perfect reach for Selene's decorative tray of crystals. They'd talk for hours.

Sometimes they'd close up shop early to head down to the video store, or they'd go to the diner up on the hill and split a milkshake. Sometimes they kicked off their shoes by the back staircase and headed up to Bo's room, opting to lie on the floor and listen to their favorite albums. It didn't really matter what they did, so long as they did it together.

"Any appointments today?"

"Nope."

"Is Selene here?"

"Nope."

"Wanna get out of here?"

Bo bit back a grin.

"Come on, summer's almost over." Andy groaned, an obvious statement neither of them could forget.

Their junior year was approaching quickly, and everyone was telling them that it was time to get serious. They would be trading beach days and lounging around with homework and SAT prep.

Bo knew Andy was dreading it more than he let on. Andy subconsciously ran his fingers through his wispy brown hair, which was always a dead giveaway to his nerves. During the summer, he had let it grow long, once falling at his shoulders. He had to cut due to the school year starting up. The Catholic school he went to, Saint Joseph's, had strict dress codes, including hair length. Andy had convinced his mother to let him cut his hair himself, resulting in uneven layers that licked the back of his neck and long strands that fell over his eyes. His mother had been furious. Bo didn't think it looked half bad. Andy was content enough.

Another thing.

Summer ending meant the separation of Bo and Andy. Bo went to the public school in the west, and Andy went to the private school in the east. Neither of them was looking forward to it.

"Maybe later," Bo said. "Besides, this place hasn't been totally dead today."

Andy raised a questioning eyebrow, which was fair considering that Selene's was always dead.

"The new kid," Bo explained.

"Ah."

New people were always big news in Whalesborough. The town had, *at most*, six thousand occupants, most of whom were older families that had lived there for generations. Unfamiliar faces weren't uncommon with tourists coming to the beaches or the supernatural, but the prospect of permanent residents had grown scarce over the years.

Furthermore, the new family had not only moved into Whalesborough but had also moved into one of their prominent haunted houses on the market.

"The old Beckham place?" Andy asked.

"Yep."

"Damn." Andy whistled low. He reached for some Big League Chew he usually kept in his pockets and offered some to Bo, who took the strands of gum gratefully. "So, what's he like?"

"Normal? I don't know, we didn't talk much. He took the job at Robinson's." Bo said.

"Yikes," Andy responded with a mouthful of chewing gum. Andy had taken the position himself three years back, so he and Bo could work right across from each other. He quit after four hours. "So, he's not the sharpest tool in the shed."

"I wouldn't say that," Bo said.

Michael was nice. Nice enough, anyway. He had to be to keep his cool after working a full day at Robinson's. Besides, he wasn't an asshole about the psychic thing, which most people were. Even though Bo didn't believe in his aunt's occupation, he despised those who made a point of putting her down for it. Discrediting her work, making accusations of interacting with evil forces, or just being plain awful to his aunt was common in Whalesborough.

"I heard—" Andy started.

"Don't. I don't want to hear it." Bo cut him off.

Bo and Andy shared many similar qualities, such as their skepticism towards the supernatural. Their unwillingness to believe in the town's ghosts had distinctly set them apart from their peers, and so they only had each other to laugh with when new crazy stories came around.

They also had their differences.

Andy Romero-Almada was of Whalesborough's blood, born and raised, which meant he had ears for eavesdropping and a mouth for blabbing.

He was always up to date on the latest news. He knew the who, the where, the how, and the what, no matter the situation. In such a small town, secrets could only *stay* secrets for so long. It was only a matter of time before Andy was bouncing into the shop, buzzing from head to toe with information.

On the opposite end of the spectrum, there was Bo Cassidy, who hated nothing more than gossip.

Bo knew firsthand what it meant to be antagonized by the town's rumors. The rumors of Selene's shop and what sinister activity went down behind the closed doors. The rumors of his living situation, why he was living with his aunt instead of with his father on the mainland. The rumors of his hand.

"Nothing bad!" Andy hurriedly explained. "You know. All good things, all good things. But also—" Andy glanced at Bo and broke off. "Nevermind."

Bo stayed silent. Andy always gave in, no matter what he said.

"Okay, but listen," Andy sighed. "The Beckham place, right?"

"I'm familiar with it." Bo could easily visualize the eerie two-story house that seemed to be on everyone's mind. He thought of the wraparound porch, ancient stylized windows, and chipping birchwood. Stereotypical creepy house.

"Okay, so it's like nine p.m. and I'm walking by—"

"Why were you walking by the Beckham place in the middle of the night?"

Andy rolled his eyes. "Okay, first of all, nine p.m. is not the middle of the night. One a.m. is in the middle of the night. Nine is like, the sixth-grade bedtime part of the night. Second of all, I was going for a walk to get my exercise in and clear my head. Y'know?"

Bo did not know. "Whatever, continue."

"So I'm walking by. I barely get halfway past the place before I hear this crazy, loud sound. Just insane crashing and banging coming from the inside. And I'm scared shitless, right?"

"Right," Bo agreed.

"I walk a little faster to get around the place when I start to see this flashing light from the top windows. And not just flickering light bulbs kind of flashing. It seemed purposeful. I could've sworn it was Morse code or something."

"What did it spell out?"

"I dunno." Andy shrugged.

The thing about Andy was that he loved to tell stories but was terrible at it.

"Okay, so?" Bo rolled his eyes.

"So? So, it was hella creepy!" Andy threw his hands up in the air. "And like, maybe the people that moved in are working on the house, trying to clean it up so they don't get lead poisoning from all the old paint or something. Or maybe some weird shit's seriously going down."

"Wait, wait, wait." Bo pinched the bridge of his nose. "Are you actually scared of the Beckham ghost?"

"No! C'mon, we all know it's like— That's not what I'm saying at all." Andy said defensively. "I'm just saying that you should stay away."

"That would be really useful advice if I ever went near that house," Bo interjected. "Maybe *you* should stay away."

"Whatever, man. You would get it if you'd been there." Andy crossed his arms and leaned his head back to look out the window. Bo went to say something else, but he was interrupted by the phone ringing at the back of the shop.

Most of the time, people called their landline to schedule appointments for readings with Selene. Once, Bo picked up a guy trying to score a second date with his aunt. Every other time, Andy was ringing in the middle of the night to complain about school or his parents.

Bo held up a hand to Andy before pushing past the curtains to retrieve the call.

"Hello?" He said into the phone.

He heard static from the other side.

"You've called Selene's Psychic and Magic Shop. Do you want to make an appointment?" Bo recited the script Selene made him memorize when he was ten.

Still silent.

Then, breathing.

Ragged and strained, like a dog panting.

Bo pressed the phone closer to his ear.

"Hello?" He asked quietly.

He was met with the dial tone.

Bo held the phone away from his ear in confusion. He stared at it for a moment before putting the phone back in its place on the wall and returning to his spot beside Andy.

"Who was that?" Andy asked.

"I don't know, the line went dead."

"Hm." Andy nodded.

"Yeah, totally." But Bo brought his hand up slowly to rub the back of his neck, his face growing pale. Andy noticed the change in his demeanor and perked up. "But maybe... Maybe some weird shit's actually going down. Maybe the Beckham girl—"

"Shut up!" Andy tossed the rest of the chewing gum at Bo to cut off the terrible impression he was making of Andy. "Next time, I won't try to look out for you. There, how's that?"

Bo furrowed his brows as he worked to suppress a smile. "Shit, dude. Did it actually freak you out that much?"

"No!" Andy shrugged. "Just... don't go there, okay?"

"Okay, okay. Got it." Bo said. Then he thought of Michael, the new kid who's living in the house that suddenly has Andy so messed up. "I think it'd be good if we showed him around."

"Who?"

"The new kid. Michael."

Andy's eyebrows quirked up. "Did you really just say that?"

Bo shrugged.

"*You* want to show the new kid around," Andy repeated.

"I don't know, man. It's not like he has any other friends." Bo said. Andy eyed him. "I'm trying to be nice."

"But you're never nice."

Bo smacked his shoulder.

It was the truth, though. Bo really wasn't that nice, which was probably why Andy was his only friend. It's not like he was a total asshole or anything. He just didn't see the point in exchanging pleasantries with people he didn't like all that much.

It's not like the kids at school were easy to talk to anyway.

"C'mon. It's not like he's gonna bite you or something." Bo said.

"I mean, we don't really know him. Maybe he will." Andy retorted.

"Let's just stop by after we close."

"After *you* close."

"You're literally here all the time. You basically work here."

"It's not like I get paid."

"I don't get paid either."

Andy stuck out his tongue. Bo tossed his Big League gum at him in retaliation.

"Fine, let's do it." Andy relented. "But I can't do it tonight. It's Jaime's last week in town, and my parents want me there for it."

"Okay, then. Tomorrow." Bo agreed.

The phone rang.

Andy jumped slightly, and Bo tried to suppress a laugh.

He picked up the landline just as he did a couple of minutes ago, only to find the line dead.

Again.

Bo turned to Andy with a puzzled look, but Andy didn't ask who it was.

He seemed to already know the answer.

Ch. Three

One thing Andy could never understand about Bo Cassidy was his disdain for Whalesborough.

Nights like these—summer evenings with nothing but the salty breeze and the calling of seabirds to keep him company—were what kept him going. Andy was leaning on the window of the trolley, resting on his forearms with his hair blowing in the wind, as the car raced on. He lived for this sort of thing.

He knew the routes of the town's trolley like he knew his own body, the streets and alleys indistinguishable from the veins on his wrist. He'd grown up on this trolley car alongside Mr. Hardy, the driver. The hours he'd spent here riding around town would accumulate to years. Mostly, he rode alone, but sometimes Bo was there to keep him company.

Andy knew it wasn't the town itself that Bo hated.

He wasn't stupid. (No, seriously, he wasn't.)

It wasn't the shores and the old lighthouse, the ancient buildings, or the obsolete systems that kept the town afloat; it wasn't any physical aspect of the town at all. Whalesborough was beautiful in a way neither of them could ever grow tired of.

Instead, Bo hated the way of life. Andy couldn't blame him completely, but he could never find it in himself to truly agree.

It may have been due to the way they were raised. Bo grew up on the outskirts of a city that resided on the mainland. Andy had never left the island. Their childhood homes carried values that were unfamiliar to each other. There was Bo's general loneliness that he'd stuck with because he didn't need anyone else, and Andy's loneliness that he endured because he didn't want anyone else. They relied on each other away from the rest of the town for different reasons.

It may very well have come from their families. The Cassidy's were few; the Romero-Almada's were many. The Cassidy's were new blood; the Romero-Almada's had lived on the island since it had been named. The Cassidy's were psychics; the Romero-Almada's were not.

Bo's family and their histories. Andy's family and their histories.

Everything in this town was intertwined with folklore one way or another. The telling of ghost stories carried the same feeling as when his grandmother recounted her own childhood. *It happened like this;* that was how it always started. Like it was truer than anything else. It always took Andy a moment before he could figure out whether the anecdote was one of the primary or secondary sources. Memory or fiction? Andy lived for that, too.

In reality, maybe it wasn't that Andy didn't understand Bo, but rather that Bo didn't understand Andy. But that's all beside the point.

"We're coming up to your stop, Romero," Mr. Hardy called from the front.

"One more lap?"

Mr. Hardy glanced back with a smile and kept the trolley car going.

It was so, so easy being out there.

Constantly moving, that's what it was. He was everywhere and nowhere at the same time. He wasn't home; he wasn't *not* home. A perfect limbo for Andy to escape.

Until it stopped.

Andy stood up from his seat to find that Mr. Hardy was already checking the main controls.

"Everything alright?" Andy asked.

"Erm," Mr. Hardy took off his hat and swatted it in the air. "Looks like something's wrong. I'll get it fixed in no time. Why don't you take a stroll around and stretch your legs for now?"

Andy nodded and hopped off the trolley. They had stopped on one of the hills overlooking the ocean. Technically, Andy's house was only a twenty-minute walk away from here, but he felt bad leaving

Mr. Hardy stranded by himself, so he only walked a couple of paces away.

Once you got away from the shore and town, Whalesborough was all tall trees and greenery. It was hard to navigate the intricate and seemingly endless forest in the dark, so Andy made sure to watch where he stepped.

Twigs snapped as he wandered. Ferns and branches reached out to him like fingers and brushed his exposed arms. Even though it was only late summer, the island was already growing colder. Andy shrugged off a shiver as he made his way through.

He knew this path well. He'd taken it just last night, and he'd known where he'd end up. The Beckham place. Now, the McKenzie household.

It loomed past the trees and stretched out into the deep, dark sky.

When Bo and Andy were eight, it had been Bo's first Halloween in Whalesborough. They had gone trick-or-treating with some of the neighborhood kids. Once the town had already been ransacked of goodies, they had decided to head off to the unsettling woods.

Andy remembered hanging back with Bo and guiding him by hand. They walked until they reached the haunted house. *Who's brave enough?* The older kids asked. *Who's gonna face the Beckham girl and come out with all their fingers?* That last comment had a clear and pointed target.

Since he was the new kid, Bo had to go first.

Andy watched as his new friend climbed the rickety steps, raised a fist at the wood to knock, and disappeared behind the door of the Beckham house. The other kids eagerly waited for the moment he came out, screaming and crying.

Andy wanted to go in after him, but this was a tradition. A test of courage and backbone. If Bo was to be accepted, he had to go in alone. To chicken out was social suicide.

Seconds ticked by into minutes. One, five, ten, before suddenly half an hour had gone by, and Bo had still not yet emerged from the haunted house. Some of the kids went home. Andy and Warren Dacre remained and waited.

"Fuck's taking him so long?" Warren Dacre was the first third grader to curse out loud, and he taught the rest of them how to swear like a sailor by fourth grade.

"Something's wrong."

"Fuck off, Romero." Warren Dacre cursed like he had a limited vocabulary, and swear words took up half his vacant spots.

"I'm going after him."

"Like hell you are, dumbass." Andy hadn't sworn much yet. He knew his mother would wash

his mouth out with soap if she ever caught him.
Warren Dacre would never wash his dirty mouth.

They regarded each other before they both went
inside.

The door creaked as the moonlight spilled in.

"Bo." Andy whispered, then more furiously,
"*Bo!*"

He sat crisscrossed right in the middle of the
foyer, where rooms branched out to the sides and a
staircase spiraled up to the second floor. Leaves swept
around their feet from the wind, and they all
shivered.

Andy drew closer and grabbed Bo by the
shoulder. His plastic Darth Vader mask had been
brought up to his forehead; the faraway look in his
eyes captivated Andy.

"Hey, you okay?" Andy had asked.

Bo turned his head to him. His eyes seemed to
focus and clear.

"She wants us to go now," he said blankly. Then
he got up and walked out of the house.

Andy and Warren watched him go with
matching shocked expressions.

"What a fucking freak."

They had never mentioned it again. Andy
wasn't even sure Bo remembered it, as he didn't
remember a lot of things from his first year on the
island. But Andy thought of that night when he

gazed upon the Beckham house. No, the *McKenzie* house now.

He shivered again.

It was only eight thirty at night, but the sun was well gone. The wind slammed a shudder from the upper window back and forth and back and forth. The window he had looked through last night had thrown up a curtain, but Andy still saw the light seeping through.

Then it flashed.

And flashed again.

He stepped into the clearing.

A flash, a flash, and nothing. Nothing for a while, then the lights flickered like a beating heart.

Ba-bump, ba-bump, ba-bump.

He heard a crash from the first floor and jumped back just as a hand gripped the curtains from above and yanked them open. Andy didn't stick around. He turned on his heel and quickly walked back towards Mr. Hardy and the broken trolley.

He kept watching over his shoulder. As he grew further and further away and lost sight of the house and its flashing light, he worked to shake off the feeling that it had been *he* who was being watched and not the other way around.

"Whoa, kiddo."

Andy yelped as he tripped over a fallen branch, almost hitting the hard ground before Mr. Hardy caught him by the shoulders and brought him back on his feet.

"Trolley's fixed. I was about to come get you." Andy tried to nod, but he was shaking like a leaf. "You okay?"

"Yeah, yeah. I'm good," Andy quickly replied. "I think I'm gonna pass on that extra loop."

Mr. Hardy nodded, clearly unconvinced, but didn't press Andy anymore as he started the trolley back up.

They finally made their way to the Romero-Almada household. A small gray house that had been torn down and rebuilt in the 50s, two stories plus a basement, lived and loved in for generations.

Andy gave his thanks to Mr. Hardy and wished him a good night before heading inside.

He knew before he opened the door that his father was waiting for him.

One hand held a glass of rum, the other held his head. No one else was around, probably out or holed up in their rooms.

"Alejandro?" His father called, not raising his head.

"Huh," Andy responded. He gently shut the door so as not to wake his great-grandmother, who was always asleep before eight. He kicked off his shoes and let them fall into the accumulating pile by the door.

"¿Dónde has estado?"

"Out."

"Hm?

Andy bit his lip and worked to tone down his attitude. "With Bo." He clarified. "Just, you know, at his house."

"Ah."

"Yep."

He turned to the staircase.

"Alejandro?" His father called again.

"Yes?"

A pause.

"El sótano."

The basement, the basement, the basement.

Andy pursed his lips and walked back out the front door, not bothering to put his sneakers back on. He went around the bend of the house until he reached the back. The cellar door was ensured to be locked shut, but Andy always had the key with him. He reached for the chain on his neck, always tucked securely in his shirt, and pulled it off.

The key slid into the lock and turned. The shackles wrapped around the handles fell away, and Andy groaned as he pulled the metal door up from the ground.

Every night, he did this.

He walked down the stone steps two at a time. He reached above for the chain to the lightbulb.

Every night.

It didn't matter how many times he changed the bulb. It always flickered.

Andy asked himself, *is this really happening?*

But he already knew it was.

Ch. Four

The nightmares had come back in full swing. Every night, he awoke with her above him. Every night, he'd look out the window and find that strange boy staring right back. Michael was losing sleep, going to bed late, and waking up early to avoid any sense of paralysis. His parents noticed, obviously, but they said nothing.

After he reached fourteen, they thought it'd be best for Michael if they pretended nothing was wrong. At first, it seemed to work, he supposed. Now it only made him feel crazy.

Don't you see? He'd think as he watched his father pour three cups of coffee, one for each of them. *Don't you see there's something wrong with me?*

"Working today?" His dad asked.

Michael picked at his food. "Yeah," he said, disinterested.

"Me too."

They all took a sip.

"Make any new friends yet?" His mother chimed in.

He thought of Bo. Then he thought of the mysterious boy watching his house. "Not really."

"That's okay. You'll find some in no time."

They drained their mugs.

Michael grabbed his letterman jacket from the coat rack and headed out the door to catch his ride to work. Everything about Whalesborough reminded him of San Francisco. From the trolley to the seaside breeze that welcomed him each time he stepped out.

If he closed his eyes in the trolley car, he could almost pretend he was back in South Beach on his way to school. A cough brought him back to reality, and he opened his eyes to see that the trolley was now crowded as they headed into town.

He looked among the passengers, who were studying him back closely. He knew it was because he was a fresh face in the tight-knit town. There wasn't any malice or ill intent, only curiosity.

It was hard to turn off the part of his brain that made him question how everyone else perceived him.

Even back at home, when he was out with his parents, Michael knew how his family must have looked to outsiders. Michael hadn't shared his concerns with his parents, though he probably should have. He knew they always felt uncomfortable when he brought up race.

After adopting him at eight, they tried their best to treat him as their biological child, which only worked so well, considering both of his parents were white and he was half Chinese. And even though he couldn't really mention it to his parents, he... Well, he missed seeing other people like him in San Francisco.

That was the first thing he made note of in Whalesborough: *There is nobody like me here.*

He tried to ignore their stares until he could reach for the bell and signal his stop at Robinson's. He slipped on his headphones and clicked play on his book.

"*Chapter Nine: Christina's Secret.*" The narrator began.

Michael shut his eyes once more.

They had caught Michael just as he was finishing his shift.

They pushed through the main door and stood in the frame like the twins from *The Shining*. Cold gazes and stiff arms at their sides. It would almost have been frightening if not for the comical height difference between the three of them. Exchanging nervous glances with each other, they looked like a set of Russian nesting dolls. Michael wasn't inclined to speak first.

"Hey, man," Bo said. "It's me from the shop, remember?" He gestured back and pointed towards Selene's.

Michael looked at Bo and then at the boy beside him.

He knew that face. He knew that creepy stance.

Michael pinched his arm under the counter, out of sight of the boys. Was this real? Did he ever get out of bed?

The sharp pain brought him back to reality.

"Yeah..." Michael said slowly. "I remember. What's up?"

Be cool. He thought to himself. *You are awake, and nothing is wrong.*

Yet. He made sure not to add the *yet.*

"We just thought we'd come over and offer to show you around properly. You know, all the good spots to hang and the places you should avoid," Bo offered. Then he added, "You don't have to if you need to head home."

Michael looked back at the other boy beside Bo.

He had spent the last couple of days playing this moment out in his head. Not this *exact* moment, but the part where he comes face-to-face with the trespasser of the night. In these fantasies, Michael was brave and demanding. *What do you want? Why are you doing this?* Or something else along those lines would be yelled.

The boy's response varied. Sometimes he managed to articulate the perfect explanation, and all of Michael's anger dissipated. Sometimes he grew defensive and rejected any of Michael's claims. Sometimes he'd disappear in the blink of an eye, leaving Michael to question whether or not he was ever really there, over and over and over.

In the real world, the shorter boy didn't break from Michael's gaze. Instead, he stuck out a fist.

"I'm Andy. I'm with Bo."

His voice was not what Michael imagined. Low and charming, like he was certain he was about to make a new friend out of Michael. Andy shook his hair out of his face and let an easy grin pass through his lips. He looked... friendly?

Michael opened his mouth and closed it. It was the most uncanny thing. This boy, Andy, was identical to the creeper in every way, except in character. The surrounding atmosphere around Andy was completely different from the mimic to the point where Michael wondered how he could have ever thought they were the same person. That is to say, the boy outside his window *was* a person and not just a figment of his imagination.

"I'm Michael." He shook off any discomfort as he met Andy's fist bump. At the last moment, Andy shot his hand under Michael's and stuck out two fingers instead.

"Snail," Andy said, grinning.

Michael stared at him.

Andy shrugged. "Anyway, you're lucky. We don't just show anybody around."

"That's because there's nobody here, like ever."
Bo rolled his eyes.

"Shh," Andy hushed him. "Don't worry, dude. I
was born and raised here, so I really do know my way
around. We should probably start heading out if we
wanna catch the trolley. Are you coming?"

Was he?

He didn't need to go home yet. In fact, his
mother would probably be ecstatic if he came home
late to hang out with some of the local kids. But was
he really going to go with some random guys around
town, one of whom Michael was a tad bit terrified
of?

"Yeah, let's go."

Apparently so.

They made it to the trolley just in time to hop
on and greet the operator, who Andy introduced as
Mr. Hardy. As they took their seats in the back and
rode along the boulevard, Andy and Bo began to
point out all the local places they had traversed over
the years.

Watching them rattle on was a thing of its own.
It was so clear from the way they talked and
interacted that their lives were deeply entwined.
Michael wouldn't be surprised if they told him they'd
been friends since birth. Even when they grew silent,
their eyes still conversed with each other in ways
Michael couldn't understand.

It was funny, he thought, that it now seemed impossible to imagine meeting Bo without meeting Andy alongside him.

Every part of this town had a place in their story.

"That's the public library. There's only, like, four authors to choose from, though. Bo hates half of them."

"That's one of the video stores, but we got banned because Andy tried to sneak into the adult section when we were twelve and got caught. The one on top of the hill is better anyway, so it doesn't matter much."

"That's the bar everyone's dads go to over the weekend to watch football, and that's the alleyway they all end up pissing in on their way home."

"That's where Andy got punched in the face for the first time by someone who wasn't his sister."

"That's where Bo—Hey, what the hell?"

Bo smirked before leaning back in his seat and turning to Michael. "On a scale of one to ten, how informative has this tour been so far?"

"I'd say about a seven-point five," Michael said, giving him a small smile back.

"We're only about a quarter through town. We'll bump that rating up in no time." Andy stretched in his seat. He seemed unable to stay still for more than five seconds. But when his shoulder slumped back down and his smile dropped, suddenly he was that enigmatic figure outside his window again. "You good?" Andy asked.

Michael's own face must have gone slack. He cleared his throat. "Yeah, yeah, I'm—"

"Really? 'Cause you've kind of been giving me a death stare this entire time?"

"Andy," Bo said in a warning tone.

Andy ignored him and leaned forward in his seat. "I'm just saying. If you have a problem with me, just come out and say it."

"It's not that." Michael began to explain, but he cut himself off. Hadn't he been waiting for this moment for the past week? He let his fingers curl into his palms. "Just— Um."

Andy raised an eyebrow.

They're gonna think you're crazy. But he had to know.

"Have you been watching my house?"

Andy narrowed his eyes. Then he leaned back in his seat. "Yeah, I guess," Andy said nonchalantly.

Michael's jaw could have hit the ground. "Wha— You've totally been stalking me!" He accused.

"Whoa, whoa, whoa. I haven't been *stalking* you. I always go by the Beckham place. It's on my way home, and sometimes I walk around the area to waste time," Andy shot back. "Also, it's not like I'm the only one. Kids go there all the time because it's haunted and shit."

"It's *not* haunted," Bo interjected.

"Whatever," Andy said. "Is that all? Or is there something else bothering you?"

Michael stuttered for a moment. "Wait, wait. Are you serious?"

"About..?"

Michael said, "All of that? It's just normal for people to walk around in the middle of the night, watching other people's houses."

Bo and Andy looked at each other and Michael, then they both shrugged. Michael gaped.

"When I said there's nothing to do here, I meant it," Bo said in a bit of a timorous manner. "People just walk around sometimes."

"Also, nine p.m. isn't the middle of the night." Bo side-eyed Andy. "What, it totally isn't!"

"I didn't see you at nine." Michael declared. "I saw you through my window closer to three in the morning."

Bo snapped his head over to Andy. Andy clocked his head to the side. "I don't know what to tell you, man. Whoever was out there, it wasn't me." Michael was about to argue back when Andy continued. "You sure you weren't just seeing things?"

That shut him up.

"No, I—" But that had been his life, hadn't it? Just because he was seventeen now didn't mean he wasn't the same scared little kid all those years ago, lying still in bed. Michael looked between Bo, confused and almost pitying, and Andy, stern and captious. He shrank a bit in his seat. "No, you're right. I probably was."

Michael was surprised to feel the tension dispersed immediately.

"If it makes you feel any better, though, people will cut it out sooner or later since it's not abandoned anymore," Bo said, clearly thankful that they weren't arguing anymore.

Andy offered, "Plus, I can find a different route to walk around if you want me to."

"No, no. It's fine. I was just freaked. Probably all the ghost stories I've been hearing." Michael laughed a bit. He hoped he hadn't just ruined whatever chance he had at making actual new friends by voicing his internal paranoia.

But Andy immediately perked up again, a grin growing on his face. Bo sighed into his hands.

"Do you believe them?" Andy questioned.

"In ghosts?"

"In all of it."

Michael regarded Andy, then smiled a bit. "Not really." He shrugged. "But..."

"But?" Both Andy and Bo said.

He thought of the shows he watched and his horror novels. He thought of his dreams.

"I think I could be convinced." Michael crossed his arms over his chest, but it didn't feel defensive. It felt like he was learning the rules of playing along with Bo and Andy.

"Oh, hell yeah," Andy said excitedly.

"Michael, why?" Bo groaned, but it was too late.

Andy was already launching into an epic tale of the local spirits. Bo made sure to cut in with a preface to ensure that both of them knew it was, as he always described it, total bullshit. Andy agreed, but not enough to refrain from retelling the story of Michael's own home.

It was built far off from town after the Beckham family was ostracized for supposedly dabbling in witchcraft. Children were warned to stay clear of the part of the woods where the family resided, lest they be taken as a sacrifice for their black magic. Only two generations of Beckhams lived there before tragedy struck.

It was 1892. Nobody had heard word of the Beckhams for quite some time, so some townspeople decided to investigate. When they approached the house, they were surprised to find the door wide open, welcoming them inside.

They cautiously entered, taking weary steps through the long hallways. One of the townsmen by the name of Ernest Calloway found a trail of broken glassware. Plates and teacups that bled into shattered gaslights and windows, leading to the youngest daughter's room.

Calloway paused at the door before placing his hand on the doorknob. He almost jumped back from the icy chill of the metal but forced himself to turn the handle. The door creaked open, and then he saw her body.

"Nobody knows what really happened. Some stories say they found her dead in a bed full of glass. Others say she was dismembered or something. But what mattered was that her corpse was left there in the house alone," Andy said.

"Wait, where was the rest of the family?" Michael asked.

"Gone. Just vanished into thin air, and nobody saw them ever again." Then Andy smiled. "My guess is it was a ritual gone wrong. But that's why it's been on the market for so long. People think her spirit is still lingering around, looking for a new family to call her own."

"Whoa."

"I know, right. It's great."

Bo scoffed. "Come on. You don't really believe this shit, do you, Michael?"

Michael shrugged. "Just because I don't believe in it doesn't mean it isn't interesting."

"See, Bo! Mikey here gets it."

Michael responded almost automatically, "It's just Michael." Then he cringed at himself, because he really should just get over it already.

Andy didn't seem to notice. "My bad, Michael. Just ignore Bo. He hates it when I go on like this." Andy said.

"I don't *hate* it," Bo said defensively. "It's just that everyone here goes on about the same five stories over and over again. It's so boring."

"Blah, blah, blah." Andy used his hand to mime a puppet yapping away. But they were all smiling together bashfully.

They moved away from the topic of the supernatural and back to themselves. Bo didn't hold back from poking fun at Andy and the less-than-wise decisions he'd made over the years. "It's not *my* fault you chipped your tooth on a brick. I told you not to do that trick." Or Andy telling Michael all about Bo's embarrassing moments. "He hit a baseball right into that window and tried to blame it on me."

"That *was* you, liar." Bo snapped.

Andy shook his head. "Even to this day, he denies it."

"Whatever, I'm not doing this with you again."

Michael told them about San Francisco. Bo was especially curious and told him that he planned on looking at schools in California for college.

"Somewhere far away. I don't think I could spend another four years here." Andy scoffed.

They told him what to expect during the upcoming school year. Michael was glad that, despite being a year older than the two, they would all be in the same grade since Michael had been held back a year. They learned that Michael would be attending the public school along with Bo. Michael asked if they could eat lunch together.

"I don't know if there'll be room at the table." Andy chipped in. "Bo's a pretty popular guy."

Bo rolled his eyes but didn't deny anything. He promised Michael he'd save him a spot.

Before they realized it, two hours had gone by, and Michael had to get home soon.

"Maybe if we get the chance, we can check out that haunted house of yours." Andy kid and nudged Michael's side.

"Would you want to?"

Andy squinted. "I mean, I haven't been inside since forever, and I'm kind of curious to see what you guys have done to the place."

"Well, if you want," Michael started, "you guys could totally spend the night or something."

"Hell yeah," Andy smirked. "Bo?"

Bo shrugged. "You know me. I'm good with whatever. Just don't expect me to play Bloody Mary in your bathroom or anything."

"Noted."

But when he hopped off the trolley, his mind drifted back to the inevitable doubts of the night. As he watched the two fall away from view, Michael's eyes couldn't help but linger on Andy and think of the stranger outside his window.

What would it mean if he saw the boy again?

He didn't want to think about it.

Michael was sure he wouldn't like the answer.

Ch. Five

Traditionally, the last two weeks of summer were spent lounging around until their limbs fell asleep. Michael's arrival had changed things.

Now, they went out every day, showing him every nook and cranny of the island. Even places Bo hadn't thought about in years, like the hidden creek he and Andy had found when they were thirteen, were rediscovered. He'd forgotten what it was like to be curious about the town. He felt like he was ten years old again, running around with scuffed knees and wild eyes, hand in hand with Alejandro Romero-Almada back when they were still just boys. They didn't do that kind of thing anymore.

It was a change of pace for Bo, who wasn't used to having more than just Andy around.

Between the two of them, Andy was far more outgoing and approachable. Selene had always described him as a *charismatic young man*, which Bo agreed was a rather fitting term for him. Andy didn't have trouble making connections with people. He was always saying the right jokes at the right times, knowing when it was time to stand his ground or let something go; he just knew how to get along with people.

Which is why it always surprised Bo that Andy never chose to hang around anyone else.

There were plenty of other kids on the island that Andy could spend his time with. He'd probably get more out of it, too. Undoubtedly better than just hanging around with Bo.

But it had always been the two of them and the two of them alone.

Until Michael McKenzie.

Bo put a finger to his lip when Michael and Andy came into the shop. They quietly came up to the desk. Like Andy, Michael had found his own spot; he'd resign at the back once he got off his shift at Robinson's. Bo sat on the stool, Andy sat on top of the counter, and Michael leaned on the wall behind them.

"Selene's giving a reading," Bo whispered. "We can head upstairs if you guys wanna talk."

They nodded before heading towards the back.

"Have you seen Bo's room yet?" Bo heard Andy ask Michael.

Michael shook his head, trailing the back.

"It's not much." Bo shrugged, but he was secretly eager for Michael to see his room. He'd worked hard on making it feel like himself. So much of the house was representative of Selene, from the hand-made artwork that hung in the living room to the scatter of dream diaries and empty teacups. And though he loved his aunt, his room was the one place that was completely untouched by Selene. It was Bo's, and Bo's alone.

Bo pushed back the sangria-colored curtains once they reached the backroom. It held any additional supplies and stock not put out in the shop, as well as Selene's work office and a set of rigged stairs that led up to their living space.

Bo and Andy kicked off their shoes before beginning the steep climb. Bo always had to keep a hand on the rail to not fall backwards. It was only when they reached the top that Bo remembered to turn back and tell Michael to take off his sneakers, but he looked down to find him already in his socks.

Andy smirked. "Don't worry. I already told him about your germophobia."

"I'm not a germaphobe." Bo huffed. "I just don't like it when you track dirt all across our carpet." But when he turned away, he smiled.

Bo guided them down the hallways, hoping to rush Michael out of the living room and away from the mess Selene had probably left behind. They pushed through his door, and Bo felt proud of himself when Michael whistled.

Bo had spent the last couple of years getting on the good side of the video and music store owners for the sole reason of getting his hands on all the posters that came through. They were plastered all along his wall and sloped ceiling. His shelves were lined with his endless cassette collection, some of which were Andy's that he had left over.

"You haven't even seen the best part." Andy raced over to jump on Bo's bed.

"Outside clothes!" Bo shouted.

"Germaphobe!" Andy called back before pulling off the curtains hung on the slanted ceiling to reveal a roof light window. He unlocked the latch and pushed the window open before climbing onto the roof. Michael looked between Bo and where Andy once was.

Bo sighed. "Just be careful. It's easy to fall off."

"You say that like you know from experience," Michael remarked.

"Not me. Andy."

"That makes more sense."

Bo tried not to mind when Michael climbed onto his bed and out the window after Andy. He was going to wash his sheets that night anyway. He followed suit.

Andy had already steadied Michael onto the flat top of the roof, and they sat with their feet dangling. "Remember when we accidentally left it open that one night?" Andy smiled, and Bo rolled his eyes as he joined them.

It was one of their first sleepovers together, and they were still so small that the bed felt huge when they shared it. Andy left the window open because he couldn't sleep without fresh air blowing in the room, but it had ended up raining. They'd woken up drenched and shivering, rapidly attempting to shut the heavy window before the water caused any permanent damage to Bo's room.

"Wow," Michael said. "You can see everything from up here."

Bo followed his gaze across town.

"It's alright." Bo shrugged. Andy shoved his shoulder slightly, causing Bo to lose his balance and almost tumble off. He swore violently and gripped onto Andy, who gripped onto Michael. "Shit, Andy!" But they were all laughing.

"I need to get started on my room. There are still boxes everywhere." Michael turned to Andy. "What's yours like?"

"It's not much." He copied Bo's words. "No, seriously. I have to share with my older brother even though he's off at college now, but he hates it when I move stuff around, so I'm basically banned from touching half of my own room."

"Isn't he going back later this week?" Bo asked. Andy nodded.

"You have a brother?" Michael chipped in.

"Two. And two sisters. I'm one of five."

"Jeez," Michael said. "I wish I had siblings."

"You really don't." Michael laughed, but Bo knew Andy didn't say it to be funny.

Bo heard the echo of Selene's voice from down below, and he called back. After a minute, she stuck her head out the window.

Bo looked nothing like his parents and everything like his aunt. Same wavy blond hair, same gray eyes, same pale skin. Just like Selene, Bo's cheeks were always flushed. All through summer from the heat and all through winter from the cold. His fair skin was still a bit pink from the days they spent lounging around the shore, but the tan would fade again in no time from the cloudy weather that Whalesborough was famous for. Unlike Bo, Andy had a tan all year long. A fact that he never let Bo forget.

"Oh! You *are* here." Selene said, but she was looking at Michael.

"Selene, this is—"

"Michael McKenzie from across the street. Thanks for all the packages." She gestured for the boys to follow. "Come on, the tea's getting cold."

Bo groaned, and Andy pretended to push him again before they all filed back down into his room, falling onto his bed ungracefully. When they met Selene in the living room, Bo was thankful to find that she had tidied up a bit.

She sat at their dining table, if you could call the worn-down desk that, sipping her tea. Three other cups sat surrounding her.

Bo knew this strange ritual well. She had done it for him on his very first night in this house after he had left home for the final time. The tea leaves were already seeped, so Bo took a savory sip. He wasn't particularly fond of Darjeeling, but it was easy for tasseography.

Andy drained his cup quickly and swirled the mug in his hand before flipping it over on a saucer Selene placed for them. Selene and Bo finished theirs not long after and did the same. Michael took the longest, clearly taking in the scene before him before trying his best to mimic those before him.

"I'll read yours first, Andy." Andy pushed his saucer towards Bo's aunt and watched as she studied it. She let a few *hm*'s and some *ah—interesting*'s before handing the cup back. "Hard work will pay off."

Andy put on a show of thanking Selene before she began to read her tea leaves. Bo took the time to inspect his own cup.

He didn't share his aunt's talent for spiritual insight, but he had picked up a few things from living with her for so long. He made note of the spiral of tea leaves near the handle—a tornado of misfortune approaching quickly. Bo frowned as he turned the cup more and looked along the sides. Small leaves speckled the rim like marching ants. Selene would remark on future difficulties that Bo would work to overcome.

He used a napkin to wipe away the message before watching Selene walk over to Michael's cup and flip it over.

Bo and Andy both awkwardly stretched across the table to peer at his reading.

"What do you see?" Selene asked.

"Um," Michael attempted, "A square?"

"There's no wrong answer," Selene said. "But think more broadly. Look at each spec. What does it make you think of?"

Michael swallowed and looked back at Bo, who shrugged. Michael examined the leaves closely. "Well, I mean—" He started. "I guess it kind of looks like a door."

"Hm." Selene tilted her head to the side.

"Is that right?"

Selene ignored his question. She took all their cups and brought them to the sink. "Are you boys sleeping over tonight?" She gave them a cheerful smile as she ran the water.

"Nah. We should probably try to fix our sleep schedule before school starts back up again." Andy said, rising from the table. Michael stood up too, rather swiftly.

"I'll walk you guys out." Bo tried to keep his voice casual, but he could feel his cheeks flushing. He watched from the steps as Andy and Michael slipped their shoes back on. "Sorry if she creeped you out. She doesn't mean to."

"It's okay," Andy responded, but they all knew Bo wasn't talking to him.

"Yeah, it's fine," Michael said. "Do you know what it means, though?"

"The door?" Bo tried to remember. "I think it has to do with something unusual. Or maybe being closed off. I don't know. It's mostly subjective. Besides, it's all—"

"Bullshit?" Michael finished.

Bo didn't say anything for a moment. "Sorry, again," he tried.

Michael smiled. "Don't worry about it. I had fun. Will she read my palm next time?"

"Or deal you some tarot cards?" Andy joined in.

"I think she'd rather interpret your dreams, if anything," Bo smirked.

Michael stiffened slightly but regained his composure briskly enough that Bo thought he'd imagined it. "Ha, maybe."

They left, and Bo clambered back up the stairs. Selene was still washing dishes.

"You embarrassed me," Bo said dully.

She looked up to watch him brush past her and towards his room. "Did I?"

"Yes." He slammed his door.

He knew he was being unfair to his aunt. He had no right to ask her to dilute herself for his sake, but he was tired of *this*.

It was like an early preview of what was to come during the school year. It was easier back when it was just Bo, when he could keep it away from Andy. But soon Michael would be roaming the halls with him, and he could only hide from his peers for so long.

And if Michael knew, then Andy would know.

He had so much love for Selene and so much to blame her for. He was forever grateful for the home she provided him with, and he would always resent her for choosing Whalesborough instead of somewhere else to live. Anywhere else.

The phone rang.

When he had turned fifteen, he had convinced Selene to let him put a landline next to his bed. Now he hated it.

He picked it up and slammed it back down. Bo was so sick of those calls.

At first, he thought they were just ghost calls, but now he's certain that it's his classmates getting a head start. He imagined what they would say when he walked into the school building.

Hearing voices again, Cassidy? Just like your psycho aunt. Sorry, I meant psychic. Is there much of a difference, though?

It rang again. He picked it up and held it to his ear. "What?" Bo snapped.

Static.

Breathing.

Nothing.

"If this is you, Dacre, I'm kicking your ass the second you walk into school," Bo threatened.

But it wasn't Warren Dacre. Instead, in the small voice of a little girl, there came a single...

Hello?

Then, the line went dead.

Ch. Six

Michael didn't get any sleep that night or the night after that. He was so exhausted he shook. So, when he met Bo and Andy at Selene's, they took one look at him and canceled their afternoon plans.

"No offense," Andy said. "But you look worse than my great-grandmother. And she's like, a hundred years old."

"It's true, she's terrifyingly ancient," Bo agreed.

"No, it's—" Michael was cut off by a yawn, which did nothing to help his case. "I really wanted to hang out today."

It was only four o'clock, but Michael was already swaying on his feet. His sleep schedule had only grown more worrying. He had tried avoiding sleep altogether. He could handle the exhaustion, but not the endless fear. His parents were pointedly ignoring the screams that tore him awake each night, but he found a pamphlet for a new psychologist from the mainland in his mother's drawer when he had gone looking for some hair gel.

Michael had to get this night terror thing under control before school started.

He wouldn't be able to make it through the day, much less pay attention in class, if he continued like this. He had almost dozed off at the register a few times, only to be jerked awake by the screaming baby like an alarm.

"It's fine, guys. What did you have planned?"

Bo and Andy exchanged a look, one that made Michael feel even more alienated.

They had been good at including Michael so far, but it was evidently clear that he was the outsider. Even if they had all been friends for years instead of a few days, Michael was sure it would be the same. It was just a founding, unspoken principle that Bo and Andy would always be *Bo and Andy*. Michael had to learn to accept that and find his place among them in a different way.

"We were just thinking of hitting up the video store and seeing if they have anything good," Andy said. "You really wouldn't be missing all that much."

"No, let's go. I haven't seen anything new in a while," Michael attempted.

"Michael. Dude," Andy said. "You look worse than death. And I've seen dead people."

Michael blinked slowly and fought to keep his eyes open.

"Joking. That was a joke. Fuck man, you're really out of it, aren't you?" Andy remarked.

Michael tried to curate a response, but whatever he said came out as a groan.

Bo said, "How about this? You go take a nap in my room real quick. We'll head down to the video store and get some snacks. Then we can all meet back up in an hour, well-rested and awake."

"Whoa. Inviting him to your bed before taking him out to dinner?"

Bo ignored this comment from Andy and turned to Michael instead. "Selene's out grocery shopping for now, but she won't mind when she gets back."

Michael opened his mouth to argue, but Bo cut him off again.

"I would make you go home. But I don't trust you not to fall asleep on the trolley ride over," Bo said. "Just go to sleep, man."

Which was easier said than done.

But when he kicked his shoes off before reaching the second floor and crashing into Bo's bed, he barely thought about the potential nightmares he'd had.

Michael woke up feeling his entire body.

He flailed so much that he tumbled out of bed and hit the floor hard enough to make him groan. When he looked up at the ceiling, he saw it was pitch black outside. *Shit*. He looked around for the time and found a radio clock on a bedside table. It was read at one o'clock in the morning. *Shit!*

Michael quietly left Bo's room and worked down the hallways in the dark, grasping at the walls to try and lead him through. He heard a crash and jumped backwards, only to realize it was some jumpscare from a horror movie left on in the living room.

He found Bo and Andy asleep on the couch together. Andy slumped across the cushions, his legs stretched out over Bo's lap, and Bo was asleep with his arms crossed and head tilted back. They must have fallen asleep halfway through the classic *Halloween* because Jamie Lee Curtis had just made it to the neighbor's house.

He heard a throat clearing behind him and turned around to find Selene in the kitchen, wrapped tightly in a bathrobe and matching slippers. Michael met her by the refrigerator, and she handed him a glass of ice-cold water.

Michael hadn't realized how thirsty he was until Selene was taking the empty glass from him and refilling it. He took the second one down more slowly.

"I'm sorry if I frightened you the other day," Selene said.

"Oh, you didn't at all," Michael whispered.

"Still, though. Bo wasn't too happy." She looked over to the two boys sleeping together on the couch. "I guess I just got a little over my head. It's been so long since Bo brought someone over. Who wasn't Andy, I mean."

"My mom's the same way." He remembered how he tried to avoid inviting people over to his house back in San Francisco. It wasn't that he was embarrassed by his parents, but sometimes he was embarrassed for them. Like when his dad asked a too-direct question that bordered on offensive, or when his mom complained loudly at a restaurant even though the waitress was two feet away.

"They tried to stay up for you," Selene told him. "They felt bad for waking you."

Michael had to admit that Selene was off-putting. Bo didn't exactly have the most welcoming or warm presence either, but he was aware of how his neutral face often came off as sour. Selene seemed completely oblivious to her uneasy aura. She didn't look mean, per se, but rather constantly macabre. Like whenever Michael was standing in front of her, she was watching an eerie stranger approach him from behind instead of looking at his eyes.

When Michael spoke with her, he had to fight the urge to look over his shoulder.

"Are you hungry?" She asked politely.

"No, I should probably be getting home and—Oh, shit!" He slapped a hand over his mouth. "Sorry. I'm so sorry. I just really need to call my mom.

"Oh, don't worry about that. I saw her at the grocery store, and I told her you were spending the night. She was excited." Selene smiled.

Michael racked his brain at the memory of Bo mentioning that Selene was out shopping before he'd fallen asleep. "Wait, but that was before..."

Right. Psychic.

"It's okay, I forget too."

"But," Michael brought a hand up to push his hair out of his face. "How does that even *work*?"

At that moment, it was all too much. The nightmares. The ghost stories. The woman who was standing before him. He didn't understand how he found himself so wrapped up in it so suddenly.

"It's more mundane than you're thinking. Look over there," Selene said softly. She pointed to the television where Jamie Lee Curtis was leaning on the door, breathing heavily. Michael Myers sat up and turned his head in her direction, but she hadn't seen him. She had no idea that it wasn't over yet. "It's just like that."

Michael furrowed his brows. "I don't understand."

"I am *you*. And *you* are Jamie Lee Curtis," she explained. "What may seem like the ending to you, I see the continuation. Not as simple as that. Or as clean cut, but in a sense, that's what it's like. A gut feeling that there's more to come. But it's not always the future."

"No?"

She shook her head. "Sometimes, they're from far back. Like flashbacks in a movie."

"Does it," Michael began, but was unsure of how he was going to ask this, "hurt?"

"If you suddenly remember you have a math quiz next period, it's more of a shock than anything. Does that make sense?"

Michael nodded and took another sip from his glass. The screams of *Halloween* echoed through the living room. He was too tired to think clearly, but a small voice in his head whispered, *If you believe her about this, what's to stop you from believing the rest?*

What if there really were ghosts in Whalesborough?

Michael hadn't had a nightmare within the nine hours he had been asleep. He hadn't so much as woken with a numb finger. It had been just like it had been back in California when he thought he'd outgrown the nightmares.

What if there wasn't anything wrong with Michael?

What if it were the house instead?

"Can you see ghosts?" He hadn't even meant to ask it.

Selene regarded him. "Being psychic and being a medium are two very different things. Though their roots of clairvoyance are similar, I suppose."

"But are they—" *Real?*

"Yes."

"You're sure?"

"I don't have to see air to know it's there, do I?"

Michael worked to process this. Then he said, "I think I'm being haunted."

"You, or your house?"

"My house, I guess. But it seems personal." He swallowed. "I have... these dreams."

"Dreams?"

"Nightmares."

"Ah." Selene paused to pour herself a cup of tea. Michael watched intently as she grabbed some loose-leaf tea and an infuser.

"Sometimes I find myself stuck in bed, completely paralyzed. My mom took me to some doctors to get me diagnosed, but I wasn't put on meds or anything. They used to only happen once in a while, so it was manageable. Just something I had to get over, you know?"

She hummed in response as the water began to boil. Selene made sure to take it off the stove before the kettle whistled.

"But now they're happening all the time. Even if I fall asleep for a little bit at home, I see her."

"Her?" She raised her gaze to him as she poured herself a cup.

Michael paused.

"It wasn't just about not being able to move. I used to see stuff. People over my bed or figures in the corner of my room. Back in California, though, it was also broad, like nobody specific. But here, I see the same girl over and over. And last night..." He pulled up his sleeve to show Selene his bandaged forearm. "I woke up with glass in my bed."

He hadn't told anyone yet. It had been around three in the morning when he could finally move again, and he felt his arm aching terribly. When he shifted out of his sheets, he was met with a sharp pain, like needles pricking and sticking in his veins. Michael had gone to the bathroom to flick on the light when he saw his arm soaked in his blood, the sparkling glass shards reflecting in the light.

He grimaced as he grabbed some tweezers to gently remove each bit. Luckily, they were big enough to be removed rather easily, and he was able to rinse away the blood before wrapping his injury carefully.

When he'd returned to bed, he realized how lucky he had been. His entire bed was littered with shattered glass. Later, Michael found some empty picture frames in the hallway that were missing the glazing over the pictures.

"I thought I was going crazy at first, but I didn't have any nightmares just now." He shook his head. "Only over there."

Selene gently placed her fingers on his wound before pulling her hand back. Michael shrugged his sleeve back down to cover his arm. She reached for the tea and began to chug it.

"I just hoped you could help somehow." He suddenly felt awkward and ashamed of himself for bringing it up. He decided to keep his mouth shut about the fact that he'd still seen Andy's doppelgänger hanging outside every once in a while. It seemed harder to explain.

Selene smacked her lips and flipped the cup in her hands. Then she brought it closer over to Michael, where they could both examine it carefully. When she revealed the inside, Michael recognized the familiar outline.

Selene said what they were both thinking.

"Doors are opening."

Ch. Seven

Andy just had to survive one more night with his older brother, then his room would be his own again.

Jaime was the last of his older siblings to leave the house and return to college off the island. Louis and Angela, the eldest twins, had stopped by momentarily at the beginning of summer before returning west to prepare for their first years of graduate school. Jaime was meant to go back to the Midwest for his senior year, but for some reason, he'd decided to stick around and bother Andy endlessly.

When the Romero-Almada household was full, it was packed like a tin of sardines.

Great-grandmothers, grandparents, parents, the occasional visiting aunt or uncle, and the five children made it difficult to take two steps without bumping into a relative. It was never a dull moment, truly.

Andy had done his best to avoid his older brother whenever possible. It seemed all they did now was argue. Truthfully, they had gotten along well when they were younger. All five of them had. But moving away had changed things. Or rather, it made things more obvious. Especially when the calls stopped coming through.

The art of avoidance was a magic Andy had perfected. Whether that be ignoring his mother's cries from downstairs when she asked him to do chores or pretending he didn't notice his father's disappointing gaze when he brought home a report card, he was able to distract and direct focus to some other problem or child, or problem child. His best act was one of disappearance. Leaving early in the morning, coming home late at night, locking himself in his room when he had to.

The last part was difficult when the spare twin bed on the left wall was occupied instead of being empty.

"Where have you been?" Jaime had been reading a textbook in the dim bedroom, clearly staying awake to wait for Andy.

Andy shrugged and emptied the contents of his pockets onto his bedside table. He turned his back to Jaime and began to strip off his dirty clothes.

"You missed dinner."

"I ate." Not really, but it's not like Jaime actually cared.

"Mom was upset."

She usually was when it came to Andy.

"She'll get over it," Andy muttered.

Andy slipped on an oversized sleeping shirt, only realizing that it was a hand-me-down from Jaime after he turned back around and saw his brother's gaze. The Romero-Almada siblings looked similar enough in particular features, but never as a whole. A set of almond eyes here, matching satin hair the color of umber brown there, and similar wide lips that lacked a distinct cupid bow across the board. In small pieces, they were identical, but once a step back was taken, the Romero-Almada siblings looked like a puzzle that had been broken into five sections.

Well, mostly they weren't identical. Unfortunately, Andy was embarrassed to say that he looked like a knock-off of Jaime. And since Andy was the younger, *he* was to carry the shame of mimicking. Their resemblance only worked to broadcast their differences even louder. Where Jaime was tall and broad, Andy was short and wiry. Where Jaime was intelligent and ambitious, Andy was...not that.

"Don't be such an asshole," Jaime snapped.

Too late, but he bit his tongue.

Andy rolled his eyes and went over to his bed. He was exhausted from the past sleepover at Bo's and the adventure-filled day with Michael's newfound energy. It was only after he reached for his sheets did he noticed the change.

Andy wasn't exactly the cleanest person, especially compared to Bo and his neat-freakness, but he was always sure to make his bed. Blanket and comforter stretched tightly across the bed and spread flat, tucked into his mattress, and topped with his aged pillows. He paused.

The top corner of the blanket wasn't folded the way Andy had left it.

"Did you—" But when he turned around and saw the papers he kept hidden under his mattress in Jaime's hand, he had his answer. "What the hell?"

Jaime began to flip through the pages of failed assignments, making a show out of taunting Andy. "Were you seriously trying to hide these under your mattress?"

Andy stormed over and reached to snatch the papers out of Jaime's hand, but his brother whipped them out of the way at the last second, leaving Andy grabbing at air. "What?" Andy worked to find a counter. "Disappointed you didn't find any Playboys?"

When Jaime was sixteen, he'd been grounded for a month after their mother had found his dirty magazines hidden in their shared closet, tucked away in Jaime's old winter jacket that he'd long outgrown. Andy had been eleven at the time, but he worked to always hold tight to the memory of his older brother's humiliation. Jaime had always been their parents' favorite, so when he screwed up, Andy made sure to take note and revisit the event. Jaime pulled a sour face at the mention of the incident.

"Disappointed? Yes." Jaime tossed the papers in the air. "Seriously, Alejo? I get that being a straight-A student isn't something everyone can do, but your highest grade being a C? It's just embarrassing."

He bristled as he bent over to pick up his old grades.

"You know what this means, right?" Jaime murmured.

He wasn't stupid. Andy wasn't smart, but he wasn't *stupid*.

"I already asked them to transfer me out." Andy crumbled the pages and dumped them in the trash bin. "They won't let me change schools."

He wasn't really sure why he kept the classwork. At first, it was to hide his failure from his parents, but they found out about that as soon as his report card came in through the mail. Over his sophomore year, he just kept adding to the pile more and more until it coated the entire bed frame.

Sometimes, he'd pull out some of the papers to try to motivate himself. Most of the time, they just left him more discouraged than before.

"Of course they won't. It's our damn heritage." Jaime said. The word echoed through Andy's mind. *Heritage, heritage, heritage.* "They'd pay whatever to make sure we all went to Joseph's."

In Andy's case, thousands of dollars.

The Romeros had been attending Saint Joseph's Private School since it was founded in the '30s. They had been some of the first students to be accepted on a scholarship, useful for their notably large family, and the school had become a tradition for generations. Saint Joseph's or nothing. Andy had been accepted on the same scholarship as his three older siblings for his freshman year. He lost it all after he almost flunked out a few months ago.

He had managed to scrape by with grades high enough to pass all his classes and continue to the next grade, but his scholarship had been revoked completely. His parents had sat him down, demanding explanations, but he didn't have an acceptable one.

He just couldn't do it.

In class, his mind grew numb. He swore he could feel his brain dripping out of his ears and onto the linoleum floor. If he wasn't fighting to stay awake in class, he was entranced by everything other than the lesson on the board. And if he was paying attention and giving his dedication to what was being taught, it didn't even matter in the end because it went right over his head.

The only class he had managed to get a foot through the door in was English, but that was because he'd always liked reading. Most people didn't believe this fact about him, but Andy often had two or three library books checked out at a time. More than that, his own collection of books wasn't exactly lacking. His copy of *The Catcher in the Rye* had been read to ruin, lines of Andy's own annotation dotting along the pages. *Language*, that's what it was. Andy wouldn't need math or science later, but his words were everything to him.

"Do you know how much money you're making them waste?"

Of course, he knew.

He begged them to put him in the public school and save them all the trouble. That way, even if he failed, it wouldn't be burning any holes in their wallets. But he was a Romero, so he had to go to Saint Joseph's.

"Alejandro." His attention snapped back over to Jaime. "There's just *no way* you're this brainless. You're clearly just not putting in the effort."

He didn't say *I'm trying my best* because Jaime wouldn't believe him. School had always come so easily for his siblings, especially their youngest, Mila, who had managed to skip a grade and join Andy as a junior a year early. He knew Jaime couldn't imagine *not* getting it. Why was it so simple for them and not for Andy? Everyone seemed to want to know but had yet to figure it out.

"Whatever," Andy dismissed Jaime and turned to climb into bed. His older brother hopped out of bed and yanked the covers off Andy.

"Listen to me, dumbass." Jaime hissed. "Things aren't looking good for us financially. So you'd better get your shit together and actually put an effort into your education, or you're gonna be stuck rotting away on this stupid island with all these fucking spirits."

Andy's face scrunched up.

Everyone was always talking about leaving Whalesborough and how much of a tragedy it would be to stick around. *This is home*, Andy thought. *Why is everyone so eager to get away?*

"And being a smug asshole is the kind of thing you only get to be if you aren't flunking your classes. You get one or the other, not both. So either be stupid and happy, or study harder." That must have been the logic Jaime lived by because it perfectly summed him up.

"How do you know I'm an asshole all the time if you don't even live here anymore?" Andy argued.

"Oh, please. Mom told me about your 'moods' lately." He crossed his arms over his chest. Then more quietly, he added, "She's trying her best to keep our family together, and you're making it harder on her for no reason. It makes her upset that you're always out and never want to see her anymore."

It's the other way around.

"También la molesta que ya no hables español en casa," Jaime said. "I told her that it's not her fault. I told her you're probably just going through a phase where you're trying to be white like your little friend. *Tonto.*"

Andy clenched his jaw at the mention of Bo. He didn't feel like telling Jaime that it had nothing to do with the fact that he was Cuban or Portuguese (or whatever else they were) and everything to do with the fact that he was a Romero-Almada. It was also especially hypocritical coming from Jaime, who insisted everyone start using the *American* pronunciation when calling his name. So instead, Andy said, "*Como se dice*, mind your own fucking business."

Jaime sighed, as if Andy had just proved his point. Which he probably had. "I can't even find it in me to be mad. I'm just embarrassed, Alejandro. Do you even realize how pathetic you look to everyone else?"

He wasn't stupid.

He blinked rapidly.

"Don't. Don't cry. You're seventeen now. You're too old to throw a tantrum," Jaime said.

"Sixteen."

"What?"

"I'm still sixteen."

Jaime let his face fall from the stern gaze he had held it in. His older brother roughly tossed the sheets back over Andy before stomping over to his bed and tugging the chain to their lamp off.

The brothers lay in silence.

Then, "Where do you even go?"

"Bo's. Or just out."

"Every night?"

"Yes."

"All summer?"

"Where else would I be?"

"I don't know. Secret girlfriend or something." He said it like it was plausible. It wasn't, not with Andy's life now. He was too busy with other things to spend time on girls he barely even liked. "I'm not trying to be mean."

"Yes, you are," Andy snapped. "You love it when you get to remind me that you're better than me. You eat this shit up."

Crickets chirped from outside.

He hadn't meant to say it out loud. Those grievances were for Bo's ears alone when it was late and Andy's chest felt too heavy in bed.

"You don't have to do it."

It.

Andy knew what Jaime refused to speak out loud.

"Just because it was Dad's life doesn't mean it has to be yours too," Jaime continued. "It was over a long time ago."

"I'm going to sleep."

He heard shuffling from the bed over. Andy closed his eyes tightly and tried to pretend he was the only one in the room.

"I just don't want you to wake up one day and realize you've wasted your life on this place."

"That won't happen."

Nobody understood it. Not his family, not his best friend, and sometimes, not even himself. His love for the town was so much bigger than him. How do you explain the vastness of outer space to someone confined to a single room their entire life? How do you place a grain of sand into someone's hand and describe how deserts and beaches exist? How does Andy defend his love of Whalesborough to people who hate it?

"Besides," Andy said, lying with his back facing his older brother, "someone needs to stay behind to look after the basement."

Ch. Eight

Michael received a call from Andy at the crack of dawn.

"Bo told me everything," Andy said. "We're coming over to yours later."

"Wait, wait," Michael rubbed the sleep away from his eyes. "Told you what?"

"About the nightmares. About the ghosts. Selene told him, and he told me."

Michael was awake enough to frown. "I thought Bo didn't gossip," He murmured, definitely bitter.

He wasn't sure what he thought would happen after he told Selene about his sleeping troubles, but he supposed he should've assumed she'd tell her nephew. And of course, what Bo knew, Andy would know soon enough. It was only a matter of time, though. Michael's eye bags didn't disappear after a good night's rest at the Cassidy's, and they'd only grown to look more sullen over time. It would've been hard to avoid the other boys' curious glances after a while.

"He doesn't," Andy defended. "He wasn't tattling on you. He was concerned."

Michael sighed and fell onto his back. "So, what are we doing?"

He could hear Andy's smirk through the landline. "Well, I just rewatched *The Exorcist*."

Michael hung up.

Luckily, his parents had left the house before Bo or Andy arrived. Andy came with a giant duffel bag that clanged and clunked, and Bo came with furrowed brows and a nagging frown. Michael brought them to his bedroom, or as Andy called it, the spirit's den.

"Damn, you really haven't unpacked anything," Andy remarked as he let his bag fall to the floor.

Michael shrugged because it was true. Cardboard boxes sat stacked in the corner. His desk had only been used as more storage for his packed belongings. His empty shelves were collecting dust. The single aspect of his space that seemed truly lived in was his bed, which was a mess in the center of the room.

"What did you bring?" Michael asked.

Andy worked to unzip the duffel and brought out an arrangement of strange objects, most of which Michael recognized from Selene's shop. Andy handed a bundle of sage to Bo, who seemed just as confused as Michael about the entire situation.

He pulled out a glass of salt, some crystals and pretty stones, chalk, candles, and a pendulum. Michael noticed how the duffel bag still sat full on the ground. When he squinted his eyes, he thought he'd seen the shine of a glass jar before Andy was zipping it back up again.

"First things first," Andy ordered, then he dumped at *least* three tablespoons worth of salt in his hand and chucked it at Michael. He had just enough time to shield his eyes before he felt the sprinkle of the grains hit him.

"What the heck?" Michael shook out his hair.

"Salt is good for warding off spirits, you know? Like how they make salt rings in movies, and spirits can't cross the boundaries. Duh." Andy worked to explain. Then he took out a matchbox from his pocket and lit one. He grabbed Bo's wrist with his free hand to bring the sage close to the flame and get it burning. Smoke began to fill the air in Michael's room as Andy told Bo to take laps and wave the bundle around.

"Should I open a window?" Michael coughed.

"Dude. Sage is good for cleansing evil spirits and energies. You want this ghost to stay here?"

"What?"

A day ago, Andy and Bo were going off about how ridiculous the town and its obsessions with the dead were. Or rather, Bo was going off, and Andy was nodding along eagerly. Now, they were acting like devoted hippies trying to bring Michael some sort of salvation.

"What's next..." Andy murmured to himself. "Oh yeah." Then he took the chalk and walked over to Michael's bed. The frame was made of wood and looked like it came from a stereotypical bedtime story. A tall and round headboard with an intricate design carved into the mahogany, long enough to fit Michael even after his latest growth spurt, sturdy enough to hold even when he tossed and turned in the night.

Andy tossed a pillow to the end of the bed and began to trace a design on the frame right where Michael's head would be when he slept. It looked like Andy had tried to draw a crowbar at first, but gave a circle at the bottom and horizontal lines across the middle. He took a step back to examine his handiwork, and after he seemed smug enough with himself, he handed the piece of chalk to Michael. "Retrace it when you need to." He advised.

"My arm hurts," Bo said from the other side of the room.

"Five more laps, Cowboy."

"What did you draw?" Michael clutched the chalk in his hand, though he despised the texture.

"It's a symbol, or rune, whatever you wanna call it. I think it's Greek?" Andy said.

"Norse," Bo corrected as he passed them.

"Norse, right. Yeah, Vikings and all those macho guys with beards. Anyway, it's supposed to help

protect you when you sleep." Andy smiled at
Michael. "I feel like I'm missing something. Bo, what
am I missing?"

Bo continued to wave the smoking sage around
wildly as he shrugged.

"It'll come to me," Andy said. "How did you
sleep?"

"Bad," Michael said automatically. Then he felt
guilty and corrected himself. "Fine. Better than
usual."

"Do you still dream of her?"

Michael rubbed the back of his neck. "It's
mostly the same. I usually just see her above my bed,
screaming and crying. She doesn't even touch me,
really. But like, I know if she could, she'd hurt me."
Bo stopped pacing around the room. Andy's smile
had dropped.

"Shit, dude," Bo said.

"Sorry, it's so stupid." Michael sighed.

Andy said, "I don't think it's stupid.

"But I know I look crazy." Bo and Andy
exchanged a look. "Stop, just— It's just my head
messing with the rest of me. I've dealt with this for a
while. You don't have to…" He gestured around the
room, then dropped his arms. "I don't even know
what this is, actually."

Bo opened Michael's window and stubbed out
the burning sage. Andy sat down on the floor and

yanked at Michael's pant leg before he finally joined him below.

"We don't think we're crazy," Andy said. "It's like a medical thing, right? Those nightmares?"

Michael tossed his head to the side. "Kinda. I was diagnosed with sleep paralysis when I was twelve. It basically just means sometimes I get stuck between being asleep and being awake, so my head is working, but the rest of my body isn't. And sometimes I get... hallucinations."

Bo joined them on the floor.

"Most of the time it's just the paralyzing part, though. I'm afraid, but there's nothing to *be* afraid of. Just general panic. But other times I see figures or shadows or, I don't even know. Just weird stuff that freaks me out."

He hadn't talked about this in years. The last time he allowed himself to describe the sensations was in therapy. His mom forced him to go to. After they'd figured out what was wrong with him, it became a sort of taboo subject at home. It wasn't exactly dinner conversation worthy, and there was no way Michael would willingly bring it up to his school friends.

For the first two years, he'd been so paranoid living with it that he'd created a system with his mother to ensure he'd never have to go to sleepovers. He'd simply cover the end of the telephone and call his mother over, who'd then tell Michael's friends that she was very sorry, but Michael couldn't go out until he managed to clean his room, and it truly was getting quite nauseating, wasn't it, Mikey? His friends were disappointed but understanding. Besides, it was better to be known as a slob than a freak.

"Fuck, man," Andy said. "But it's all like, mental stuff?"

Michal shrugged.

"Okay, I can work with that." Then he jumped right back up and began to darken the room. Andy shut the window and drew the curtains, closed the door and turned off the lights, and worked to make the bedroom as dim as possible. Then he brought over the candles and used them to create a circle.

He lit each wick one at a time as he spoke. "I'm going to be so honest with you. I don't think you're crazy about the nightmares. I *do* think you're crazy over the ghost stuff. The Beckham girl isn't real."

"But Selene..." Michael murmured.

"Bo, wanna take it from here?" Andy turned as he began to place crystals as well.

Bo groaned but complied. "I love my aunt, Michael. I really do. But the psychic thing is all just an act. The entire practice focuses on being broad enough that it triggers something in your brain, like a certain memory or thought, which has you connect the dots in a way that makes it plausible. Like when she tells me that today will be a day of bad news, and I find out I bombed my chemistry quiz. Did that happen because she said it would, or do I just suck at chemistry?"

"Bad example, you've never failed any other quiz before," Andy said.

"Whatever. The point is, you can't believe what she tells you. Not because she has some ulterior motive or anything, but because she's always been paranoid, and this is the best way she can cope with it. By turning it into something like magic." He turned away at this last sentence, eyes fixed on the candle.

"I still don't understand what *this* has to do with *that*," Michael said. Andy had just finished sprinkling some extra salt in Michael's and Bo's hair before adding some to his own and taking his place on the floor.

"This is a counterattack," Andy explained. "You said it's all in your head?"

Michael nodded.

"Ever heard of a placebo effect?" Andy said. "It's a treatment that's a total sham. Faking it until you make it. Usually, it only works if the patient is none the wiser, but..." Andy reached out to grab Bo's hand, who seemed taken aback but held it nonetheless. "If the issue also lacks reality, how do you treat it? Can you fake a fake?"

"Two negatives make a positive," Bo commented.

Andy smirked. "The problem is your head making fake hauntings, fueled by fake ghost stories, emphasized by fake psychic readings. But if we treat it like it's completely real and take the right measures, then maybe you'll finally be able to get a good night's rest."

It was the kindest thing anyone had ever done for him. Besides his parents choosing to raise him, but they had always told him that they didn't want him to feel like it was an act of service, so he disregarded the thought.

"We cleansed and protected, and basically boobytrapped your room in case there *was* a ghost. And now we're going to hold a séance to prove there isn't one."

The candles flickered out.

Ch. Nine

"Oops," Andy said before reaching to light them again. "Anyway, where was I? Oh yeah, séance."

"Are you messing with me right now?" Michael asked. "Because if you are, I'd prefer if you'd cut it out."

Andy went for Bo's hand again, who pulled it away. Andy sighed and said, "Hear me out. It's not serious, remember? It's to ease your subconscious. If we do this and prove there's no ghost, maybe you'll be able to relax and get some sleep. And if some spooky shit *does* go down, we took prior precautions all around your room so you'll still feel safe. Make sense?"

Unfortunately, Michael could follow Andy's logic. It didn't make it any easier to understand, though. This was *Andy*. Mostly, Michael was wondering how Andy even knew about all this cleansing and communicating with spirits if he rarely indulged in the town's obsession.

"I just," Michael began. Then he got a closer look at Andy in the dark and saw something flicker in his eyes. A sort of desperation. "Okay, let's do it."

"Seriously?" Bo mumbled.

"As if you weren't gonna go through with it," Andy said.

"I'll do it if you guys are, but *come on*."

"We're not doing it because we believe. We're doing it for Michael."

"Yeah, Bo. We're doing it for Michael," Michael mimicked. "For me."

Bo sighed and grabbed Andy's hand in his right and Michael's in his left. Michael could feel the smooth, flat edge of his middle finger. Over the past couple of days, he caught himself staring at it and pondering but was unable to make himself ask. Andy had noticed his gaze and pulled him aside to ward him off, but still. Michael tried to focus his thoughts on the issue at hand. Hands. Bo's hand. Dammit.

"Start us off, Bo?" Andy said as he closed his eyes.

"What? Why me?"

"You're the one with the psychic aunt."

"Being psychic isn't the same as—"

"Whatever, just say some kind of heebie-jeebie BS to get this ball rolling."

Michael stifled a laugh. This was supposed to be serious, after all.

Bo took a breath before staring. "So, um."

"Be confident," Andy whispered. "And close your eyes."

"Close *your* eyes."

"Everybody, close your eyes," Michael said.

Silence, once more.

"We're here to speak with the Beckham girl. We welcome any spirits to join us and make their presence known."

Michael heard the wind pick up outside his bedroom window. Even though he knew it wasn't real and that there was some underlying humor to the entire situation, he could feel his heart picking up pace in his chest. With it thumping against his rib cage rapidly, he wondered if Bo could feel his pulse through his hand.

"Are you with us?"

They all held their breaths to keep the room quiet. Michael wasn't exactly sure what they were listening for. Would they hear whispers? A shatter of glass? The sound of a pin dropping? How do the dead reach out from beyond the grave?

He felt Bo squeeze his hand quietly and hiss something out to Andy, who whispered back furiously.

Michael ignored them and shut his eyes tighter.

Are you here? He thought. *Are you real?*

He wanted to believe Andy and Bo. He wanted to believe Selene, too. He wanted to believe that everything was in his head and that he was in no true danger. He wanted to believe his gut and that there was something more going on.

Michael McKeznie wanted to believe that he wasn't out of his mind.

Would I even know? Would I know if I was crazy?

Everything was so much easier back in San Francisco when ghosts were just something limited to his cassette tapes.

"Andy," Bo warned.

"What?"

"Be quiet."

He *was* breathing rather loudly. Michael thought perhaps he wasn't the only one nervous between the three of them and felt some relief in that.

Maybe it had nothing to do with the ghost. Maybe it was just the house. Strange and old and unhaunted, but definitely rebarbative. Something is wrong at a physical and aesthetic level, but not spiritual. Maybe it was the lead paint getting to him. Maybe it was the howls he heard from the outside when he lay in bed. Maybe it was the creak of the stairs, the constant tapping of the bathroom sink, and the scurrying of mice he heard under the floorboards.

Maybe, maybe, maybe.

He felt Andy jump back violently.

"Shit!" Andy exclaimed. Michael's eyes shot open to see Andy rubbing his forearm. "Ow, fuck."

"What happened?"

"I don't know. I must have accidentally gotten too close to the flame or something." He took his hand away to reveal a small burn the size of a penny on his skin. It didn't look that serious, but Michael wasn't going to judge. "Sorry, we probably shouldn't have broken the circle. It's supposed to allow bad energies to— *What the fuck?*"

Andy suddenly leapt across the spiritual circle and gripped Bo's face in two hands. In the dark, it was hard to tell what had captured Andy's attention. With everything lit in the dull orange of the candles, Bo appeared as a wax figure. He was the palest of the three of them, by far, but he'd appeared sunken from the shadows. Diluted, in a sense. His blonde hair looked dusted, his gray eyes appeared clouded, and his thin lips seemed blue from the cold. The only color of his that remained was his pink cheeks, which looked like rose buds blossoming from his skin.

The red matched the blood coming from his ears.

"Shit, man. Are you okay? Can you hear me?" Andy was frantic, practically buzzing.

Bo reached his own hands up to Andy's wrist and slowly brought them back down. "Yeah, I can hear you, what—" But then he got a look at his blood coating Andy's fingertips, and his face morphed into confusion. "Oh."

"*Oh?*" Andy echoed back. Bo shrugged. Andy was exasperated. He dragged his friend up to his feet by the armpits and steadied him, though Bo seemed to be completely fine. "Yeah, no. Screw this."

Michael felt his stomach drop briefly before Bo squirmed out of Andy's grip and spoke up. "Seriously? Five seconds ago, you were so into all this supernatural stuff. Now you're calling it off?" Michael tried not to show his agreement.

"Dude, you're bleeding out of your ears. Isn't that like, cancer or some shit?" Andy said.

"It's *fine*." Bo crossed his arms.

Andy opened his mouth, but only a strangled noise came out, as if Bo had completely stumped him.

"Fine? Fine?" Andy kept repeating.

Michael stood up then as well and began to turn on all the lights. "Do you need a doctor or..."

"No! It's not— It really *is* fine." Bo paused. "I used to get them as a kid."

"That's not true," Andy interjected.

"Before my mom died, smartass."

Michael knew there was a reason Bo lived with his aunt and not with his father on the mainland. Andy had told him briefly about how Bo moved when he was eight. He never told him why. Michael had never asked. It just seemed like one of those things that he would learn if Bo ever decided to tell.

Of course, his time at Robinson's had gotten him acquainted with some other kids his age by now. He didn't enjoy their company as much as Andy or Bo. Besides, Bo was right when he said everyone in Whalesborough liked to gossip, especially when they caught Michael working across the street from the town's most haunted shop.

It made him feel dirty when he'd listened to other kids go on and on about the Cassidy's as if they weren't a door over. Most of the gossip was told as if an urban legend, like any other ghost story in the town. Other comments were made in ways Michael could only assume were purposely derogatory.

It was strange, he thought, that nobody said the same things about Andy or his family. Bo and Andy were always hanging around, yet while the Cassidy's were ostracized, the Romero-Almada's seemed esteemed. It wasn't wealth, not so much as a snipe at the family, but more of an objective fact. Michael knew that they were one of the *old* families, those who had resided on the island the longest.

"I don't know. Doctors said it was ruptured eardrums or something. Sometimes I hear a buzzing or ringing in my ear, or even a high frequency. But mostly they're just like a nosebleed. Nothing serious, I promise," Bo explained.

Michael relaxed, but Andy did not. "I still think I should take you home." He turned to Michael. "Sorry, man. But, you know..."

Michael did know. Bo came first, obviously.

Bo and Andy. Andy and Bo. Michael, somewhere distant but in arm's reach.

He didn't feel as bitter about it as he thought he might have.

"Yeah, yeah. Thanks for everything, though. Maybe I'll actually be able to get some sleep before school starts." Michael smiled.

"Ugh, don't remind me." Andy reached up to bring a hand down his face, but remembered his fingers were still covered in Bo's blood and flinched. "Can I use your bathroom real quick?"

Michael pointed to the way of the bathroom down from his room. Bo helped him finish tidying up from the ritual. He had attempted to rub the blood away, smearing it along the side of his neck until it dried flaky. He seemed fine. Seemed.

"Thanks again," Michael said, because he couldn't bear the silence any longer. "I know you don't like this kind of thing."

"It's okay. Andy was excited about helping you out. I mean, obviously, I was, too. But he was ready to go the extra mile, I guess." Bo rubbed his eyes. "He really likes you."

Michael paused for a moment. "Yeah?"

"Yeah. I do too. He doesn't really hang out with other people, which is weird because he's so good... You know, at talking and making friends. Andy usually kept to me, though. Or to himself. I'm glad he made an exception for you."

Michael felt himself grow flush. "I don't know if what he did is gonna work, but it's the thought that counts. He seemed very... equipped." They both laughed.

"It's so like him to be totally serious up until the moment it actually matters." Bo bit his lip to stop himself from grinning.

Michael smiled too, but was a bit confused. "You mean when he dropped it to make sure you were okay?"

"Nah, before that. During the séance. He couldn't keep his mouth shut." Michael furrowed his eyebrows at this. Bo caught on. "He kept whispering."

But he hadn't. It was silent.

Completely silent.

And though he knew it was terrible, Michael felt some sort of relief at that. Bo had heard whispers coming from none of them. The thought that Michael wasn't the only one imagining things in the house was a welcome one.

Andy called out for them in the other room.

When Michael got there, the first thing he noticed was Andy's hands. Unwashed, still stained red with Bo's blood. "I just came in, and it was like this," Andy said nervously.

The second thing Michael noticed was that the bathroom mirror was completely shattered.

Ch. Ten

"I look so fucking stupid." Andy's voice came muffled through the closet.

Bo rolled his eyes but smiled. Andy's mother had finished tailoring his school uniform, and he had decided to come over and try it on at Bo's just as he always did on the night before the first day of school.

This year was different, though, because it was no longer Bo and Andy, but Michael as well. The new boy sat on the floor, his back pressed against Bo's bed frame. His head was tilted back, and his eyes shut wearily. Unfortunately, Andy's placebo effect had only been ineffective in helping Michael, especially since the shattering of the bathroom mirror had remained a mystery.

At the angle Bo found himself at, sitting on his bed, he had a perfect view of the thin scar that went through Michael's left eyebrow. Bo absentmindedly pressed a thumb on the flat part of his missing finger.

Andy came out of the closet with his hands picking at his blazer cuffs. Saint Joseph's dress code included pretentious uniforms of deep maroon and brown. Andy had decided to bring over the entire outfit, made up of a button-up undershirt that Andy always managed to wrinkle under a knitted vest, and a purple blazer passed down from his elder brothers. The school's crest was polished on his breast pocket. Bo couldn't help but find some amusement in the shorts that went down to Andy's knees, the same color as his blazer, while watching as Andy scuffed at his brown socks with his foot.

Bo pressed his lips together.

"Don't laugh," Andy said.

Bo responded, "I'm not."

"I'm talking to Michael."

Bo averted his gaze at Michael, who had opened an eye and brought a hand to his mouth to hide a smile. "I'm so glad I'm going to the public school."

"Fuck off." But there was little bite to it. Andy went over to Bo's desk, where he slung his tie over the wooden chair. He tossed it around his neck and put effort into completing the uniform.

Michael smirked. "You like using that word a lot."

"What? Fuck?" Andy struggled with the knots. "I don't know, I guess. Do I say it that often?"

"A bit," Michael said. "I don't have a problem with it or anything. I was just saying."

"Yeah, well..." Andy still worked to make the tie when Bo came over to help him. He let his arms fall to his side as Bo undid his fruitless efforts. "It's just so versatile, you know?"

Bo scoffed.

"It is! It's an exclamation or an interjection, and a noun or an adverb," Andy rambled on. "There are so many ways you can use it."

"You don't have to defend your dirty mouth, Andy," Bo said as he finished with Andy's tie and brought it tighter to his neck.

"You're not any better," Andy said.

"I barely use the word 'fuck'."

"No," Michael chimed in, "but you use shit plenty."

"Bullshit," Bo responded instinctively. He realized his error as the others started to laugh at him. "Whatever," he playfully shoved Andy back and flopped into his bed.

In less than twelve hours, the three of them would be waking up and getting ready for the first day of school, but for now, it was the last night of summer, and they had nothing better to do than laugh at each other.

Bo tried not to think of tomorrow. It would come regardless of his endless dwelling and would sweep him off his feet in the current that was high school. Summer was a time of pleasant limbo, when days blurred together and everything was simple, and he wasn't ready to leave quite yet.

School brought piles of work, deadlines, and people who weren't Andy.

The thought of Michael being there wasn't exactly soothing either. For so long, he had been able to keep school separate from the rest of his life. Like a small box that was rotten on the inside, but as long as he kept the lid shut, nobody else would be able to notice the stench.

He knew word had traveled around, as it always did. But the thing about Andy was that, despite being a sucker for gossip, he only believed what Bo told him directly. Lying to Andy had never been his intention, but it was easier to weave stories of Bo's many friends who welcomed him to school each day with open arms than the truth. It was better this way, anyway.

However, he wouldn't be able to hide it now. Michael would be right there with him.

Bo wasn't *ready* for summer to be over.

He let Andy and Michael talk about their plans for the upcoming school year. Andy jabbed at Bo's side when Michael mentioned track. "I knew it. You're a total jock," Andy said.

"Track doesn't make someone a jock," Bo quipped. "*I* do track."

"Oh, yeah," Andy said and stuck his tongue out at Bo. Michael was obviously the most fit of the three of them. He had a square shape to him and thick arms, which would have been threatening if not for the way he always shrank in on himself.

They began to talk about the single school bus that ran through the town. Saint Joseph's didn't have a bus, so Andy had always taken the trolley with his sister. Bo told Michael it was better to walk or ride a bike instead of waiting for the bus, as it never showed up on time. It was always thirty minutes early or thirty minutes late. Michael told them he didn't have a bike, and Bo offered him his own while he worked to get one.

"When did your parents want you home?" Andy asked Michael.

"It doesn't matter. They're off on the mainland, so my dad could write an article," Michael told them.

Andy said, "So your parents just left you home alone before the first day of school?"

"I mean, yeah?"

Bo and Andy exchanged a glance, as they often did.

"What?" Michael said. "They trust me not to do anything bad. Besides, I don't really do *anything* at all."

"I didn't say anything." Bo raised his hands in surrender.

Michael leaned back and sighed. "I'm just hoping I'm able to finally sleep tonight. I don't want to go through tomorrow like a zombie."

The bags under his eyes stuck out less now that they were frequent. Bo had almost forgotten how he'd looked when he first came into the shop. Starry-eyed, fresh, and awake. Michael seemed not just exhausted, but worn out. Like a baseball glove left out in the sun to wither.

The closest Bo had seen him recharged was the time he slept for nine hours in his bed.

"You could stay over," Bo offered.

Andy and Michael turned to him.

"Since you have so much trouble sleeping in your place." He further explained. "And since your parents won't notice you're gone."

He felt awkward offering, like he was crossing an invisible boundary with Michael. Before, when Michael slept over, it was just him. Bo and Andy were still downstairs in the shop, or at least across the hall in the living room.

It's not that sleepovers made Bo uncomfortable. He's been having them with Andy since he first moved to Whalesborough. Usually, it was Andy sleeping over at Bo's since the Romero-Almada household was always packed.

Andy once told Bo that sometimes he felt like he had two bedrooms. The one in his house and the one above Selene's shop. It made sense. Half the stuff that lingered in Bo's room was either from Andy or of Andy's. Bo was pretty sure he was wearing Andy's flannel, but it didn't really matter since Andy was undoubtedly wearing his socks.

"Are you sure?" Michael asked.

"It makes sense," Andy said, sticking his fingers between his tie and his neck to loosen it. "You definitely can't sleep in your own house 'cause of all the heebie-jeebies you get."

"Heebie-jeebies make it sound so stupid." Michael frowned. "As long as you're okay with it, and Selene, I'd appreciate it."

Bo shrugged, trying to come off as nonchalant. "I don't really care, dude. Are you cool with sleeping in the living room? If not, I can set up an air mattress here."

"I'm good with whatever."

"You let me sleep in your bed whenever *I* sleep over," Andy added.

"That's because *we* can both fit. Michael has, like, a foot on you." Bo tried to hide the flush in his cheeks.

Andy sized up Michael, who sat awkwardly beneath him. "It's not a *foot*. How tall are you?"

"I don't know, like 6'2?" Michael guessed.

"So it's only a couple of inches, since I'm 5'8," Andy said.

Bo laughed. "You are *not* 5'8. *I'm* 5'9."

"Stand up right now," Andy ordered. Bo dragged himself out of bed to stand beside Andy.

They stood face to face at first, Andy's forehead close enough to Bo's lips that his breath could be felt on Andy's skin. Then they stood back to back, so Michael could judge the difference.

"Well, if Bo is 5'8—"

"Which I am."

"Then Andy's probably like... 5'4?"

"Your eyes are *broken*. Bo, get that tape measure from your desk."

They each took turns letting the tape measure drop to the floor and examining their heights. Michael was a bit taller than 6'2, Bo was exactly 5'9, and Andy stood at—

"Stop getting on your tiptoes."

"I'm not!"

—Around 5'5 and a quarter. Which, he informed the other two, was average height, apparently. "Bring the measuring tape out again. I bet I got you beat in something else." Which caused Bo to shove Andy so hard that he toppled over.

Selene came up with complimentary hot chocolates, which the boys accepted gratefully. It was such a picturesque evening. Bo had put on some Pavement on his cassette player, Michael was telling stories of San Francisco, and Andy tore off his uniform piece by piece until he was down to a tank top, his schoolboy shorts, and a single sock.

Bo was laughing so hard he was choking on his hot chocolate. Andy had an arm slung over his shoulder that Bo didn't bother pushing away. Michael had stood up and begun to wave his arms around wildly as he described what was happening in *The X-Files*.

He had almost forgotten that by this time tomorrow, he'd be trying to ignore the issues school would bring him. Almost, but not entirely, because the phone rang.

"Don't bother picking it up." He told Andy, who had detached himself from Bo. "It's probably another prank call."

"Another?"

"Yeah, I've been getting them for days. Some asshole just calls the line but doesn't say anything." He paused. "Well, sometimes they say stuff, but it's all cryptid and shit."

"Like what?"

At first, it was just breathing, then the little girl's voice, then words he could barely make out through the static. *Help,* or *please*. Or even *cut*. Cut? Cut what? The line? Bo always did; he had begun to be the one who hung up first.

"I don't know, just the typical bullshit." He let his head hit the wall. "Just let it ring."

The phone echoed through the silence; even the cassette player had fallen quiet due to the album wrapping up. Bo made a point to stare out of the skylight. The gray clouds that always haunted Whalesborough shielded any sight of stars above him. He could feel Andy's eyes on him, but then again, that wasn't unusual at all.

When the phone finally went quiet, Andy stood up. "I should probably get home. It's getting late and Mila won't bother waking me up in the morning." It was only around nine, but Bo knew Andy wouldn't willingly go home early unless it was important.

Over the past year, Andy had spent the better part of his time wandering around town or hanging out at Bo's. A clear effort to avoid whatever was going on with him at home, Bo assumed. They didn't talk about it, though. Bo knew Andy preferred to be distracted, so Bo would allow it, whether or not he thought it was what was best.

"You can just borrow some of my stuff for tonight, so you don't need to go home. Then we can head to your place early in the morning so you can get ready." Bo told Michael, who agreed.

As Michael grabbed some old pajamas that would fit him, Bo walked Andy to the door.

Andy busied himself with his shoes but didn't bother making small conversation with Bo. It was like that with them sometimes—comfortable silence where enjoying each other's presence was enough to fill the air.

"Did you," Bo began, "want to stay the night too?" He had just realized he had offered an invitation to Michael, but not to Andy. Did he really have to? It was just as much of Andy's home as it was Bo's.

"Nah," Andy said. "I really do need to get home. I need to get ready and stuff."

"And stuff," Bo echoed.

"What do they say when they call you?" Andy changed the subject.

Bo let him. He always did. When Andy pushed, Bo let himself be pulled. It was their thing.

"Don't worry about it. They're just messing around. They just breathe or whisper random shit about getting cut."

"Cut?"

"Yeah, like I said, it's nothing. Why? Does it mean something to you?"

Andy shrugged, but he seemed dulled. "No. I need to go. I have things I need to take care of. Family things."

Bo didn't really understand, but he nodded. "Call me when you get home, okay?"

Andy hummed in acknowledgment and went on his way. Bo watched him go out the door and catch the trolley. The landline rang, and he pulled it off the wall and slammed it back down to silence it.

Ch. Eleven

When they were younger, they believed in ghosts. Andy remembered crouching under bed sheets stretched across chairs and coat hangers, with Bo holding a flashlight under his chin to illuminate stretching shadows across his face, bodies so close that as they whispered, they could feel their breaths on the other's cheek.

Bo would aim the flashlight at the white cloth, and Andy would make puppets with his hands in the dark. They would spend hours coming up with stories, *ghost* stories, and work to scare each other. Sometimes, they both came up with such grotesque and frightening tales that the only way they could sleep was tangled with each other, tucked into layers and layers of blankets. For some reason, they thought that if they were close enough together, the monsters of their tales couldn't drag them away during the night.

Despite the daunting stories they put so much effort into, it was those nights that Bo was less afraid than ever. When he had first moved to Whalesborough, he was such a quiet thing. Always trying to blend into the pale wallpaper and disappear, and though Andy stuck to ground him and bring him back to reality, it didn't always work.

With the disguise of a ghost story, Bo was able to talk about why he had moved.

Andy remembered when Bo first started making up stories about his hand. He would wave the shortened finger in front of Andy's face. Bo even let Andy press his own finger against his. Andy remembered that the skin gave, and he realized that the distal phalanx (as Angela would later inform him of the proper term) was gone. Bo would let his voice go low, or as low as it could go at eight years old, and pull Andy into his past.

Each time it was a bit different. A monster bit it off. He lost it to a witch for a potion. He gambled it away with a ghost, and so on.

Andy doesn't remember when or what Bo said exactly, but one day he figured out the truth.

Bo had been prepping carrots and accidentally chopped his finger off after his mother abruptly collapsed in the kitchen. Bo had cut his finger off while he watched his mother die.

Back then, his finger was still pink and red from the fresh wound. Sometimes, the skin would break and it would bleed. Andy would take band-aids and cross them over Bo's finger and kiss it better, just as his mother would whenever he got injured himself.

Bo stopped talking about his finger soon enough. Selene confirmed the story to Andy when he was twelve. Bo's mother's death. The missing finger. They still refrained from talking about it.

There were some things that Andy and Bo just didn't talk about. Bo's finger. Why Andy was at Bo's place more than his own. Bo's mother. How Andy was spiraling toward failure in school. Bo's father. That time Andy dated a girl for two weeks.

And now, the fact that they used to believe in ghosts.

He didn't know why he was thinking about that as he came home. His hair was slicked to his forehead with sweat. His school uniform was damp from the humid and salty air. Andy stuck his fingers down his collar and pulled the tight shirt away from his neck in order to breathe better.

He went to kick off his shoes, but his eyes landed on his great-grandmother, who was sitting quietly in the kitchen. Andy was fairly certain that his great-grandmother was never going to die. Not that he was complaining, of course. He loved her dearly, but her ancient age was as impressive as it was disconcerting. He thought that perhaps his great-grandmother was the oldest person in Whalesborough.

At her age, she mostly resided in her bedroom or the living room, sucking on peppermints and binging Spanish soap operas. Her legs had stopped working a while ago, so she always sat in a wooden wheelchair. It seemed like someone had placed her in the kitchen and forgotten about her.

Andy went over and turned on the kitchen light. His great-grandmother startled awake, bleary-eyed and babbling. He rested his hand on hers. She turned her head to him and pursed her lips, as she always did whenever her relative sat near her. Andy crouched so she could peck at his cheek, then got up to fetch her a glass of water.

He helped her take slow sips. She kept opening her mouth, and Andy kept bringing the glass to her lips, but it wasn't until she was shaking her head did he realize she was trying to speak. His great-grandmother wasn't much of a talker, nor was Andy particularly in the house, but when she did speak, it was in a gravelly voice through broken Spanish.

"¿Cómo puede ser tan frío?" She asked.

"It's autumn now, almost winter," Andy said. "Invierno."

She said again, "¿Cómo puede ser tan frío, pero tan brillante?"

Andy was puzzled by her words. "I— uh, don't get what you're saying. ¿Qué quiere decir?" Andy tried to ask.

"De todas formas," she said, "me recuerda de esos días. Con tu padre."

"My dad?" Andy perked up. "What about him?"

But the talking must have tired his great-grandmother out, because she closed her eyes and let her head fall back as she murmured. Andy lightly tapped her shoulder to get her attention, but she swatted him away. "Abuela—"

"Don't bother your bisabuela, Alejandro." A voice said behind him. He turned to find his mother wiping her hands on a washcloth before tossing it on the counter.

Andy swallowed and stepped away from his great-grandmother. "I wasn't," Andy defended meekly.

His mother gave him a look that told him to watch his tone, and he shrank away. The thing about his family, Andy thought, was that they had learned to communicate in silent ways. When translating between Spanish and English became difficult, they exchanged looks and touches to converse. Entire arguments and lectures could be given through glare. Resolutions and apologies were conveyed through glances.

When Bo would come over for family dinners— before everyone had gone off to college and back when Andy still felt he had a place at the dinner table—he would get lost. Especially since Bo wasn't used to the Spanish. It took him a while to realize *Hi-*

meh was who he knew as *Jay-me*. After, he'd ask Andy how he dealt with it—so much going on in such small exchanges. Andy had shrugged because it didn't seem like something he had learned to *deal* with, just something that *was*.

Right now, the look his mother gave him told him that it didn't matter what he said because she had already made up her mind to be pissed at him. "I told you not to go out tonight," Andy's mother said.

Oh. Yeah. Andy had forgotten about that.

"You have school in the morning. I don't want you going around town at night with Bo." She reminded him. "Y debes centrarte, ¿vale?"

Andy brought his hands behind his back so his mother wouldn't see his clenched fist.

"Mila is already in bed," she continued.

Sometimes, Andy really hated his little sister.

"I need to check the basement."

"No, it's too late now." She paused before walking over to him. Over the years, Andy had grown taller than his mother. It was most apparent now, as she brought her hand to his cheek and tilted his head down so he would meet her eyes.

"I spoke to your father. We want you to step away from the work here and focus on school instead." Andy grabbed his mother's wrist and took her hand away from his face. "We've already decided, no more. Your father will take care of it. And if not, Mila—"

Andy pushed past her and left the kitchen. "I'm going to bed."

"Alejandro," His mother warned.

"Night!"

He stomped up the stairs. Jaime had been gone long enough for his scent to finally fade. Andy's room should have been empty. When he opened the door, he almost sent his fist through the wall at the sight of Mila snooping through his stuff.

He had the door completely ajar, catching her red-handed as she fumbled through his closet, her eyes wide. She at least had the decency to look guilty.

Andy looked from her to her hand, where she held a cassette recorder. He jumped at her.

"Get the hell off me!" Mila hissed.

"Get the hell out of my room!" Andy bit back.

They kept their voices to a whisper to avoid being reprimanded by their parents, a lesson they all finally learned once Mila grew out of her tattle-tale phase. It was far better to deal with arguments, no matter how petty, on their own. Getting their parents involved only led to punishments for all parties involved, and that kind of justice always tasted bitter.

He shoved her slightly, not to hurt her but to knock her off her feet, and she fumbled onto his bed.

Once she was distracted, he yanked the recorder out of her hands and shielded it close to his chest.

"Whatever, it's not even yours!" Mila quipped. Technically, she was right. The cassette recorder belonged to Jaime, who bought it with birthday money when he got into a phase of making scientific journals for himself. Andy suspected his brother just liked listening to his own voice spout impressive words that even Jaime didn't fully understand. Whatever the case was, once Jaime left for college, he forgot about the record. Which meant that, logically, it should go to Andy, the next one in line for the inheritance.

"Doesn't give you the right to snoop through my stuff, rat." He inspected the recorder for damage or disturbance, but it seemed he caught Mila right as she found it. So much for already being in bed.

"I just wanted to record some songs off the radio." Mila pushed herself off Andy's bed to cross the room and sit on Jaime's instead.

"You don't even have a Walkman to listen to."

She scoffed. "I'm gonna get one."

"Yeah, right. With what money?" Mila had just blown all her birthday money going to the salon to get her hair cut by a professional instead of their mother. Her brown hair was cropped to her chin, curling in odd places against her jaw and neck. She had yet to get used to her brand-new bangs, still

clearly uncomfortable with the hair getting in front
of her eyes as she constantly pushed strands away.
"Can you get out of my room now?"

"I'm not in your room." She splayed out on the
bed. "I'm on Jaime's side."

Andy resisted the urge to smash the recorder
against his head.

"He'd be pissed if he knew you were on his bed,"
Andy said.

"Nah, I'm his favorite."

It stung because it was obviously true. It seemed
everyone besides Andy let Mila get away with all
kinds of bullshit because she was the baby of the
family. Especially Jaime, who was notorious for not
discriminating against who he snapped at.

"Why do *you* even need it? You don't have a
Walkman, either," Mila pointed to Andy's chest.

Andy groaned and turned his head. "It's not for
me, smartass. I record stuff for Bo all the time."

Mila rolled her eyes. "Shouldn't you be at his
place, like usual? Or did you guys break up or
something?" Andy tossed the recorder on his bed
and went for Mila. She scrambled out of Jaime's bed
and made her way to the doorway. Before she fully
stepped out, she said, "Is that a yes?"

Andy shoved her out and slammed the door.
Then he immediately regretted doing so, because his

parents would definitely have heard his little tantrum.

The thought of his parents giving Mila *his* job made his skin crawl. It was Andy who spent night after night in the basement, hours of fruitless efforts spent in the cellar of their home. The fact that his parents brushed over his hard work so casually felt like those days when he would be sent to timeout for mischief he wasn't even a part of.

In the morning, he would be woken up by a screeching alarm and pushed into the hell that was private school, surrounded by people who only worked to remind him that he was stupid. Tonight, though, he would lie on his bed and listen to the cassettes he recorded over the past few weeks.

Andy closed his eyes and let the sound roll. Silence, and silence, and more silence. The whirling of the tapes. The static of the audio. The wind working to build tension. Andy's own jagged breathing. The part where he nodded off.

A hiss.

A whisper.

A voice.

It cuts into me

He paused the tape and went back. Over and over and over.

He couldn't imagine giving this to Mila.

Ch. Twelve

The week before, Michael checked out the school so it wouldn't be completely unfamiliar to him. Thank God he had.

In the dawn, the tall trees still concealed the carved-out paths that Michael rode through on Bo's bicycle. He knew where he was headed well enough not to stress. Michael was especially grateful for the hours of sleep he managed to get, as Bo made sure they hadn't stayed up too late the night before.

He had set out his clothes before he headed over to the Cassidy's anyway, eager to make a good first impression. His prior school's track letterman, deep red with the number seven embedded on the breast pocket, faded jeans and tennis shoes, so he didn't seem like he was trying too hard. Michael was a bit disappointed that all the effort he put into his hair would be ruined by the wind.

As the woods cleared, he heard the bustling of the front of the school. W.B. High School was old-fashioned but well-maintained. A brick building with an open courtyard where students lingered and had pointless summer catchups.

Michael hopped off and wheeled over to the bike rack. Bo also let him borrow the matching bike lock, swearing Michael to secrecy as he taught him the four-digit code that even Andy didn't know. Oh, five, one, one. He quickly secured the bicycle and stood back up to see some of the students looking at him.

He tugged at the straps of his backpack and awkwardly stuck his hands in his jacket pocket as he scoured the courtyard for Bo. He caught a group of girls pointing at him and giggling, and he realized that his hair was probably messed up from the ride over. Michael quickly began to pat and part his hair, hoping the gel might help more, when a kid his age stepped towards him.

He stood tall, shoulders back, and a bag slung casually over his arm. He raised an eyebrow as he scanned Michael up and down before extending his hand. "You're the McKenzie kid, right?"

Michael tried to subtly glance over the kids' heads, watching as more students piled off the school bus that finally managed to arrive. "Uh, yeah. Michael." He watched Bo bounce off the final step.

The kid stood on his tiptoes to garner Michael's attention again. "I'm Warren. I think we have homeroom together," he said. "I could show you to your class if you wanted."

Bo looked up at Michael and gave a smile. Then, his eyes drew to who Michael was talking to, and his face grew blank. Michael watched as Bo paused, doing some sort of math in his head as he examined the scene. Michael was just about to wave him over when someone shoulder-checked Bo so hard that he stumbled.

Michael took a step towards him, but Warren clasped a hand on his shoulder and pushed him towards the entrance. "C'mon. The layout of the school is a total mess. You definitely need a tour, or else you're gonna get lost."

Bo regained his composure enough to watch Michael being pulled by Warren. Michael had just enough time to see the pissed-off look on his face before he entered the school.

He didn't have any classes with Bo before lunch. He had most of them with Warren and his endless number of friends. Michael swore they couldn't get more than two steps before Warren had to stop and say hello to somebody new. He'd make a point to introduce Michael. "This is the new McKenzie, kid. Isn't he crazy tall? No, no, he does track. Yeah, yeah, totally. No, yeah, definitely."

Michael's mind had gone numb with the dull conversation.

"Cheer up, Mikey. You're the most interesting thing in this town since the Carpenter's hauntings," Warren teased.

"It's just Michael," He corrected.

Warren eyed him, then scoffed. "Okay, then, *Just Michael*. You need to chill, man. There's no need to be so tense." He reached up to squeeze Michael's shoulders playfully, but it wasn't exactly comforting.

His first couple of classes were boring enough. The teachers handed out the syllabus and went over future courses. He tried to bullshit his way through icebreakers, everyone eagerly hanging onto every word he said, even the teachers.

He felt himself sweating through his letterman jacket, despite it being freezing in the school. He mentioned it to Warren, who laughed and said that the ghost of the lazy janitor back from the '70s always messed with the temperature.

It was then that Michael truly realized that everybody in the town *actually* believed in ghosts. He had people talk his ear off about it enough when working or out in town with his parents. But it was at the school, passing through the hallways, that he fully grappled with the magnitude of the town's belief.

As he was passing by a girl drawing a pentagram on the inside of her locker, Warren grabbed him again. Something about Michael's new acquaintance reminded him of Andy. The easy smile and friendly demeanor, how Warren managed to get along with just about anyone. Yet, there was just enough of an underlying difference to make Michael hold himself at a distance. When Andy touched Michael, he was always careful and spirited. Andy touched in a way that felt like he was sharing a part of himself. Warren's touch was heavy and demanding, like it was there to garner attention more than anything else.

Michael didn't like it very much.

"I guess you can eat lunch with us." Telling, not asking. "I'll make space for you."

"That's okay. I want to meet up with my friend." Michael wondered how Bo had managed throughout the day so far.

"Well, sit with us first. Maybe there will be room for your friend, too." Warren pushed him into the bustling cafeteria. The school was small enough to have one lunch period, unlike the four different ones Michael was familiar with in San Francisco.

He had wanted to scope out the lunch meals before committing to buying them for himself, so he let Warren sit him down at his lunch table before wandering off to the lunch line. Michael slowly ate his sandwich as Warren's friends pestered him with questions, some way more personal than he would have preferred. By the time they were drilling him about his dating life (which was totally dead), Michael had pretended to be completely enamored with his food to avoid talking with them more.

One girl, Bailey, particularly bothered him. Not because she was mean or anything. In fact, she was probably the sweetest one there. But she looked almost identical to Bo, to the point where it was creepy. When he approached her from behind, he was extremely disappointed to find that it wasn't, in fact, his friend. Just a girl with flushed cheeks and short-cropped, pale curls.

Finally, he watched Bo come out of the lunch line with a plastic tray in his hands. Michael could have sworn he heard a choir of angels singing. He was suddenly realizing how lucky he was to have stumbled upon Bo and Andy compared to the tedious and dull crowd he was currently surrounded by.

Michael stood in his seat, sticking out like a sore thumb in the crowd from his height. Bo noticed him immediately and gave an awkward nod. Relief flooded through Michael. It seemed like Bo had cooled off from whatever had managed to make him so heated earlier.

Suddenly, Warren emerged from the line behind Bo and rammed right into him. For a second, it seemed like an accident. As Bo fell, food spilling off his tray and arms outstretched to catch himself on a nearby lunch table, Michael saw Warren smirk.

From so far away, he couldn't hear the words that were exchanged. He could only watch as Warren leaned in and murmured to Bo. Bo stood passive, eyes shot to the floor, as Warren grabbed Bo's wrists and slipped a banana into his hand. It seemed like a kind gesture, Warren offering his food to Bo after the accident, but the flash in Bo's eyes confirmed that this was far from innocent.

Bo pushed past Warren and tossed the fruit into a nearby trash can before fleeing the cafeteria. Michael wanted to race after him, but his feet stayed in place. It was like waking up in the middle of the night, unable to move.

Warren reached him before he had the chance to urge himself to leave and pulled Michael back down to his seat. As they chattered away, Michael gripped his knees. "What was that?" Michael asked, trying to keep his voice low and even.

Warren smiled. "What? Cassidy? Relax, man. It was an accident. Not my fault that he's always such a buzzkill."

"No, totally." A girl chimed in. "He's borderline mental. Like, there's something seriously messed up in his head that makes him incapable of taking a joke."

"Please. If you're gonna talk about Cassidy, don't sugarcoat it for the new kid." Somebody else said before turning to Michael. "His aunt's a total nutjob, and obviously he is too. Honestly, you're better off staying away from him."

"Oh, come on. He's not that bad. He hangs around with Andy Romero." Bo's doppelgänger,

Bailey, noted. "Andy doesn't hang out with total freaks."

"You're only saying that because you still have a thing for Romero," Warren scoffed. Bailey blushed but didn't deny anything.

A boy who was chewing on some tobacco spit into his water bottle before adding his thoughts. "I don't know why he bothers hanging around him. People are gonna start thinking they're gay for each other or something." He smirked. "Probably not too far off. In Cassidy's case, anyway."

Michael stood up abruptly.

The rest of the table looked at him.

He stuttered out some excuse about needing the bathroom and rushed out. He wasn't even sure where he was going. He just couldn't stand another second of them listening to them talk shit about Bo like that.

He found himself in a stretched hallway lined with lockers. He'd been assigned one himself but hadn't gone to take advantage of it yet. As he walked through, he noticed that the students' names were printed and taped under the locker numbers.

He skimmed through, each unfamiliar name blurring together. He paused at number sixty-six. The first thing he noticed was an extra six carved into the metal, probably by a knife. Then he noticed the scrubbed-away graffiti, faded but still legible. The word *FREAK* had been messily written out.

Finally, he noticed Bo's name taped to the locker.

Michael shut his eyes tight. He was right back in that bed.

Ch. Thirteen

B o Cassidy was used to feeling like a freak. He wasn't used to having someone make note of his torment. As much as he appreciated the sympathetic glances he caught from Michael across the classroom, it was killing him.

He wished he could go back to when he didn't share a class with Michael. At least he also got out of sharing a class with Warren Dacre.

Warren sat behind Bo and made an effort to pester the back of his chair. At each knee bump or full-on kick, Bo gripped the edge of his desk. It was almost pathetic how desperate Warren was for his attention. Bo would have commented on it if he thought he'd be able to avoid getting his ass kicked.

Of course, Warren wouldn't lay a hand on Bo himself. But he'd get Trevor Campbell, who'd taken up getting wasted during school, to get the job done. He might even be able to get Bailey Tait to do it, who's hated him ever since Andy dumped her their freshman year. She's convinced Bo talked him out of dating her (he didn't) and decided that the heartbreak was entirely his fault (it wasn't).

The bell rang, freeing him from his sixth period. He only had to get through one more.

Luckily, the seventh period landed him in Study Hall. Which basically meant doing nothing until he could go home. Ideally, he would be going over notes for other classes or studying for the SAT, but after today, he just wanted to take a nap.

Michael tried to reach him before he got to the door, but Bo managed to dodge him and make his way to the media center. If Michael was going to be eating lunch with Warren and his band of merry assholes, Bo would probably have to hide out in the library for the rest of eternity.

He made a point not to glance at his locker. His sleeve was stained from attempting to wipe away the word. He would need to stop by the convenience store down the street and pick up wipes for the future.

When he finally got situated in a tight corner of the media center, Bo let his head crumble onto his desk. His peers around him had already dispersed into tight gossip circles. Nobody was even bothering to get any work done.

When Bo heard someone setting their bag down beside him, he thought it was Michael. When he looked up, he didn't have it in him to be displeased.

"Can you just fuck off for five seconds?" He told Warren.

"Careful, Cassidy. Or else I'll tell Mrs. Hallewell you're using foul language in her library."

Bo let his head slam back down onto the table.

Warren Dacre was the worst kind of asshole because he was arguably the most attractive guy in town, which might not seem like that much of an issue, but it was. He could do no wrong with such a charming smile that even the teachers seemed fond of. Bo was pretty sure that Warren could set the damn school on fire, and the town would blame the building for being so cold in the first place. Not only that, but even Bo had trouble resisting his charisma. Whenever Warren extended a helping hand to pull Bo off the ground, he had to remind himself that Warren was the one who had tripped him in the first place.

Warren reached over and tugged at Bo's hair. Bo quickly shot up and smacked his hand away. "What are you doing, creep?" Bo snapped.

Warren pulled his hand back to cross his arms, a bored expression on his face. He leaned his chair back far enough to kick his feet onto the table. "You know McKenzie?"

"No," Bo said. "Barely." He corrected. Even though he was kind of pissed at Michael for ditching him for Warren, he knew that revealing their true closeness would only drag Michael into Bo's hell.

It made sense. Michael was not only the new kid, but also athletic and laid back. Even his geekier obsessions, like *The X-Files,* would captivate their peers' pathetic addiction to ghost stories. Honestly, Bo was surprised Warren hadn't managed to mark Michael as his before the school year started. Not that Michael was something to be had, of course.

"You seem close," Warren commented. His eyes were an alarming shade of blue, startling and repellent. When he narrowed them at Bo, he immediately felt his palms sweat.

"Yeah, well..." Bo trailed off. "He works across the street from my place, so I've seen him around. Sometimes he stops by to deliver package mix-ups."

The simple truth must have satisfied Warren because he cut his gaze away. Suddenly, Bo felt furious with him. Who the hell did this guy think he was, bugging Bo when he'd done nothing to him, calling his line all night long, claiming his friend?

Bo knew he couldn't call Warren out for all the bullshit he put him through over the years, so he chose one.

"If that's all, then could you stay off my landline?" He shifted his head forward so he wouldn't have to look at Warren. Just because he was pissed off didn't mean he was brave.

"I don't know what you're talking about." Warren's voice was always condescending when he spoke to Bo.

Bo still refused to look at him. "Don't play dumb. I know it's you calling in the middle of the night. I don't get what's so funny about it. It's not even fucking scary. It's just *annoying*. But maybe that's your whole spiel, huh?" Bo tilted his head over. "One half-assed attempt at getting my attention after another? Were you seriously that bored over the summer?"

Warren took his feet off the table to glare.

"You know, you say all this shit about how much I bother you, but last time I checked, *you're* the one going out of the way to find me," Bo said. "If you missed me that much over break, you could've just stopped by."

Warren stood up and slammed a hand on the table. The sound of the slap made Bo flinch. "Don't go projecting your delusions onto me, *freak*. I haven't been ringing your house, so you can quit flattering yourself by pretending I'm obsessed with you or something. Honestly, you should be thankful I take the time out of my day to acknowledge you, because otherwise the only social interaction you'd be getting is from your psycho aunt and playing lapdog for Romero." Then he kicked Bo's backpack and stormed off to join his other friends.

Bo watched him go. He realized that Warren had seemed defensive, not because Bo had called him out for the prank calls, but because of the assumption of his obsession. It brought his mind back to the phone calls.

As school drew closer, he became more stressed at the idea of going back to this than the calls themselves. The truth was, he hadn't actually recognized Warren at the end of the line. He hadn't even recognized the voice of the girl, who could have been one of his friends' little sisters but evidently wasn't. But if Warren really had no ties to the phone call, then... Bo didn't even know.

Almost as if he manifested it into existence, he heard a phone ring.

Bo glanced up to see if anybody else had noticed, but everyone else seemed absorbed in their conversation. The call echoed through the media center, so loud that Bo thought the singing of the phone would cause him to go deaf, yet nobody so much as moved.

He looked towards the source of the sound and noticed it came from the payphone right by one of the library exits, out in the hallway. Bo didn't particularly feel like going after it. It's not like he was expecting a call from Selene for anything, but the ringing was driving him crazy.

He quietly stepped out. No one paid any mind to him as he slid into the hallway and he reached for the buzzing phone like Pavlov's dog. He paused, holding it away from himself for a moment, before bringing it to his ear.

Bo silently prayed for it to be somebody, *anybody*, besides who he thought it was. A mother trying to reach her kid but got the time wrong, or a misdial from somebody else in town. He was desperate for anything.

"Hello?" He whispered.

That goddamn breathing.

Bo knocked his head back against the payphone box.

"Who are you?" When there was no response, he added, "Please?"

He heard a whimper on the other line. Long and painful, like it was being dug out of the stranger. It stung Bo, despite not even knowing this mysterious person.

"Are you okay?" He asked without thinking. "Do you need help?"

Yes

Bo exhaled. It was the girl again.

"Who—" They wouldn't answer that. "Where are you?"

Home

"Where is that?" Bo leaned closer to the phone. "I can't call for help unless you tell me where you are."

No

It was so stark, Bo jerked back.

Nonononononono

"Okay, okay." Bo hushed. "I get it. You don't want me to tell anyone."

Youyouyoujustyou

"I—" He felt a pain in his head. He pulled back from the phone to lean on the wall for support, feeling unsteady on his knees. Black spots dotted his vision, and he worked to blink them away. After a deep breath, he brought the phone back to his ear, but was met with static. "No, wait."

He slammed the phone booth, but the signal was lost.

There was somebody out there, somebody who needed help. He knew he should tell someone, his aunt or maybe even the police, but what would he say? He didn't know who they were, where they were, or even what kind of danger they were in. Were they in any danger?

They sounded painful each time he answered the phone. They always pleaded for someone to hear them. They were... cut?

Bo set the phone back on the wall and leaned back. When he looked ahead, he realized there was a classroom right across from him. Through the window on the door, he made eye contact with Michael. Bo hadn't even realized he was being watched.

He didn't want to seem like an asshole despite being exhausted, so he raised a slight hand to Michael.

Michael raised a hand back, but brought his hand higher until he touched his ear. Bo mimicked the gesture and brought his hand to the side of his head. He felt his fingers go wet and slick.

Bo stared at his hand, now laced in his blood. He kept blinking.

When he looked back up at Michael, they wore matching hopeless expressions.

Bo didn't waste any more time standing around. He rushed back into the media center to grab his backpack and give a hurried explanation to Mrs. Hallewell about going to the nurses' office. He headed down the hallways, the pressure in his head unbearable and the sensation of blood dripping down the side of his neck and through his shirt clamant.

He shot through the school doors into the courtyard and quickly got to his bicycle. Part of him recognized that it wasn't in his usual spot, but he was too desperate to get away to pay any mind. He tore off the lock and hopped on, pedaling as fast as he could back home.

Selene had screamed at the sight of him. The stained blood. The grim expression.

He couldn't blame her.

Ch. Fourteen

Andy tried to find some humor in the fact that honesty had only lasted a couple of weeks within the three boys' friendship. They sat behind the counter at Selene's. Andy was on the floor, back to the wooden panel of the table, silent and reticent. Bo, with his face beside the register, but Andy noticed how the skin from the side of his face down to his neck seemed intensely scrubbed, making him appear unusually flushed. Michael leaned on the counter opposite Andy, studying his own hands nervously as he clenched and unclenched his fists, a remorseful expression lingering on his face.

None of them spoke first, because they each knew that asking about each other's day meant recounting their own. So they sat in the quiet, opening and closing their mouths as they tried to urge themselves to speak up.

Bo finally spoke to Michael.

"Sorry about the bike. I forgot you needed it."

"It's fine. I don't mind walking."

"You can take it back home. It's yours, for real."

"Cool," Michael said.

"Cool." Bo agreed.

Cool, Andy thought.

He had never so desperately wanted to go to the public school to find out what had happened to make Bo so jittery and Michael so guilty. He kept this to himself, though.

"Are you feeling better, at least?" Michael asked. Andy snapped his head up to look at Bo, who seemed to have already been looking down at Andy, though his head turned away, leaving Andy uncertain. Bo closed his eyes and hummed a response.

"You don't have to worry," Bo said.

"I—" Michael began.

"It was just a headache."

Andy watched Michael's brows furrow together as he looked at Bo, and then, subtly, his gaze shifted down to Andy. Michael tucked his hands into his jacket pockets.

"Right," Michael said.

"Right," Bo agreed.

Right, Andy thought.

He had never so desperately wanted to understand Bo Cassidy.

Despite being best friends for almost a decade, there were some things about Bo that Andy would never understand. When he got like this, despondent and tepid, Andy felt completely cut off from him. Sometimes, Andy thought he was Whalesborough and Bo was the mainland. His ever-fluctuating moods served as the ceaseless waves that kept the lands apart.

Whatever the cause of this particular tenor, it was a mystery to Andy and known to Michael. Though after watching the latest exchange between the three of them, Andy wasn't sure if he'd get Michael to talk about it.

Michael was similar to Bo in that way. While Michael let Andy ramble about the latest happenings to their neighbors, he only added minor quips. He preferred to listen rather than give his own opinions. Andy thought that perhaps gossiping made him uncomfortable, maybe violating some kind of principles Michael held, so he started to refrain from dragging him into his whispering sessions. Instead, he went back to talking Bo's ear away, who always ended up telling Andy off for being such an eavesdropper and blabbermouth without any true judgment behind it.

Bo definitely wouldn't tell Andy what was wrong.

He could be as stubborn as a brick wall when he wanted to be. Andy had learned that over the years the hard way. No matter how much he pestered or nagged, Bo was resolute in his stance. Unwavering and absolute. It was as honorable as it was annoying, and Andy hoped Bo never changed.

Even in times like this, when he knew a small part of Bo was hurting and Andy wanted nothing more than to work to fix it.

The desire was entirely hypocritical coming from Andy.

He pushed himself off the ground and latched his arms under Bo's shoulders to yank him up. Bo let himself be dragged until he slunk backward, his head landing softly on Andy's shoulder as he curiously stared at him. "No more moping."

"I'm not moping," Bo said unconvincingly. Andy scrunched his face in a way that made Bo smile. Not beaming and bright, but a shy grin spared for Andy alone. Lopsided, almost like a frown, and meek. There were often these moments between the two of them that stuck out to Andy for no particular reason, like those simple smiles from Bo Cassidy that seemed to belong to Andy Romero-Almada.

"One done," Andy said, "only a hundred and sixty days ago. Let's celebrate getting through the first one."

"But I'm *tired*," Bo emphasized this point by faking a dramatic yawn and stretching straight out of Andy's grip. Then he fell back onto the table and snored away.

"Nope. It's tradition. We gotta do it. Come on, Cowboy," Andy said and shook him awake.

"What's tradition?" Michael asked. Andy looked over, almost forgetting Michael was there at all, and offered a smile.

"Oh, man. We have *so* many rituals we need to get you in on. Isn't that right, Bo?"

Bo looked between an eager Andy and a bemused Michael before sighing in defeat.

"I'll grab my swim trunks."

It didn't matter that summer was over. It didn't matter that it was freezing. It didn't even matter that this was obviously a ploy to distract them from their issues of the day.

What did matter was that they had survived the first day of school, and the dock was barren.

Over the summer, there were some waters that were much more crowded than others. Most of the beaches were dominated by families looking to sunbathe and relax. Rivers and streams belonged to the fishermen who preferred freshwater systems. The lakes and creeks were marked territory for the teenagers who wanted to let loose and carouse.

The dock, though, belonged to spirits. That's why Bo and Andy preferred them.

Not actually, of course, but since the town was convinced that anyone who went swimming there would be drowned by vengeful spirits, it had been practically abandoned by the '80s. *Friday the 13th* had its effects on Whalesborough.

The lake wasn't all that big, probably the size of a swimming pool. There were a couple of fish that would nip at their feet and parts where their legs would sink into the muddy floor. A wooden dock was built decades ago, now venerable with age. On one of the pillars that held up the platform, Andy had sat on Bo's shoulders at twelve years old and carved their names into the wood with a pocket knife, forever marking it as theirs.

They had come for all sorts of occasions, not just traditions like this. They'd go when they wanted to get away from everyone else. Andy remembered the endless days full of swimming and floating flat on their backs in the murky water, or letting their feet dangle over the edge of the dock and skipping stones to pass the time.

It was at these docks that they said things they used to be too afraid to discuss.

Andy's house always carried a weight of onlookers, a place where they worried about being overheard and judged. Bo's bedroom was too familiar to risk contamination from the things they couldn't say out loud. The trolley was always rocky, the diner was always too loud, and the streets were always too demanding.

The dock was a place where they felt shielded from the rest of town. The stillness of the water, the echo of nature, the steadiness of their surroundings. It was where Bo had told Andy that he didn't call his father anymore. It was where Andy told Bo that he had started failing all his assessments. It was where, when it got chilly, they would huddle close under Bo's flannel because Andy always forgot to wear an extra layer.

Now they brought Michael.

For some reason, it felt like a sort of violation. Andy knew Bo felt similar, but they didn't want Michael to feel excluded. It seemed unfair to keep their new friend out of their strange patterns for the simple crime of showing up too late.

They had managed to find three pairs of swim shorts. One of Bo's, one of Andy's, and one (which could've belonged to either of them but couldn't manage to remember who) that now belonged to Michael. Not without Bo smacking Andy's shoulder to silence his laughter at the obvious tightness of the shorts, though.

He heard Michael ask Bo, "Why does he always call you Cowboy?" before Andy kicked off his sneakers and tore off his shirt, diving into the lake without care. The shock of the freezing temperature made him gasp underwater and forced him to spring back up to break the surface. He beat his fist against his chest as he coughed, and Bo and Michael laughed at him from above.

Bo sat on the edge of the dock as Michael slowly waded through the water. Andy sat below his best friend, grabbing at his legs and trying to drag him into the water. Bo kicked him away, pushing Andy back underwater with his playful attacks.

Michael kept his arms crossed over his bare chest, clinging to his shoulders as he shivered. Andy decided to leave Bo, letting him lie flat on his back with his baseball cap tipped down over his eyes, and dragged Michael deeper into the lake.

Michael kept jumping at each piece of grass that touched his leg, certain that a gator would pop out to bite his leg off. Andy assured him that he'd only have to worry about gators down in Florida, and the worst nips he'd get were from small, curious fish.

They tread water in the deep parts, splashing and dunking each other into the water until their bodies acclimate to the chill. As they floated on their backs, Andy watched as the sun crossed further into the west.

"Do you know Warren?" Michael asked.

"It's Whalesborough. I know everyone." Andy reminded him.

"Right, but..."

Andy let his arms splay out like he was making snow angels. "Dacre."

"Yeah."

Andy thought of the boy. "He's alright, I guess. We were close when we were younger. Like, pre-school friends. Kinda drifted apart once Bo came around. Not from any falling out. We just ran with different crowds. Why?"

Michael stopped floating and let himself sink into the water a bit. "I don't know. I met him today. I guess I was just wondering what you thought of him." He seemed rather nervous. Andy thought that perhaps Michael was waiting for his character judgment on Warren.

Earlier, when Bo and Andy were hanging out before Michael got off his shift at Robinson's, Bo told Andy to lay off while discussing their peers. He thought it would be a good idea for Michael to have his own opinions on the other kids in town instead of just listening to what Andy picked up from whispers on the streets. Andy thought that was fair enough, so he was careful when choosing his words.

"You know, we get it if you want to hang out with other people now that the school year has started," Andy said.

Michael glanced. "Is this your way of casually telling me to bug off?" He joked, but his voice sounded strained.

"No, not at all." Andy swam off his back. "I'm just saying, Bo and I usually stick together. We wouldn't mind if you wanted to go off with others sometimes. We don't want you to feel pressured to hang around if you want to... You know, make other friends."

"That's not what I'm getting at," Michael assured. "Honestly, meeting everyone else only helped me realize that—" He cut himself off.

"What?" Andy asked.

"I don't know. Maybe that I've already found my people? That's what my mom's always saying. You gotta find your people that get you and stuff." Michael said bashfully. "Ugh, that sounds so dumb."

Andy grinned. "No, I totally get it. That's what it's like with Bo. Nobody else really compares, you know?"

"Yeah. No, yeah." Michael nodded. They fell onto their backs again to float. "I mean, I guess it's also because Warren was kind of an asshole."

Michael's use of language surprised Andy, though he tried not to show it. He was far more focused on Michael's opinion of the town's golden boy. "Really?"

"You don't agree?"

"No, I do. I definitely do." He thought of Halloween. "He gives Bo shit sometimes."

Michael shifted quickly enough to send waves into the water. "You know about that?" Andy realized that Michael was tall enough to stand in the deep end while Andy struggled to face him vertically in the water. Michael's tone drastically shifted like a light switch, as if he was suddenly troubled. "Have you talked to him about it?"

"Who? Warren?"

"No, *Bo*."

"I mean, it was a long time ago. So, why not just let sleeping dogs lie?" Andy said, then pondered for a second. "Bo holds grudges, though. He's probably not totally over it, if that's what you mean."

"That's not—" Michael began to shake his head, but he cut himself off when his eyes landed on Bo, who was waving them over. "Nevermind." His abrupt cut-off sent Andy into a spiral. The promised good time at the dock made him forget about the sour mood they started in, and he was quickly reminded of Bo's restrained attitude.

He grabbed Michael's wrist. "Are Warren and Bo..." But he wasn't even sure what he was trying to ask.

Michael pulled his arm back, and Andy let him. "If Bo hasn't brought it up, then I probably shouldn't." Then he made his way back to the dock to meet Bo. Andy stayed behind to watch the exchange between the two of them. A friendly, but tense, chat from what Andy could read from far out. But that wasn't what they were there for. That wasn't what *he* was there for.

So, Andy just dunked his head under the water and let the water freeze him from the inside out.

Ch. Fifteen

School was miserable. Home, even more so.

The Cassidy household proved to be some kind of safe haven for Michael. Even though Bo and Michael had yet to talk about the bullying, Bo still offered his bed whenever Michael needed it. Michael thought he understood Andy a bit better. Sometimes, there was no way to talk with Bo, even when the desire to do so became a constant static behind his ears.

They had made a routine of sorts. Michael rode Bo's bike after school to Robinson's, worked a couple of hours, then took a power nap before he had to go back home for dinner. It wasn't ideal, but better than the alternative of getting no sleep at all.

Sometimes, he'd overhear Bo and Andy laughing together in the living room and grip the sheets tighter.

The days were getting shorter and colder, and night approached more rapidly. Michael found himself racing to beat the setting sun on his way home, pedaling as fast as he could to catch the final minutes of sunlight.

Tonight, however, he lost track of time. It was the first Friday of the school year, so he'd stuck around with Andy and Bo a little longer. Andy decided to head out first, as he usually did now, and Michael followed after him half an hour later.

He tugged his letterman jacket tighter around his core as he biked through the empty streets and into the woods. His Walkman bouncing in his pocket, the words of W. Flick echoing in his ear.

"*Henry slowly stepped towards the door, the chanting of the nursery rhyme luring him closer like a siren's call from the other side. His heart was pounding in his chest, so powerful he thought it might break out of his ribcage.*" The narrator had set the scene. Michael felt his heartbeat racing inside of himself.

He wasn't afraid of the dark, but the looming shadows weren't exactly creating a welcoming atmosphere. He tried to lose himself in the horror stories instead of the unsettling forest. Michael gripped the bike handles tightly as he rode over a twig, the snap of the wood making him flinch slightly.

The story continued. "*He rested a hand on the doorknob, a voice from the other side begging him to turn it and release them.*"

Michael had tried to get away from Warren, but the junior class size was so small, he shared all his classes with the same forty kids. It didn't help that Bo would always disappear from the cafeteria completely, not even bothering to show up to purchase lunch. Michael had trouble rejecting Warren's offer to eat with him when he couldn't find Bo to sit with him instead.

Michael was beginning to realize that he had trouble getting himself out of uncomfortable situations. Maybe all the guidance lessons on peer pressure actually served a purpose.

"Pressing an ear to the door, Henry listened more closely to the song of the strangers."

He arrived at his house. He hopped off the bike and decided to walk the rest of the way. By now, his parents had been back from their trip from the mainland and had been bugging Michael nonstop, asking about school and friends and work and anything else they could think of.

"It was then that Henry recognized one of the singing voices."

He heard the loud crunch of dead leaves from behind. Michael slipped off his headphones and rested them on his neck as he turned. In the dark, he couldn't see the source of the sound. Perhaps a squirrel or some other small woodland animal.

"It was a familiar voice," the muffled voice from his headphones said.

A sudden movement from the corner of his eye caught his attention. He snapped his head over in the direction and saw a figure, still but aggressive. Michael stopped breathing.

Short and lanky, hunched in the shadows but no longer hidden.

Michael recognized the way that the stranger held themself. Though their features were concealed in the dark, the schoolboy's uniform was immensely visible.

"It was the voice of a friend."

"Andy?" Michael murmured.

Then Michael remembered that Andy had gone home earlier. He remembered that Andy had told him he'd stopped walking past his house. He remembered that he had already realized that the figure outside his house at night wasn't, in fact, Andy at all.

The mysterious creature turned on its heel and ran into the woods.

For a moment, Michael stood paralyzed.

He dropped the bicycle and began to chase after it.

At first, he struggled to find his footing. From the uneven terrain of the forest to the loose rocks and twigs working to trip him up and the ditches and rabbit holes, each step threatened to capture his shoe and hold him in the ground. Deeper into the woods, the trees grew thicker, branches residing closer to the ground that swiped at Michael's head and shoulders. He brought his hands in front of his face to protect himself.

His audiobook kept feeding tension to the chase, as the story of Henry and the mysterious chanting cult only made the scene more frightening.

It had been a couple of weeks since Michael had put effort into running. The track season ended last spring. He didn't have any trouble keeping up with the stranger, but his lungs had begun to burn and his legs began to ache.

As he drew closer and closer to the figure, Michael could hear their ragged breaths and grunts of exertion. He reached an arm out, trying to grasp the back of the uniform blazer. His fingers kept barely grazing the fabric.

It came to him that it wasn't just the figure he was chasing, but his sanity.

Though he had been seeing less and less of Andy's doppelgänger, there were still some nights he caught them lurking outside his house. It was worse than the screaming girl above his head. When he saw the stranger outside, he was fully awake and alert.

There was no excuse.

The paranoia was killing him more than the lack of sleep at that point. The disappearance and reappearance, the unnatural occurrence of this being—it made Michael feel like he truly was losing his mind.

If he could only grab it, prove it's real, reveal its true nature...

Suddenly, there was a hitch.

Michael blinked for a second, then he was tumbling down. He drew his arms and legs close to himself as he rolled. The fall of the stumble made him gasp in pain as his body bounced along the slope. He hit the ground once, twice, and now three times before collapsing at the bottom of a hill.

The pain in his head was blinding. Bringing a hand up to his forehead, he looked around for the person he had been chasing, but he was alone in the ditch.

Michael took his gaze to the edge he had fallen from.

The stranger wasn't above, either.

Michael brought himself to his feet and made the slow but steady climb back up to the path he had taken. As he walked back, he noticed the branches he had broken through and the shrubs he had kicked. It stuck out to him that all the damage had been caused by his track and not by the stranger. As if only one of them had been running through the forest.

His father was waiting on the porch.

He clapped Michael on the shoulder when he approached him. "Getting some extra practice for sports?" His father laughed. "Your mother told me she saw you run off into the woods alone."

Alone, alone, alone.

Michael McKenzie could very well be crazy.

Ch. Sixteen

Michael was making faces at Bo from across the street. Bo had parted the velvet drapes to let some light in, which created a clear view between the two shops. The thing about Michael McKenzie was that he was able to keep a neutral face, but he had very expressive eyebrows. His features were usually so careful. Round face and soft cheekbones; a long, flat nose Bo caught him tapping at with a pencil whenever he worked to concentrate in class. His eyebrows contradicted the rest of his face. Sharp and dark, a light scar running through his left one, constantly shooting up or down, furrowing or easing. A dead giveaway that revealed his true feelings on a matter. Andy had joked that Michael would get wrinkles by the time he was twenty. Michael had scrunched his eyebrows in response.

Now, Bo watched as the boy across the street reacted to whatever was happening at Robinson's. It was like a game of charades as Bo tried to imagine what could have had Michael's face twisted in such a way. It was probably one of the Robinson kids giving him a hard time.

"What are you giggling about?" Selene asked as she came into the shop.

Bo swerved on the counter chair. "I'm not giggling." He spared a glance back over to the grocery store and cracked a smile at Michael rubbing his temple.

"Hm." Selene smiled with him. "I need to head to the back, so if anyone comes in for me, tell them to hang on. Are you still avoiding the telephone?"

"I'm not—" Selene shot Bo a look that told him not to bother with lying. "Yeah, I guess so."

When he had thought it was prank calls, Bo would simply pick up the phone, only to set it back down to quiet the ringing. Now he found himself waiting for a call like a rooster waiting for the sunrise.

It was an abrupt switch, from dreading the landline to pleading for a ring. He felt ashamed of himself for treating the caller like an inconvenience. Somebody out there was suffering, in one way or another, and Bo had been too busy absorbed in himself to notice.

The longer he sat in radio silence, the more he worried. What if he realized too late?

He didn't want to think of what the lack of calls could mean.

"Take note of anyone who calls. I'm expecting some appointments to roll in," Selene said. Bo waved her away in a *yeah, yeah* sort of manner. Once she had left the store, Bo found himself staring back at Michael again.

The past week had been awkward between the two of them for obvious reasons. After the disastrous first day of school, Bo had decided ignoring Warren (and, by extension, Michael) was the best course of action.

Skipping lunch to stay behind in class and work on homework or eating in the media center had been successful so far. The only thing Bo had to deal with was couples making out in the corner and the teachers' side-eyeing him.

By now, Warren had definitely picked up on Michael and Bo's history, which only made him cling to the new boy tighter if anything. It was almost embarrassing how much effort Warren was putting into claiming Michael as his. Bo refused to say this to either of them, though.

Another thing: Bo hadn't spoken out about the calls besides the night before school started. Andy seemed curious enough about them but decided to let Bo be. Michael was blissfully unaware.

Bo couldn't decide if he preferred it that way or not.

He was so used to keeping things to himself, even from Andy. They talked about most things—minuscule and intricate details of themselves that seemed unimportant in the grand scheme of things but only worked to deepen their friendship. But they were also used to ignoring certain topics that they had dubbed too delicate to broach.

At first, he thought it was strange for best friends not to talk about everything. As the years went on, it was something that made their friendship formidable. Bo never felt pressured to reveal more than he wanted when he was with Andy, and he knew Andy felt the same. Being able to comfort each other in silence and at a distance proved to be invaluable.

It seemed like everyone wanted Bo to talk about himself and what he was feeling, especially his aunt and Andy. Yet Andy never pushed like everyone else did. He knew when to leave well enough alone.

For so long, Bo had thought this made Andy different from everyone else in Whalesborough. Michael was working to prove this theory wrong.

The other boy had yet to actually confront Bo about the deal with his peers. He also hadn't told Andy, which Bo had become aware of. It made it feel as if Michael had chosen Bo over Andy in that context, even though Bo knew it wasn't like that at all.

Bo had made up his mind that the next time the girl called him, he would try his best to find out as much information as he could to help her. Then he would tell Michael and Andy to hear their thoughts on the matter. After that, he wasn't sure what he'd do. He probably wouldn't be able to handle it on his own, but the idea of getting the police involved made his stomach twist.

When the phone beside him rang, Bo jumped to grab it.

"Hello?" He urgently said. When he heard heavy breathing on the other line, Bo felt his throat tighten. "It's you, isn't it? Listen, I want to help you. I really do. But you *need* to tell me who you are and where your house is so I can... I don't know. Call somebody else to take care of—"

"Who the hell is this?" A gruff voice said.

Bo's mouth fell open. The recognition of the voice was blunt and bare to him. Bo hadn't heard it in years, the dialect and tone working overtime to jog his memory. He wiped his eyes with the back of his hand.

"Dad, what—Why are you calling?" Bo answered.

He didn't really remember when he last spoke to his father. After he briskly moved to Whalesborough with Selene, his aunt organized nightly calls with his father so Bo wouldn't feel homesick. Then, nightly calls turned to weekly calls, and then weekly calls turned to monthly ones. Before Bo knew it, he had only heard from his father on his birthday or holidays, with the occasional card and five-dollar bill to accompany the dull efforts. He thought, perhaps, that the last time they spoke to each other was when his father called the line drunk and babbling, not so much looking to reach Bo but too out of it to care who he talked with.

Bo couldn't say he missed his father. They had never had a close relationship to begin with. It was his mother who took care of him. When she died, Selene had come as soon as possible to take him off his father's hands.

He had some photos of them together in his room, but he didn't leave them out. It made him think of a time he barely remembered in a solemn sense. He knew his mother more than his father, but some days the absence of his dad hurt him more than the death of his mom. Could he truly miss someone he barely knew?

At first, he did, greatly. Then, Selene had given him the classic "the phone works both ways" pep talk, so Bo worked to convince himself that he wouldn't allow himself to miss his father if he wasn't going to miss Bo back.

"Oh, it's you." His father at least seemed surprised to hear from him. "Hey, kid."

"Hey..." Bo rested his back against the wall and brought the phone closer to his ear.

There was a moment of silence.

"So, how have you been?" His dad asked.

Bo brought his thumb to his flat middle finger and tapped. "Fine. Good, I've been good. Um, and you?"

"Ah, you know how it is." But Bo didn't, not really. "Is your aunt there, kiddo?"

For a second, Bo had the terrible thought that his father had forgotten his name.

"She's busy right now. I can take a message, though."

He heard his father take a long sip of something, and Bo wondered if he was drinking. Back when they lived together, his father worked long hours during the day, leaving Bo alone with his mother. His mom would go off, maybe to her room or outside. Bo wasn't always sure. He'd find himself alone in the small home, playing with toy sea animals and listening to the radio. If he found the remote tucked between couch cushions, he'd put it on the National Geographic Channel or reruns of the classic Westerns.

When his father came home late, his mother would be in the kitchen. She used to cook, but after Bo turned six, his mother decided it was time for him to learn how to make his own plate. She'd watch him pull out ingredients and instruct him on how to make meals. Nothing that actually required the stove, of course. Just some microwavable dinners his father always stocked up on.

His father would sit on his reclined chair and drink a couple of beers before falling asleep on the couch. In his final years at home, his parents rarely slept in the same room. Bo only realized that fact after his mother had died and he had moved far away.

His father coughed into the phone. "Yeah, okay. I just wanted to know if she was planning on coming up to the mainland."

"For what?" Bo asked. His aunt wasn't known to leave the island. If she wanted to get away from town, she fled to the sea just as Bo and Andy often did.

The question seemed to quiet his father. He took a careful second before answering. "She usually comes up to visit your mother's grave around this time of the year. For the…"

"Anniversary, right. Sorry, I—" Forgot. He didn't say that to his father, though. Bo curled in on himself, embarrassed and apologetic. "She always comes up?"

"For a couple of days or so. Just for that, not to see me or anything." His father cleared his throat. "I thought— Well, I guess I just assumed you went with her."

"No, I don't," he said. "I haven't."

"Neither have I, kid."

Bo wasn't a kid anymore.

The conversation seemed over, but Bo wasn't ready to let his father go just yet. He wasn't sure what it was. Was it hearing his voice again after so long or the mention of his mother that made him ache more? If he closed his eyes, he could remember what it was like in that house.

Brown, peeling wallpaper. Art pieces from his mother's hand, just like the ones Selene hung in her home now. The ruffled carpet that would tickle Bo's bare feet. The howling neighbor's dog that would keep him up at night. The musty smell

He remembered how quiet it was. How the silence seemed to cover the house like layers of blankets over his creaking bed. The soft buzzing from the light bulbs could be heard if he focused. He remembers that his mother always spoke in a whisper and that his father never spoke to begin with unless to reprimand him.

"If I go this year, will you come down too?" Bo found himself asking.

He heard his father sniff. "I don't think so, Bo."

It felt good to hear his father say his name. Neither of them said goodbye when they hung up.

Bo stood by the phone for a second. Not doing anything, just staring at the floor and thinking.

When Selene came back to the front of the shop, he was still standing there. She stood beside him for a moment, taking in the scene. Then she carefully tucked a piece of hair behind his ear. It reminded him of what his mother would do when she wished him goodbye at the bus stop to school.

"It was your brother," Bo said. For some reason, it was hard to acknowledge his father out loud. "He was talking about—"

"Yes, I know. I'm sorry, I should've been here to pick it up myself."

"You knew he'd call?" Sometimes he forgot his aunt had hunches about these kinds of things.

She shook her head. "No, no. Just... I'm sorry. How was he?"

Bo shrugged because neither of them had actually given a real answer when they asked. "I didn't know you went up to visit her."

Bo suspected that his aunt loved his mother too much, and that's why they never talked about her. Bo thought he was like his aunt in that way. Their grief was something so personal, something to keep for themselves away from others. It was something to keep quiet, not to be heard.

Bo wondered how normal it was to think about it. Some days, it felt like it was all that was in his mind, and he would find himself touching the photographs of his mother and thinking, *I've forgotten how your cheeks pull when you smile.* On other days, he only thought of her when he saw his reflection in the mirror.

"Yes. I used to go more often during the first couple of years. Then you..." She trailed off. "It became more difficult. Between you and the shop, it's hard to find time to get away."

"Sorry."

"It's just a fact, not something to blame you for." She swept her hair over her shoulder.

"Can I come?" He asked her. If he had known it was something he could have done, visiting his mother's grave, he would have been doing it for years. The idea of taking a boat ride up to the mainland on the weekend, picking up flowers, and sitting by his mother's grave... It made him think that he wouldn't be so lonely. And maybe, if he'd grown brave, he would have brought Andy up with him.

He was almost mad at Selene for not inviting him before. Then he realized that he had never asked in the first place.

"Of course," Selene said, before falling silent. She seemed careful then, like she was unsure of how to speak to him in the moment. "I know it's hard for you. To think about her."

But it wasn't. Sometimes, thinking about his mother was the easiest thing Bo could do.

Ch. Seventeen

Andy was throwing rocks at Bo's window like he was in some sort of rom-com. He blamed it on his sisters' summer obsession. He's probably seen every Meg Ryan movie known to man. Not that he was complaining.

Bo opened the window just after another rock hit the glass.

"Dude," Bo said.

"Get down here," Andy responded.

"It's like, ten p.m.?" Bo rubbed his temple. "We have school tomorrow."

Andy shrugged and pulled his arm back to throw another rock at Bo. His best friend quickly slammed the window shut. Andy leaned against the brick wall as he waited. Bo appeared from the back door in his pajamas and Converse he had yet to lace up. Andy bit back a laugh.

"Why are you already dressed for bed?" Andy said.

"I'm sleepy." Bo rolled his eyes.

"Well, go ahead and tie those laces. We're heading down to the dock." Andy pulled on the collar of his sleep shirt.

"Now?" Bo swatted Andy's hand away. "Seriously?"

"Seriously."

"Is Michael meeting us?"

Andy kicked a pebble. "I was thinking it could just be us."

Bo seemed to consider this. For some reason, Andy was afraid he would say no. Bo shrugged and said, "Michael has my bike."

"I know, you're riding with me." Andy pulled his bicycle off the wall. He remembered the Christmas when they convinced Selene and Andy's parents to get them matching ones. He swept a leg over and placed a foot on the pedal.

Bo stared at him.

"Oh, come on. We've shared a bike before." Andy rolled his eyes.

"Yeah, when we were like, ten. You sure we're both going to fit on there?" Andy could tell Bo was trying his best not to laugh at him.

"You haven't even tried to get on yet." He reached over and pulled Bo behind him. "Check it."

"Hm." Bo hummed but complied with Andy's demand. He sat down at the back edge of the bicycle seat, his feet on the peg. There was just enough room for Andy to squeeze in close. "I'm gonna fall off."

Andy grabbed Bo's arms and wrapped them around his waist. "Just hold on." He kicked off and began to pedal down the road.

There was something about the dark that made him feel invincible. He knew it seemed dumb, but Andy thought there was power in the shadows and moonlight. At least, that's how it worked according to the stories. He saw it in life, though, too. The way the night shielded some things and emphasized others. Everything was stronger then.

The breeze almost knocked them off the bike, causing Bo to grip onto Andy tighter. The ocean waves they rode by were terrifying and all-encompassing. The cool of the approaching autumn worked to push Andy and Bo closer to share body heat.

When they got closer to the dock, they hopped off and decided to walk the rest of the way. Andy had brought a flashlight that he kept pointed at the ground, though they could have navigated their way through well enough without it.

Andy dropped the bike by the water's edge and climbed onto the dock with Bo. The croaking of toads was the final lullaby of summer nights. Soon, they would bury themselves in mud to hibernate for the winter.

Bo walked far enough to the end of the dock to rest his legs over the side of the pier. Andy joined him without a second thought.

Andy couldn't stop thinking about what Michael had said. He'd gone to Michael once more, but the other boy had simply said, "You need to talk to him about it."

But Andy didn't know how to get Bo to talk about stuff he didn't want to. To be fair, Andy didn't know how to get himself to talk about stuff he didn't want to, either. If he was being completely honest, being able to function in silence wasn't so much something he picked up from Bo, but rather from his family. Bo had only made it easier to manage.

"If you," Andy started, "were having trouble, you'd tell me. Right?"

Bo shifted. "What do you mean?"

"Like, if you were having issues with Selene," Andy prompted. "Or at school."

Even in the dark, Andy watched Bo still. He decided to give Bo some privacy and turned his gaze to the lake. As he shone the flashlight onto the water, he watched insects dart around in the night.

"I'd tell you," Andy said. "If someone was bothering me."

"I know. You already do that." It was true; Andy had already talked Bo's ear off about the boy who sat in front of Religious Studies, who kept sticking chewed gum under the desks.

"Yeah, but..."

"You know what it's like for me, Andy."

It was harder for Bo. That was common knowledge.

Harder for him in the sense that he was always alienated from the rest of the town for not being a native, for being off-putting, for being reclusive. Selene's reputation didn't help. Despite the town getting plenty of use out of her shop to aid in their supernatural obsession, they treated the Cassidy's as ghosts themselves.

Not only that, but Andy thought it was harder for Bo to be a kid than it was for others.

Bo was always so serious as a boy. Reserved and quiet, like the soul in him was already old. Andy remembered dragging him along with the other boys in town by the creeks after school. Where Andy and the guys worked to grasp fish in their hands and put worms down each other's shirts, Bo would sit with his feet in the water and stack rocks into towers.

He minded getting dirty, always so clean and tidy. Andy had the skill of tracking dirt anywhere he went, but Bo made sure to keep all his spaces neat. When Andy first ate dinner with the Cassidy's, Bo made him sing "Twinkle, Twinkle, Little Star" as he washed his hands thoroughly.

Another thing was that Bo was always so good at being anodyne and docile to the world around him. While everyone else would throw tantrums and argue with adults, Bo always accepted what he was told. Whether that was an unfair punishment from a teacher or nasty words thrown at him by neighbors on the streets, Bo was able to take it with little response.

It always came as a shock when Andy remembered he had never seen Bo cry.

Not when they had crashed their bikes into each other, and Bo had a gaping wound on his forehead that made Andy burst into tears, despite being completely fine himself. Not when the people in their town were cruel and unjust to him for the small crime of being who he was. Not when he was surrounded by death, from his mother's departure to the dead animals they'd find on the side of the road.

Andy was the opposite. Always crying over movies or homework. He got better at choking down his feelings as they got older. Louis and his father would lecture him because boys don't cry, especially over stupid things like bruised egos. Jaime put up with it.

Andy was better at being a kid, but Bo was definitely better at being a man.

Even now, in the way he carried himself, Andy saw it.

The nonchalant way Bo held himself, how he could walk through life unbothered and unscathed by judgment and change. Bo was what Andy was supposed to be now. Confident and steady. Finding success at school. Growing up. Andy was jealous of Bo in this way.

No, that wasn't it.

Andy wasn't envious of Bo for being able to grow up. He was just craving the days of their youth.

"This was so much easier," Andy began, "when we were boys, and all I had to worry about was what would be for dinner."

Bo turned to him. Andy looked back.

Nights like this, he missed it so much it hurt in his chest.

The days when they didn't have to care about grades or where they would end up. When school was only an interruption of summer fun instead of the deciding factor of their future. Back when Andy still belonged among his family, and Bo couldn't understand the mean words directed at him.

When Andy could touch Bo without eyes on them. When being so close wasn't a thing to judge but rather a thing to admire.

Andy doesn't remember when it was, but one day they realized that they were being best friends wrong to everyone on the outside. It didn't matter how the two of them felt on their own anymore.

He missed when being together was enough to make everything right.

"I know what you mean," Bo murmured.

That didn't change anything, though.

Andy wondered if it was possible to lose sight of somebody sitting right next to you, because it felt like Bo was getting further and further away from him each day.

"You'd tell me, right?" He tried to bring it back to the reason he brought him there.

They could say things at the dock that they couldn't anywhere else.

"Yeah, Andy. I'd tell you."

Andy waited for Bo to continue. It took a couple of minutes before he realized they had both gotten better at lying to each other.

Ch. Eighteen

Not to be dramatic, but Michael was certain that Warren Dacre was causing him to lose Bo. Michael had already confronted Bo about it, a rather meek attempt, but Bo had simply brushed him off and told him to do whatever he felt like. To say the least, both of them felt defeated.

He had stopped sitting with Warren at lunch. When he asked why, Michael had stumbled over his reasoning. As a stammering mess, Warren must have decided to go easy on him, and he'd waved him away. Michael was unsure if he was trying to save face or if he actually lacked strong feelings towards their relationship. Either way, it was clearly over with.

Michael started trying to talk to Bo during class, but he was still being ignored. He wasn't sure if Bo was doing it for Michael's sake or his own. Whatever the case was, it was proving to be very inconvenient to Michael's efforts. He spent the entire lunch period roaming the halls and peeking into classrooms looking for Bo. A teacher had called him out, and he had to play the new kid card to get out of punishment.

So after the final bell rang, Michael didn't head straight for the courtyard and to his bicycle. Instead, he went to find Bo's seventh-period class and meet him somewhere in the middle. As he was shoving past students, constantly pushing against the flow of the crowd, Michael noticed an opening towards a wall. A small group of students had stopped in front of the locker banks, murmuring and snickering at something.

He felt a pit form in his stomach when he realized that they had crowded around where Bo's locker was. Tall enough to see above their heads, Michael caught the fresh words scribbled aggressively on the metal door.

HOMO

And Michael... didn't know what to do.

But he stepped forward anyway.

Some students yelped at him as he pushed past them and approached the locker. He took his sleeve off his wrist and spat on the cuff of his jacket before scrubbing away at the writing. It wasn't coming off, only smearing along the door and staining his fabric. Michael still worked tediously at it.

He kept swiping at the words, trying to erase them without any success. Eventually, he tugged off his backpack and pulled out his water bottle to help, but nothing seemed to work.

The thought of Bo seeing his locker terrified Michael for some reason. He knew that Bo was used to such comments. Freak wasn't the only 'F' word that was thrown around when people talked about him. Michael thought, though, that the speculation about Bo's sexuality was something that was especially judged.

The way that his classmates talked about Bo and his friendship with Andy was always a sort of recurring joke at the lunch table. For some reason, those words felt more vile than when they poked fun at his living situation or even the state of his hand. They felt pointed and sharp, and the way those words made Bo flinch proved to Michael that they were beyond effective.

He didn't know how long he had stood attempting to clean the locker. Most of the kids had cleared out by then, and even some teachers had passed by without any concern for him. It made Michael work even more furiously, knowing that nobody even cared about the obvious harassment Bo went through.

By the time his arm was aching and his sleeve was drenched, the letters had only partially faded. Michael sighed and wiped the sweat off his forehead. Too focused on catching his breath, he didn't realize Bo was gently putting a hand on his bicep and urging him out of the way.

Michael watched Bo open his locker and pull out a dry-erase marker. "It's a permanent marker," Bo said. "It won't come off that way."

Michael stood silently, too nervous to move in the moment.

Bo uncapped the marker and carefully copied the words. He slowly traced each letter, mimicking the handwriting as perfectly as he could. When he finished, he wiped it away with his sleeve, and Michael noticed that the word had faded drastically.

He watched as Bo did this over and over.

Michael thought it must have felt like some sort of hell. He wondered how many times Bo had done this.

Bo kept rewriting and erasing.

HOMO HOMO HOMO

Until finally, with a final swipe, the words were gone. Bo put the cap back on the marker and tossed it into his locker. Michael listened to the way it clung against the metal. When he slammed the locker shut, Bo shut his eyes and quietly exhaled. Then he turned to Michael and said, "I missed the bus."

Michael stared. It was well past when school got out by now, but he wasn't even thinking about that. All he could focus on were the words and Bo.

"Can I walk back with you?"

They walked with the bike between them, Michael pushing it along the path by the handles. He still hadn't managed to make himself speak up, instead waiting for Bo to start the conversation. Michael was worried that saying the wrong thing at that delicate moment would finally push Bo over the edge.

He noticed how every day at school wore on Bo, like stretching a rubber band tighter and tighter. Flexible and ductile, but when constantly put to the test, they only become more high-strung and ready to snap at any given second. Michael didn't know what it would mean if Bo broke.

When they made it halfway through the hike, he couldn't take it anymore.

"Do you know who wrote it?" Michael asked, his voice cracking due to lack of use.

Bo shrugged but kept his eyes fixated on his own shoes. "Doesn't matter."

Michael wanted to argue, but Bo was right. Anyone in the school could've been responsible, because everyone was against him in one way or another. Even if they found out who wrote today's insult, someone else would step up for tomorrow.

"We don't have to talk about it," Michael began. "I know that's how you and Andy like to do things."

Michael wasn't used to the idea of banned topics in relationships. In the books he read or the movies he watched, best friends were always portrayed as keepers of each other's secrets, pairings that told each other everything. Even his parents had a code of honesty. They were always talking about their feelings, whether they were positive or negative.

There wasn't an argument they couldn't talk into a compromise.

Michael wondered how long Bo and Andy had been withholding themselves from each other. Had it always been like this? A constant tightrope walk across uncomfortable discussions? Or was it something they learned over the years, something that built up behind their walls like water behind a dam?

However, it began, it wasn't working anymore. Michael thinks they all knew that, even if in the back of their minds. The biting of tongues and adamant avoidance did nothing but build a steady tension. Michael was still new to the friendship, and he even felt what must have been burdening the two of them for years now.

But how to fix it?

"I used to be in therapy, you know." He tried to mention it casually but failed. "For my nightmares. I was still pretty little. I remember the first meeting I went to. I was so humiliated. 'Cause, like, who wants to sit down and talk about being afraid of going to sleep for a whole hour with a stranger? Especially since... You know, we don't do that sort of thing. We're supposed to just man up and push through it, right?"

He remembered it clearly. His mother dragging him down to the office, the Kit-Cat clock in the lobby, and its blinking eyes, perfectly matching the rhythm of Michael's anxious foot tapping on the ground. His father had an arm slung around Michael's shoulders to steady him, but it did little to soothe him. He knew his father noticed the embarrassing flush creeping up to his cheeks. They avoided eye contact with each other.

"Then, when I actually sat down and faced the psychologist, I was more scared than anything else. I feel like every book I read portrays those kinds of doctors as evil. Or at least portray the patients as beyond saving. I didn't want to be another screwed-up person from the movies."

He hadn't wanted to be another crazy person. He had just watched *The Silence of the Lambs* against his parents' wishes, and his brain was rotted with nightmare fuel. When he had left the theater with his friends, they went on about what they'd do if they came across such disgusting psychos.

In retrospect, Michael shared literally nothing with Hannible Lecter or Buffalo Bill, but the judgment of those with disturbing mentalities had stuck with him in the moment.

Michael paused and turned to Bo, only to find him looking right back.

"It wasn't like that, though. The lady I talked with was really nice, and she didn't pressure me to open up right away. Instead, we talked about movies or sports. When I finally loosened up, I was able to talk about what was going on. What it felt like when I was waking up with no control of my body. The things I would see that would terrify me. Even the time I wet the bed." Michael watched Bo pursing his lips. "It's okay, you can laugh."

"It's not that," Bo muttered and let Michael continue.

"I guess what I'm trying to get at is that it actually helped me a lot. Having someone to listen to me without judgment, just to hear me out for *my* side of the story. It made me feel like I wasn't going crazy," Michael said. "I mean, the nightmares never stopped. I stopped going after a couple of months. But honestly? I kind of think everyone should have a chance to try it out, even if they don't have any mental problems or anything. I think everyone should be able to talk about stuff that's bothering them, no matter how... trivial."

Michael stopped in his tracks at the edge of town. They were coming out of the woods now. Any concealment they had from the trees would be broken away by the bustling streets, and Michael knew that it was always more difficult to talk about stuff in the open.

"At the end of the day, I realized that it hurt a lot more to keep the stuff inside of me. Letting it bounce around the walls of my head, building up until it was all I could think about, making me paranoid that people could sense my thoughts off me... " He didn't know if anything he was saying was getting to Bo. He didn't know if he was rambling on for no reason. But even if Bo didn't react to his words, it felt better to get them off his chest and out there. If he couldn't convince Bo, Michael was convincing himself of the truth of his own words. "I think people need to talk about things, even if it scares them. *Especially* if it scares them."

Michael watched the rise and fall of Bo's shoulders through his serrated breath. He couldn't tell if the flush of Bo's cheeks was from the cold or embarrassment. His mouth was a fierce red, and Michael wondered if he'd been biting back words the entire walk.

"Is there something you want to talk about?"

Finally, Bo took a quivering breath. "Your arms look tired." He pointed to Michael's grip on the handles. He hadn't realized that his knuckles had gone white and started shaking. Bo gently took the weight of the bike away from him. "I guess I've been able to convince myself that if I talk about it, it makes it all true. Right now, everything is like Schrödinger's cat. If I don't acknowledge it, it can't... hurt me."

He glanced at Michael before quickly looking back down at the ground. "I know that I should be used to it by now, after years of living here, but I just—I just can't. It's like I'm able to *feel* every word. What people said about Selene, about my parents, or why I moved here in the first place. My hand." Bo seemed to register that he was tapping his thumb against his missing finger and stopped. "People have spent so long building the story up on their own that if I told them I'd just accidentally cut it off myself, I don't think they'd believe me. It's like one of our ghost stories."

He smiled a bit at that before his face became stone again. "But it's harder when they aren't too far off. When they actually say the right things to get under my skin. Things that, you know, I never even realized about myself. Then suddenly it's like this slap in the face. Like this fucking wake-up call. And if they were right about—" His voice cracked, and he cleared his throat.

"You know, if they were right about me being gay, what if every other shitty thing they've ever said about me is true, too?" Bo looked back towards Michael. He was blinking quickly. "What then?"

Bo dropped the bike. Michael watched as it clambered into the dirt as Bo stalked off to the woods.

It was that feeling of seeing Bo's locker earlier that day. Being able to feel the blood pumping into his fingers as his hand grew heavy, the way his mouth went dry, and the ache in the middle of his chest.

When he closed his eyes, Michael saw the word on the locker. *HOMO*.

Michael glanced back.

Bo had sat down, his back resting against a tree, and his head pointed towards the sky. Michael took the spot next to him. Bo had his eyes shut tight. Michael watched him inhale through his mouth and exhale through his nose over and over. Michael reached a hand out to touch Bo's shoulder, but he was shrugged off. He stuffed his hands in his pockets instead.

"That doesn't matter to me. At all." Michael said. He needed Bo to know.

"But it matters to *me*." He scoffed. "I know it's not like it's going to fucking—go away or something. I know I'm stuck with it. It's just like... it was never *mine* to care about. Everyone knew before I did. Something about me that I still have no clue about. It was like they could just smell it. I was being called a queer before I even knew what that word meant. Do you even know what that's like? To have everyone know this huge fucking thing that you could barely even grasp onto without feeling like you're throwing yourself off some sort of cliff."

"No, I don't," Michael said. "I don't know what that's like at all."

Bo let out an exasperated sigh. He turned to Michael wearily. In that gaze, Michael *felt* it. The exhaustion and frustration, the humiliation and dread.

"I didn't know," Michael confessed. "I never even... I mean, people talked, but I never really believed them."

"Maybe you should have."

Michael shook his head. "No," he said simply. He hoped Bo understood.

He must have, because he kept going. "I only realized it a couple of years ago, once I started high school. Before, it was such a faraway concept. I'd see stuff about AIDS or shit on the news, and it didn't even feel like it existed in the same world as me, you know? Then, it was like I couldn't get away from it." Bo gave a short laugh. "I kind of thought I got super-hearing or something, because suddenly every time someone mentioned it, I noticed. Someone could just say the word 'gay' or 'fairy' across the room, and I'd have to stop myself from snapping my head in their direction. It didn't matter if they yelled it or whispered it. It didn't matter if it was about me or not. I mean, in some way, it was always about me anyway. I guess. That probably doesn't make any sense."

Suddenly, Michael couldn't take it anymore. He reached over and grabbed Bo by the shoulders, pulling him into Michael's chest. He wrapped his arms around the other boy, letting Bo's head bury in the crook of his neck. At first, Bo's arms stayed limp at his side, but then he clung back.

He wondered how Bo had managed to keep it all inside. It was like Michael could see the heaviness of it seeping out of him. The loneliness was a noose around Bo's neck, one he couldn't loosen. Michael thought he knew what it was like to feel alone, the nightmares dragging him out of touch with everyone, but at least he had people to talk to, people to listen to him.

"You know, it's probably not a good thing to hug me like this. People talk."

"Let them."

"But you're not..?"

"No, no. I'm normal." He cringed at his own words. "Sorry, not like—"

"It's fine." Bo shrugged. "I get it."

Which only worked to make Michael feel even worse.

Bo pulled back to bring his knees to his chest. "There's nobody here like me."

It was strange hearing his inner thoughts spoken out loud by somebody else. When he was people-watching out of Robinson's window or walking down the hallways of W.B. High, it was so apparent that he was alone in his identity. Unlike Bo, though, Michael's race was the first thing people noticed. If it came down to it, Bo could always try to deny the rumors of his sexuality. Michael couldn't hide the shade of his skin or the shape of his eyes.

"I know what that's like."

"Yeah?"

"Yeah, I really do." Michael crossed his legs and leaned back against the tree. "I mean, obviously. There's no other Asian people here, Bo."

Bo blinked and then seemed embarrassed. "I never even thought about that. Shit. I'm sorry, man."

Michael shrugged. "I mean, there's not really anything I can do about it. I don't think my parents thought about that, either." In his mind, Michael kept thinking, *I have never said this out loud before.* Sometimes, certain thoughts felt like betrayal. Like thinking poorly about his parents was spitting on everything they'd given him. Except Michael was tired of keeping things in, too. "I'm thankful to them for everything. They picked me when nobody else would. But I think that pretending that I'm, you know, white has... messed me up or something. I used to hop onto the subway and ride down to Chinatown, just to be around people like me, just to be able to see people that I looked like. Except, it was so hard."

Michael laughed a bit. Bo wasn't, though; he was completely focused on Michael, and it felt good to have someone clinging onto every word he said. "I still felt like I was doing it all wrong. I heard this language I never learned, ate these foods I never grew up tasting, and watched this culture I never got to be a part of. Even when I was with people like me, I was still so disconnected." Michael smiled at Bo. "I miss it, though. I think you would have liked San Francisco."

Bo scoffed. "Why, because it's like the gayest city in the country?" But there wasn't a bite to his snapping. He was joking, Michael realized.

"Oh, come on. Do you know how many gay clubs there were? Dude, you'd be having the time of your life." Michael was smirking. He tried to imagine Bo sneaking into one of those places. Everyone he'd seen entering was wearing tight pants and mesh tops, glitter spread across their skin, and a wicked grin on their faces. It seemed like a good enough time.

"I don't think so." But Bo was smiling. "It's like what you said about feeling disconnected. Even if I were surrounded by other... gay people, I still don't know if I'd find people like me there. I think I'd like to visit, though. Maybe you could take Andy down to the coast while I get shitfaced to Mercury and Bowie singing sweet nothings into my ear."

"Sorry to break it to you, Bo, but I'm pretty sure the gay clubs up there only play EDM."

"Why the fuck do you know so much about what's going on in the gay clubs?" Bo laughed.

"Hey, hey. I'm secure enough in my masculinity to like—"

"What, experiment?"

"All I'm saying is you know where my feelings land on David Duchovny."

Bo was shaking his head, grinning from ear to ear. "I can't believe you right now."

Michael raised his hands in surrender and stifled a laugh. Then he cleared his throat. "Speaking of Andy... does he know?"

Bo's smile immediately dropped. "We don't—"

"Talk about it? Right."

Bo groaned. "Michael, cut me some slack here, okay? Shit, man. I've never talked about this with anyone. This is probably the first time I've even said it out loud."

"Seriously?" Michael furrowed his brows together.

Bo shrugged. "Not technically. I went through a phase where I would just say it to my reflection in the mirror over and over. Trying to get used to it or something. But this is the first time I've said it out loud to somebody else. I never really got the chance before." Michael felt something blossom in his chest at that. Ever since he was younger, he had always been a stand-in kind of friend. Someone to talk to while waiting for somebody else. He was never the first person to tell a secret to. Even though the circumstances were muddled, he felt honored that he was the first person Bo had chosen. Bo said, "Andy knows."

"He doesn't listen to the stuff people say about you. You know that, right? Obviously, he doesn't mind the gossip, but when it comes to you, he's like a guard dog. The only thing that matters is what *you* tell him."

"It's not that, not the rumors. It's—" He cut himself off. Michael saw something flash across his face, like he was remembering something unpleasant. "There's no way he *doesn't* know. So now we're in this sort of stalemate, and I don't know what's gonna happen to us when one of us finally acknowledges it."

Michael noticed the way Bo gripped onto his arm to stop himself from shaking. He was suddenly struck by how truly terrified Bo was. It made him think of every time Andy reached out to touch him and how every time Bo pulled away, like his touch was an open flame.

"I know he makes jokes, but Andy wouldn't care. He's not like that."

"I know."

"He's your best friend, Bo."

"I *know*."

"He cares about you."

Bo closed his eyes. "You don't get it."

"Then help me understand."

Bo stood up. "I can't—I can't talk about this anymore."

Michael was reminded that this wasn't normal for him. That Bo wasn't used to being pushed and pushed for answers. That Andy had always let him be—never straining, never asking too much or going too far. Bo wasn't used to someone listening to him like that. More importantly, Michael was beginning to realize how suffocating the town could be.

"Maybe another time?" Michael tried.

"No."

So Michael let it rest, and they walked back in silence.

Ch. Nineteen

B o had a history of miserably lounging around in his room and listening to Slowdive's *Souvlaki*. When he hit Track 5, he decided he had spent enough time feeling sorry for himself and got out of bed. Besides, the further he got into the album, the further he spiraled into his thoughts.

Every cassette he owned could be tied back to a single moment. He remembered the day he picked this album out of the clearance bin at Teddy's Tunes, his preferred music shop out of the two in Whalesborough. It was further out of town and catered to less mainstream genres. Teddy Jr., who went by Theo, had taken over the shop from his father by the time Bo started going there. They had bonded over their shared love of cassettes, despite CDs becoming a more popular medium.

Every time Bo got a new album, Andy would come over to listen with him. They'd lie on their backs and listen to each song, sharing their thoughts or interrupting the lyrics by saying, "This reminds me of that time..." until they'd gone through each track and then some repeats.

Bo didn't want to think of the memories tied to the first time he listened to this album with Andy.

Some things were better left untouched in his mind. He clicked off the cassette player and carefully slipped the tape back into its case before returning it to its place in his bedside table.

The compact drawer mimicked the corners of Bo's mind. Trinkets of a past Bo would rather not remember, but too intertwined with him to part with. Cassette tapes that hurt to listen to, pictures of his mother whom he barely recognized, birthday cards from his father in rushed handwriting, a small pin with a pink triangle he'd found in the trash years ago in a frantic haze. Each item cluttered the tight space, collecting dust in the darkness. When he was feeling especially desperate and alone, he'd take each one out one by one and trace the rough edges.

His eyes scanned across the drawer. Bo had thought about moving the items somewhere more secure, like in a shoebox hidden in the closet. Whenever Andy came over, Bo's heart would always pound in his chest when he stood by the table. He imagined what Andy would see if he opened it and wondered if his friend would even realize what he was looking at. Would he see a mess of strange objects, or would he find Bo raw and unraveled? Sometimes, Bo thought of just dumping out the drawer to Andy and saying, "Do you get it now?" He thought of Andy picking through each hidden treasure and holding it up between himself and Bo.

"Do you get it now?" But he could never bring himself to do it.

He thumbed a photograph of his mother. It was a little after he was born, though he wasn't in the shot. It was candid, forever keeping her in a moment of laughter. A strand of her mousy hair caught in her mouth, freckles prominent on her cheeks and nose from the summer blaze, lip curled, and eyes shut. Only at angles did he find her in himself.

The structure of their ears, their knobby knuckles that grew deep red in the cold, the matching shade of their lips. Little things that could only be noticed upon closer inspection.

He didn't have any of his father in him besides his inability to talk. Instead, the Cassidy he took after was Selene. It was difficult to imagine that his father and his aunt were siblings. Growing up, he always thought Selene was from his mother's side because they were always so much closer. Always linking arms and giggling with each other.

If he tried, he could almost remember the first time he came to Whalesborough with his mother as she helped Selene open up her shop. His legs dangling off the counter as they blasted Fleetwood Mac on the radio, his mother pulling a broom out of Selene's hand to drag her into a dance.

He even remembered his aunt picking him up and holding him between them. His grip on her shirt collar, her chin on his head, looking up to see his mother and Selene's foreheads knocked together.

He thought his mother was happiest when she was with her.

A knock on the door interrupted his thoughts. He closed the drawer but kept the photograph in his hands as Selene entered. His aunt carefully stepped over a pile of clothes by the door to take the spot next to him. She looked down at the photograph and smiled softly.

"I took that one," she said softly. "You kept squirming in my arms. It was tough to keep the camera steady." Selene carefully reached over and touched the smile on his mother's face. Then she drew her hands away and clasped them in her lap.

Bo flipped it over so neither of them would have to keep looking at it. "Did you want help with dinner?" He asked even though he knew the answer. Selene never let him help out in the kitchen, probably because of his notorious accident. He also suspected it was to prove to herself that she was a better fit to take care of Bo than his parents had been. Though Selene loved Bo's mother and father, he didn't think she'd ever forgive them for how they handled raising him

"I was looking into buying ferry tickets for the anniversary." She faltered in her speech slightly. "I wanted to know how long you felt comfortable staying up there for. I usually only stay for a day or two, but if you want to visit your dad—"

"No," Bo said quickly. Then he cleared his throat and looked down at his hands. "I mean, probably not. He sounded busy, so I don't want to bother him."

"He would make time for you."

Bo wasn't sure he would, though. Not when they lived together, and especially not when they lived apart.

Bo suspected that it was his mother who wanted a baby, not his father. When she died, there wasn't really a reason for him to stick around anymore. It's not like his father put up much of a fight when Selene took him away.

Bo tapped on his flat finger rapidly.

He shut his eyes as he was brought back to the day his mother died.

She was watching him cut vegetables, singing along to a song on the radio, when she abruptly fell silent. A canary in the mines. He turned, and she was on the floor, her face contorted and unrecognizable in the moment. She didn't even look like a person. Back hunched, limbs warped, mouth agape for a scream that never came.

He didn't even register the knife coming down on his hand.

He just stood there, staring at his mother twitching and jerking on the ground as the blood splattered out of his finger. It could've been minutes, it could've been hours, it could've only been mere seconds.

He finally snapped out of his frozen state and reached for the telephone. His blood-soaked hands slipped on the dials, but he was able to call emergency services. His words slurred as the pain finally caught up to him, his hand and head pounding in unison. Bo tried his best to tell them about his mother, twitching and dying on the kitchen floor before him.

A stranger came into the kitchen yelling. Strong hands gripped the knife out of his hand and pinned his arms to his side. His body was lifted off the chair he had pulled to the side of the counter, allowing him to reach the surface. His eyes kept on his mother. He realized that he had been misunderstood and tried to explain that he hadn't called for help for himself but rather his mother. It was like they hadn't even seen her. He began to scream at them as they dragged him out of his house and into an ambulance, drawing further and further away from his mother's forgotten body.

The doctor held him down as they closed his wound with stitches. They had left the missing finger with the carrots, and it was too late to go back. His father was unreachable, so Selene was called. He remembers a police officer waiting with him, holding Bo's good hand tightly but providing little comfort.

Hours in the waiting room. Hours alone with a stranger and a half-empty carton of chocolate milk. The officer kept telling him how brave he was and how good he was, and that it was okay if he needed to cry. Bo brought the shortened finger to his palm, distracting himself with the itching cotton.

He asked the officer if they had gone back for his mother, too. He had looked away from Bo.

Selene burst into the room. When Bo saw her tears, he knew that his mother was dead. She fell to her knees in front of him, head in his lap, as she soaked his bloodstained clothes with her sobs. He gently placed a hand on her head and stroked her hair. It was what his mother had done whenever he cried.

His aunt took him in her arms and held him tightly. She tried to speak to him, but her apologies kept getting broken by hiccups. As she took him back home to pack his belongings, Bo heard Selene screaming at his father, already drunk after a long day at work.

His father took every vile word, not disputing a single thing. When Bo came out of his room, a suitcase gripped in his wounded hand, and his father turned to him, slack-faced and a bottle held close to his chin.

Bo said, "What about Mom?"

"Take him." His father turned away from him.

Selene cried the whole way home.

Now, as they sat side by side, Bo knew they were both thinking about it.

"Sometimes," Bo began, "I think you loved her more than my dad."

She took her shaking hands and brought one up to brush a strand of hair behind his ear. "Just because love looks different doesn't mean it isn't there."

Growing up in that house, more haunted than Whalesborough, he realized why it hurt so much. His father's absence, his mother's silence. Barely talking, rarely touching, never acknowledging.

He remembered why he didn't talk about his mom anymore.

To everyone else, it was like his mother was already gone, with only Bo to remember her.

The way her tongue peeked out in the corner of her mouth when she was concentrating. When she would bend Bo over her knees and blow raspberries onto his stomach. How she danced like a river stream, how she sang like it was bursting out of her.

When he talked about her, Selene would get a far-off look on her face like she was reminiscing about a long time ago, even when Bo was still little.

His mother was always such a faraway thing, pulling further from his grip.

He couldn't bring it up, couldn't mention it, because Selene was always so dismissive about it. She acted like Bo was too young to truly remember her, like he lost her too quickly to ever love her. It used to make him feel like he was losing his mind. It still does.

"You always talk about her like she never had a place next to me," Bo said. "Like she was always…"

Selene's hand fell.

He shut his mouth and closed the drawer in his mind.

Ch. Twenty

They were always the last to get off the trolley. Mila was kicking at their bags on the ground, and Andy was pretending like it wasn't bothering him. He tried not to look at his backpack because then he thought about the graded quiz crumbling at the bottom. Only two weeks into school, and the losing streak had already begun.

He sighed through his nose and let his head hit the wall of the trolley.

"So this is the phase you're going through this year?" Mila asked. Andy looked at her, and she mimicked his stance in an exaggerated way. "Being super angsty or whatever."

"What are you talking about?" He decided she reached her max for a smartass attitude for the week.

"Every year, you try on a new persona. Last year you were, like, in your bad boy phase where you skipped school and flunked basically all your classes."

Andy narrowed his eyes at her.

"And then before that, you tried out being a manwhore."

"Excuse me?" Andy sprang up defensively. "I kissed a total of three people. That doesn't make me a manwhore."

"Three?" Mila's eyes widened. "I only knew about two. Wait, wait, wait. There was Bailey Tait, who you went out with Freshman year, and then you swapped spit with Lesley Galleger at the Winter Formal—"

"Don't say *swapped spit*. You make it sound disgusting."

"It is disgusting," she deadpanned, then her mouth fell open. "Wait! Was it Marissa?"

"What! Ew, no! She's like our cousin." Andy grimaced. Marissa Aguilar was a family friend from the mainland. They came down every couple of months to stay with the Romero-Almada's to catch up, but as the kids all got older and moved out, the visits became more infrequent.

"I *know*. That's why I'm mortified. Duh," Mila said. "Then who was it?"

"If you honestly think I'm going to talk about this with you, you need to get your head screwed on tighter." He pulled the bell on the trolley to ring for their stop. Mila was pouting as they stepped off to walk home.

"Look, all I'm saying is that you've been in a pissy mood lately. I just wanted to know if this is going to be your thing for the year," she told him.

He cut a glare towards her.

"Okay, so I guess it is." Mila shrugged. "But do us all a favor, Alejo? Be nicer to Mom. You're ruining it for all of us."

Andy didn't have time to respond as Mila rushed inside and headed to her room. When he entered the house, he found his mother washing dishes in the kitchen.

For a moment, he just watched her.

When Andy was growing up, his family was the one constant thing in his life. In every corner he looked, he could find a relative. Someone to hold him and listen to him. Someone to just be there with him in that moment. There was a time when the best part of Andy's day was sitting down at the dining table and passing food between his siblings, listening to his grandparents talking about Cuba and the communist party, watching his mother and father exchange glances with each other from across the table, and reaching for the other's hand.

But among his siblings and cousins, his aunts and uncles, even his grandparents and his father, Andy loved his mother the most. It wasn't ever a question. Those days when all he would do was stand by her side and cling to her leg when she was busy doing work around the house, even if he only got in her way. She'd pick him up and hold him as he grew heavier and heavier. While siblings kicked the soccer ball around the backyard, Andy sat on the kitchen counter, swinging his legs back and forth as he watched her cook or clean.

At night, he'd try to stay up late with her. When she finally sat down on the couch to relax, he'd climb next to her and lay his head in her lap. She'd drag her fingers through his hair, her nails scratching along his hairline and neck, until he fell asleep right there.

His older siblings used to make fun of him for it, calling him nene de mamá, but he didn't care back then.

Andy slowly entered the kitchen and took a place beside his mother. She had the radio playing boleros, old hits from the '60s that even Andy knew the words to. She was humming to herself as she took a wet cloth to clean off the porcelain plates. Andy remembered the days when he helped her. It had been his job to dry the dishware when she was done with it.

As the station played the next song, "Espérame en el Cielo" by Celia Cruz, he took the plate from her hand and set it down in the sink before dragging her into a dance. She didn't put up a fight.

He was taller than her now, but only by a little bit. He held onto one of her hands, still warm from the dishwater, and let his other arm wrap around her waist. She brought her arm up around his shoulders, her hand falling in the space between his shoulder blades. His mother's head rested against his neck, and he shut his eyes as they swayed.

Dancing was a language in the household as much as Spanish was. He remembered the unofficial lessons his grandparents instructed him through, mambo and bachata. They'd count each step with a clap of their hands and make him spin around the room until he was dizzy. There were times he found himself tapping along the street instead of walking.

As he held his mother, he realized that the last time he danced with her was when he was still shorter. And in that moment, he missed her so much.

He didn't remember the day he stopped clinging to her skirt or the last time she carried him back to bed after falling asleep in her lap. He doesn't remember when he stopped trailing her like a shadow or when he last helped her bring in the groceries from the car. Andy didn't even remember the last time he told his mother that he loved her.

He tried to push away the shame of that, but he couldn't. Instead, he held his mother tighter and told her right then. She murmured into his shoulder. He didn't catch her words, though he could imagine what she had said. Lo sé. I know.

Andy started singing along to the song, not very well, but enough so that he felt his mom smiling. She took her hand off his back and to his hair and gently patted where it was long on his neck. "You need a haircut," she said.

"I like it like this," he responded.

She shook her head. "I don't get the style these days."

"I don't think I do, either."

"Jaime always kept his hair so short."

Andy faltered.

Suddenly, he remembered *why* they didn't do this anymore. Why he skipped out on dinner and instead stayed in his room, pretending to be busy with homework. Why he had stopped spending time with his mother, stopped doing mundane tasks for the sole reason of being with her. Why he started pulling away and staying away.

Andy's mother was his favorite person, but he wasn't hers. More than that, he was nobody's favorite. The realization cut him deep, carved him hollow, and left him empty. It hurt to watch everybody walk past him to reach somebody else.

He spent so long wondering why that was. The question that echoed in his mind, refusing to pass his lips at the kitchen table each night, but deafened him nonetheless—*Do you even like me?* Glancing between his mother and father, his sisters and brothers, everyone who shared his last name but refused to meet his eyes. *Do you?*

He knew it was more fun being around him when he was a boy. Back then, he was allowed to be messy and tumultuous, brash and loud. It was part of his charm, the family troublemaker. As he got older, though, he found that everyone was waiting for him to grow out of that part of himself, but he never did.

That silent doubt was heavy under his skin. Was it enough? To be of their blood and have his height marked along the kitchen wall; was that enough for them to keep putting up with him? Even now, he knew how he tested them without trying. He had thought that maybe if he pulled away on his own, locked himself in his room at night, or stayed out of the way during the day, he'd spare them. But that still seemed to piss them off as well.

Nothing he did could ease the tension.

The failed test was burning a hole in his backpack.

Andy pulled away from his mother. She still had her arms around him, raising her head to look him in the eye.

In that gaze, he felt it all at once. Self-conscious and ashamed, but most importantly, completely embarrassed by who he was at that moment. He wanted to ask her if she loved him because he was her son or because he was Andy, but he wasn't sure if he actually wanted to know the answer—if he needed the answer at all.

She took his face in her hands, her eyes crinkling. He thought she was reading his mind, and he worried about what she would think of him. Worse, he was scared that if she knew what he thought of himself, she would agree. Quietly and carefully, she spoke. "A veces, te miro y me pregunto dónde fue mi niño feliz."

Perfect moments with his mother only existed in childhood.

Andy brought his own hands up to cup her wrists and held her for a second.

He didn't know what he was supposed to say. Or if there was even a proper way to respond.

For so long, he felt like a shell of the boy he used to be. Like every attempt to get back there—to those endless days with nothing but laughter and ease— was futile. Working to find it in his old hobbies, he would set down his baseball mitt, realizing that nothing was fun like that anymore. His room held an atmosphere of disconnection, even when buried under his sheets. He worked to avoid the gaze of his family and classmates. Bo was far away. But even more apparent, Andy had lost himself along the way, too.

Looking in the mirror at night, the lights dim and the shadows on his face elongated, he pinpointed each feature that belonged to somebody else. He was made up of people who loved him disproportionately to how he loved them. He touched his eyebrows, his nose, his lips, and his throat and wondered, *who is this kid?* Only to find he would be met with no answer.

Sometimes Andy went through photo albums to look for him.

He wondered if his mother said things to hurt him on purpose. He had moments like that, too. But her gaze looked too earnest, too sincere, and he realized that she only said it because she truly meant it, which somehow wounded him more. Nothing hurt more precisely than when his mother's cruelty was meant to be love.

Andy took her hands off him.

"So do I."

Ch. Twenty-One

Almost a month in Whalesborough, and they had yet to clean the attic still. While his parents were busy modernizing the rest of the house (which included connecting landlines, tearing down walls, and adding new wallpaper), Michael was left to clear out trash and organize the leftover clutter. He finally made his way to the south hallway and was greeted by the scuttle hole to the attic hanging above him.

He tightened the bandana around his mouth and nose so the dust wouldn't bother him before reaching for the rope to pull the drop-down ladder. The wood creaked as it fell. Michael frowned at the splintered steps. As it rested on the floor, he tested his weight on the bottom step. The wood gave slightly.

Michael sighed. It was going to be a long day of cleaning.

He scurried up the ladder, ignoring the uneasiness of the structure, before pulling himself up to the attic. Michael immediately felt the stickiness of a spider web hit his face and swatted it away, groaning. He pulled a headlamp out of his pocket and tied it around his forehead.

Clicking the light on, he scanned the attic. Dusted crates stacked in corners, old wooden

furniture like rocking chairs, and toy horses swung
back and forth as a breeze swept through the attic.
Somewhere, an old wasp nest hung from the low
ceiling like an omen. It reminded Michael of every
single horror movie he'd ever seen. He stifled a chill
going up his spine.

He'd decided he'd try to spend as little time as
possible in the creepy place, so he quickly got to
work. Going through different antiques and judging
their quality—what his mother could salvage or what
his father could donate to local shops. Then he
started going through the crates, ripping off the
wooden lids and brushing the dust off the trinkets
inside.

Some held fabrics and old winter gear; others
held things like old dolls or silverware. One box was
filled to the brim with broken glass, and Michael felt
his stomach plummet. He'd gotten around to
wearing shoes throughout the house (Bo would be
shaming him if he knew) due to the glass shards
littering the crooks of his floorboards. He hadn't had
another intense experience like the time he woke up
in his bed with a bleeding arm or when the mirror
had shattered when the boys were over. Now it was
just small things that could be brushed off as normal.
Whatever normal meant now.

Don't think about it, Michael told himself. *Not
during the day*.

He closed the bin as he heard someone else enter the attic. His father popped through the scuttlehole. "All good up here, Mikey?"

Michael shrugged. "I think there might be bats up here. I really don't feel like getting rabies."

His father laughed and joined him. Michael was pleased with the company.

He remembers the first time he saw his father. He had come to the care home to write an article on the foster system. While he observed, jotting down notes as the kids went through their everyday activities, Michael perched next to him and peered over his shoulder.

His father had asked him if Michael wanted to be interviewed, and he agreed passively. At first, they talked about what it was like living there, sharing a sleeping space with the other boys, and the strict schedule they followed. Then, Michael told him about going to the different homes, all the different people Michael had lived with, and all the different towns he'd traveled through. When Michael ran out of stories to tell, he started making stuff up.

He remembered his father asking him if he thought about his biological parents, which seemed like a bit of a loaded question to spring on an eight-year-old, looking back. Michael confessed that he knew enough. From hours spent looking at the government papers kept secure in the system and what he learned from his caretakers, Michael knew a good enough story of how he ended up in the home. Young mother, young father, poor planning, and a regretful nine months.

Sometimes he'd sneak in to see his birth certificate, just to see their names. He'd trace his finger over the print, *James Hughes* and *Susan Kuang*. They felt more like characters than people, faceless figures in his head that Michael tried to picture. He'd bring a hand to each part of his face and think, *Are these my mother's or my father's?* Well-aware that he'd never know the answer.

Michael wondered how much they had talked it through. How many nights did they stay up, questioning whether they'd give him up? A bitter part of him hoped they lost sleep over it, that they cried over it, and regretted their decision just too late. Another, softer part of him hoped they only did it for the best, that they did it because they wanted him to have a life they wouldn't be able to provide for him.

He'd told his (soon-to-be) father some of this. Other parts he kept to himself. Michael remembered that his father had set his pen and notebook down to listen to him, not writing anymore. After, Michael had smiled and shrugged before thanking the stranger for his time and wishing him luck with his article.

A couple of weeks later, he came back with his wife, and they'd taken Michael home with them and given him the name McKenzie.

"How's the cleaning?" His father asked. He kicked at a spinning top Michael had dropped from the bin.

"Eh..." Michael said as he glanced around the room. He'd only gotten through a quarter of the attic.

"Welp, it's a good thing I'm here to lend a helping hand." His father clapped. "Definitely not avoiding your mother's questions about paint and kitchen tiles."

"Oh, so you're not here for me." Michael turned back to the boxes. "I'm just an excuse to escape Mom's nagging. I see."

"You're kidding."

Michael frowned. "My feelings are *very* hurt."

"Yeah, you're kidding." His father rolled up his sleeves. "What are we doing here, kid? I don't need to tell you not to touch anything cursed, do I?"

"Shoot, I forgot about that rule. I've touched about five different haunted dolls, so if they start showing up in corners, that's my bad."

"You joke about that now, but our neighbors might actually kill us if we unleash evil upon the town."

"Oh well," Michael said flatly, but a smile escaped him.

His father took the left while he stuck to the right, going through the boxes one at a time. They were used to working together like this in other spaces, too. Michael was on the right side of the table working on homework, and his father was on the left working on his writing. It was the same when they were cooking meals together or cleaning the living room before his mom came home. Even back at their old house, when the three of them shared a bathroom, brushing their teeth side by side before they had to hurry out the door, they had an order.

In the past couple of weeks, they had all been so busy with their own things. His father buried himself in his work, taking full advantage of the opportunities the East Coast was providing him. His mother worked to replace her past job as a notary in San Francisco. While that was in the works, she instead put effort into building relationships among the island residents. Whatever free time they had, they spent on the house.

Michael had thought about mentioning the severity of the nightmares, about the stalking, about the constant state of paranoia he was living in, but when he saw them exhausted from their troubles, he'd bite his tongue. Besides, he was too old to get scared of his imagination now. If his parents knew the true extent of his... disorder? It didn't really matter. He just didn't want them to panic and send him away to some sort of ward. He heard them talking about that late one night when he was younger and first started having nightmares.

Furthermore, his parents didn't seem nearly as affected by Whalesborough's supernatural roots as Michael was. They joked about the townsfolk enough for Michael to realize that they were aware of the stories, but they always brushed them off. If his parents weren't going to bring it up, Michael wasn't going to either.

So to say he was furious with himself when he screamed after opening the final crate was an understatement. His father immediately dropped whatever he was holding to race over to Michael's side and place a reassuring hand on his shoulder.

Michael had backed away from the box, hand gripping his shirt as his heart beat rapidly. His father looked at him curiously before approaching the box and pulling out the photographs littered around.

His father held a heavy portrait framed in gold. He carefully brought it up to face Michael. "Is this what gave you a fright?" Michael knew he meant it to sound playful, but he could hear the concern in his father's voice.

Michael tried to hide his fear as he gazed into the face of the girl above his bed.

She looked perfectly identical, except more... lively. Like she was present, like she had truly been a person. A lace collar and silk blouse, her blonde hair braided back with ribbons. The photograph was sepia, but Michael noticed the shade of blush on her cheek and a sparkle in her eyes. He had to stop himself from reaching out for the photo.

It was so startling to see her in a different context. She belonged in his nightmares, in the shadows of his room, and in the corners of his mind. She...

"I mean, I get it. Victorian children always give me the creeps, too. Yeesh." His father dropped the photo back into the crate. "Seems like you've been getting all the spooky bins. I can take them from here, kid. Why don't you go downstairs and indulge in your mother's comparisons of white shades? Save me the trouble of choosing between eggshell and linen sheets, would you?"

"Dad..."

How could a girl who had his mind made up to scare him exist in a photograph? How could this preservation of her life reside in the house all along?

No, no, no.

Those weren't the right questions at all. Michael was beginning to realize that now.

"It's okay, Mikey. Let me take care of it from here." His father smiled, but it didn't reassure him.

The name engraved in the frame was burned in his mind.

EDITH BECKHAM

The right question was this: How did Michael know the face of a girl who died a hundred years ago?

It was a terrible, terrible thing to realize that Michael McKenzie may not be crazy.

Ch. Twenty-Two

The ringing never stopped.

The rain pounded down on the roof like bullets. The wind slapped against the window, wet and arduous. It felt like the entire house was shaking. Maybe it was just Bo.

But the ringing never stopped.

He kept picking it up, pulling it close to his ear, and sticking a finger in the opposite one to drown out any other noise. The storm outside was ceaseless, demanding his attention, but Bo stayed focused on the call.

When he first picked up, he was met with a terrible screeching. A scream that rivaled metal against glassware or fingers against chalkboard. He thought his ears might burst, but he had yet to bleed. Bo hung up and waited for the next call.

Five minutes later, he picked up again. This time, he heard her sobbing. Violent and interminable, getting louder and louder with each heave of a breath. It was worse than the screaming. Bo blinked tears out of his own eyes as he listened to the cries before slowly placing the phone back on the wall.

Again, he picked up on the first ring. Bo pushed the phone as close to his ear as he could to pick up the whispers. The murmuring of desperate sentences was inaudible, Bo only managed to pick out a few words here or there. *Hurt* and *home* stuck out to him. He kept trying to talk back, asking them to speak a little louder, but it was Bo who was now met with a dial tone.

The storm raged on. The weather in Whalesborough was never subtle. If it were hot, it would scorch the entire island. If it turned out to be cold, it would freeze you from the inside out. If it were going to be dry, the air would taste like static. If it rained, it poured for hours and hours.

From miles away, Bo could close his eyes and picture the roaring sea. Waves as tall as buildings, as powerful as cannons, more ruthless than the storm outside. Even in his room, Bo shivered.

The ringing returned.

"Please," Bo whispered. "Please."

His head rested on his knees, his voice strained from choking down his fear, his eyes blurring from exhaustion. Bo couldn't stop, though. Not until he helped her, whoever she was.

"Who are you?"

He waited for the screaming, the crying, or the silent pleas he could barely make out. He wasn't sure how much longer he could take this before he broke.

It must have been some kind of torture, listening to someone in agony and not being able to do anything.

Until, "*I don't know.*"

Bo sat up straighter. A voice, clear as day, of a young girl, probably no older than twelve. He gripped the phone in two hands.

"I—" What to say, what to say? "You don't know? Do you mean you don't remember?"

"*I don't know.*"

He swallowed. "Okay. That's okay. Do you know where you are?"

He listened intently to the other side of the line. Bo heard a squelch. He bit back a whimper.

"Do you know—"

"*Home.*"

"Where is that?"

"*Here.*"

Bo let his head slam back against the wall. The sound of his frustration must have been picked up because she began to cry.

"I'm sorry, I'm sorry," Bo said urgently. "I want to help you. I just need you to tell me where you are so I can do that. I can call the police to send them over or—"

"*No.*" So loud it made him flinch.

"Okay, okay. No police. I can come over by myself. Does that work? I can help you."

"*You can't.*"

Bo squeezed his eyes shut. He didn't know what he was supposed to do. He didn't even know how he got to this point in the first place.

"Then why did you call me?" He didn't even mean to say it out loud.

He was met with silence. The only indicator that she was still on the line was a sniffle. Bo's lip quivered, and he jerked as lightning flashed past his window.

"*You're the only one who can pick up.*"

Confusion stewed inside of him. "That doesn't make any *sense*."

"*You can hear.*"

His ears grew hot, and he felt the tickling sensation of the blood building up and trickling down. He reached his finger between the phone and himself and spared a glance at his stained fingertip. He wiped his hand on his jeans before pushing the phone back to his ear.

"I don't know what you mean," he admitted.

The girl began to make noises with her lips. Pushing out air in puffs, hissing, shushing, and making painful noises as she stretched out vowels. Listening to her work to sound out a word was far stranger than anything he had heard before.

"*Buh- Ahh- Eee-*"

The heat of the blood dripping down his neck burned. There was a pain building up behind his eyes, and he screwed them shut to fight it. His grip tightened and tightened around the phone until his hands were shaking unsteadily. He bit down on his lip to stop crying out.

"*Bo C-Cassidy.*"

The lights in his room went down as a shock from the phone made him drop it. He brought his hand up to his cheek to meet the flickering sting as if he had been slapped. He quickly shook his head and yanked the phone back to him, but the landline must have been knocked out because there wasn't even a dial tone.

His heart was pounding in his ears. He sucked in breath through his teeth. Bo raked a hand through his hair, only to remember it was wet with his blood. He felt the thickness of it coat the strands of his hair, tangling his curls. He stifled a choked gasp in his throat.

Bo stood on his shaking legs and made his way across his room in the dark. The storm, he realized, must have taken down the power along with the lines. He reached for a box of matches tucked into his desk and lit a candle Selene had picked out for him.

The glow from the fire illuminated the dark. He brought the candle close to his chest, trying to take in any heat he could. One hand holding the bottom, the other cupping the flame, he brought it higher to his face. His hold was loose due to the blood making his hands slippery.

Even now, he could feel the pooling sensation from his head. He wasn't sure how much blood he had to lose to grow worried. Unlike other kids on the school playground who got nosebleeds, Bo had only ever bled through his ears during his childhood.

He remembered being six and sitting with his mother when they started. She had taken him to the bathroom and used a wet cloth to dab away the dried blood. She told him not to plug his ears with tissues when they started.

When his father came home, he'd reluctantly taken Bo to the doctors. They couldn't find any sign of a cut or infection of any kind, so they chalked it up to a ruptured eardrum. His father scoffed but didn't argue. Bo realized that his father should have. They both knew that their house was always silent. What loud noise could have done the damage?

He got them frequently all throughout the first grade, until after around a year, they ceased. It was decided that he just had sensitive ears. The only other time he got earbleeds was when his mother sang too loudly in the kitchen.

Once he moved to Whalesborough, he never got them again.

Until now, that is.

Bo took a careful step back, making sure his shaky breath didn't blow out the flame. He stumbled over his steps, lurching forward. He caught himself with his free hand and turned to the wall to face a mirror he had hung up.

Cast by the light, he caught his reflection. The bags under his eyes were only emphasized by the long shadows on his face, his hair and neck bloodstained with drying flakes clinging to his skin and curls, his lips parted and blue.

For a moment, his reflection frightened him. He blinked slowly, as if waiting to see this warped copy of himself fade away, but it stayed. It hurt to keep his eyes open. He let them fall shut.

In the darkness, Bo felt a breeze graze the back of his neck and heard a hushed whisper in his ears. He sucked in a breath as he opened his eyes.

In his reflection, he saw hands cupping his ears.

"Fuck—" Bo spun around, so quickly the flame blew out. "Shit, shit, shit!" He quickly grasped the matchbox on the desk and desperately lit the candle again. He waved it in front of him, looking for the figure who was behind him just a second prior, but he was alone in his room.

He wiped the blood and sweat from his forehead, his entire body quivering in the dark.

He let out a yelp as he heard his radio click on. He heard the whirling of the mechanics, the static change of stations; he even saw the glow of the technology on his desk. He stood back, not daring to move from his place as the sound poured into his room.

Bo neurotically listened as the radio distorted and sang. He heard the cackling of a woman's laugh, drawn-out strings, a baby cooing, and a man's voice echoing in the dark. He didn't mean to. He dropped the candle. It went out before it hit the floor, and Bo was cast in darkness once more.

As the voices of arguments broke out through the radio, Bo realized that it was a song that was playing. He almost laughed when he finally recognized The Beatles' "Revolution 9." The feeling of familiarity soothed his nerves.

Even though the song sent shivers down his spine, he was able to take a deep breath and calm himself down. He told himself he was alone and that nothing else was there to hurt him. He swallowed down the rest of his fear and picked the candle off the floor, setting it down on his desk before creeping out into the hallway.

"Selene..." He called out. It was late—almost past one in the morning. He didn't think his aunt would be up, but if she was, he didn't want to startle her in the dark. "*Selene!*" Bo hissed louder.

When he came into the open, he found a circle of thin candles lit around the dining table. It reminded Bo of the day Andy had set up the séance at Michael's place. He looked in the kitchen to find a kettle boiling water, the bubbling providing ambiance in the dark.

As Bo stepped closer to the table, he felt his sock grow damp. Lifting his feet off the floor, he found a puddle of tea. Selene must have accidentally tipped over the mug at some point, but she wasn't anywhere to be found anymore.

Reaching for the spilling cup, Bo's hand paused at the single tarot card illuminated by the dark.

The Devil stared back at him.

The teapot began to scream as the blood from his ears dripped onto the red man.

Ch. Twenty-Three

To be a Romero was to be a falsifier. To be an Almada was to grin through the lies.

Falsehood was passed down by fathers, something tied to the Romero name. Misleading came from his mother's side, an Almada trait more than the latter. Andy Romero-Almada had been born to spread cheap smiles like butter and let lies roam around like fruit flies. Give just enough away to satisfy others, but never the truth.

His family was as ancient as the island. Where there was a corner of Whalesborough, there was a Romero or Almada. They were well respected, a vital part of the local community, without an exact reason. Other families had an obvious purpose. They came from wealth and worked to keep the town afloat with charities and donations. While the Almadas came later, the Romeros had always lingered. Though they had few physical contributions, their history was a thing of sacred mystery, something among the whispers of the town's gossip. *Romero*.

To be a Romero-Almada was to lie and lie and lie.

Andy thought perhaps that he was a Romero, through and through. More than anything else.

In his blood and his home. He had the face of his father and the tongue of his mother. A contagious smile with words that could talk his way out of anything. The Romero-Almada siblings were all similar enough in looks and different in charm, but shared the identical trait of being confident prevaricators.

Andy had learned that there was little difference between a lie and the truth and that it was his job to correct the order of the world with his mouth in whichever way he deemed fit.

When Michael had asked him if he had been watching his house, he had responded with a hindrance of the truth, just as he had been taught to.

Almost, but never enough.

The truth was this: Andy was running out of time. Watching the old Beckham place at night wasn't enough anymore. He was going to find a way to get inside one way or another.

Tonight, though, was not the night to do it. The ground was unsteady from the storm, the power was still out around town from the strong winds, and the static electricity was still in the air. Andy shouldn't even have snuck out to hide beyond the woods of the Beckham property, honestly. Especially not after being chased out last time.

It was risky.

He was desperate.

Andy didn't want to think about it.

He turned on his heel to head home.

The cold bit at him each step of the way. When he made his way out of the woods, he opted to walk along the trolley's road. How many times has he taken this path? How many hours, how many nights?

He'd been going to the Beckham place long before the McKenzie's moved there. The creaking steps, the chipping walls, the chill of the building—all of it was his before it was Michael's. Even before it became a nightly ritual to visit the property in the dark, Andy was always drawn.

He remembered going back as a boy after the Halloween fiasco with Bo and the other kids. He sat where Bo had sat, cross-legged in the center of the foyer, waiting for something to happen. He wanted to hear what Bo had heard, see what Bo had seen, and know what Bo had known. Nothing came to him, but he didn't give up.

Something in the back of his mind told him he had to do it—that it would be his *purpose* to find what was lurking in the house. He never understood that deep desire that carved out a home in his chest until he was ten, when his parents gave him the key to the basement.

He thumbed at the key now. There were times he gripped it in his hand, letting the rigid edges of the key cut into his palm and leave dents. Other days, he did everything in his power not to touch it.

It was a conflicting thing being Andy Romero-Almada.

He had realized that he wasn't so much of a liar as he was a hypocrite.

He steered away from his usual path and walked down to the shore instead. The sea was the only part of Whalesborough that he hadn't managed to corrupt yet. Unlike everything else in his life, he couldn't take the ocean in his hands and squeeze it past a breaking point. Its magnitude was completely unfathomable to him—exactly what Andy needed.

Andy felt as if he still loved like a little boy.

He remembered when a small bird had fallen from its nest in their backyard. His grandmother had opened his palm and gently placed the creature inside. "Gentle," she had warned. "So you don't hurt it."

In his hand, it felt almost nonexistent. As heavy as a paperclip, too soft to seem tangible, the only indication of its reality was the steady beat of its heart against Andy's skin. In his hand, it was too perfect to be palpable. Even at his young age, he was aware of the purity of it.

He fell in love with it in those seconds, immensely and absolutely, just like he loved everything else in his life. His family, his friends, his home. All of it.

Before he could even comprehend what he was doing, he was squeezing his hands close. The bird squawked in pain, and his grandmother quickly snatched it from his hands and began to scold him. She ranted about his inability to be careful with fragile things and that if he didn't pay attention, he would break something beautiful without realizing it.

Somewhere along the reprimanding, Andy understood that it wasn't just about the bird anymore.

The moments he'd held his baby sister too tightly to him and ended up hurting her. When he'd grip his mother in such a fierce way, he sometimes left marks. Each time he dragged Bo around town and he'd squint in Andy's hold.

Andy was incapable of loving something without suffocating it.

The ocean, though, was too big for him to grasp onto. Andy couldn't break it. Maybe that's why he loved it in a way unfamiliar to him.

He kicked off his shoes and peeled off his socks before walking into the water. He let the waves overlap his legs, the chill stinging him. Under his feet, he felt the sand give way, slowly dragging him deeper and deeper into the center of the earth. He kept his feet planted on the ground so the tide couldn't drag him away. That's what everything was like recently, he thought. Sinking and pulling, sinking and pulling.

Andy let his shoulders mimic the waves, lifting and falling, rising and crashing.

I should go home, he thought. Picturing that house, though, he couldn't bring himself to want to go back. Andy was in a constant state of limbo between loathing and loving every aspect of his life. Sometimes, he thought it was too good to belong to him. Other times... he didn't even know.

It was ironic, in a way, that Andy felt like he was haunting his own house.

He forced himself to drag his eyes from the violent waves to the abandoned lighthouse that resided on the cliff to Andy's right. Back when Whalesborough was bustling, ships would often harbor in the small town before reaching the mainland. During the mid-80s, though, fewer ships passed through. There wasn't much of a point to the lighthouse anymore, and some of the townsfolk began to complain about its endless creaking and blinding light, so it was abandoned.

On nights like the Fourth of July or New Year's Eve, someone would go up and work to start it up again, if only for a short while. Abhorrence was stalled by nostalgia.

Andy forgot what it looked like when it was shining.

As he gazed upon it, his vision tunneled. Goosebumps crawled up his spine. There was a building static in his ear that grew louder the longer he stared, but he was unable to turn away.

For a split second, he could've sworn the waves stilled.

Then they came crashing down onto him, and the lighthouse lit up like a damn firework.

He fell, his back slapping onto the wet sand. The shock of the wave had punched the breath out of his lungs, and for a split second, he thought he was dying. As the water came over his mouth, he spat out the taste of salt. Even as the waves drew back, he stayed put on the ground.

Sand in his hair, salt on his lips, his clothes soaked and clinging to his bony limbs.

He turned his head in the sand and looked up at the lighthouse, but it was dim as if it had never been on in the first place. He heard a faint buzzing, like when holding a light bulb up next to an ear, but maybe that was from hitting his head on the ground.

On the cold Earth, he couldn't bring himself to lift out of the sand. He stared above, right at the moon, and sniffled.

He could feel it.
It was happening.

Ch. Twenty-Four

Michael McKenzie was selfish when he invited Bo and Andy over for a sleepover.

He just couldn't do it anymore. The constant back and forth in his mind was like watching a tennis match, the ball passing left and right and left and right and left and right, and Michael was losing it. He was actually losing it this time.

He didn't even bother to sleep anymore. He was terrified of pulling the sheets off his bed and finding his mattress full of glass. Against his will, he found himself dozing off in other places, like class or the back rooms at Robinson's. He'd jerk awake sour and disheartened because the ease of rest outside his home was no longer comforting. It was a reminder that maybe the thing haunting him wasn't his nightmares.

When he was younger, it didn't matter where he fell asleep. He could get the paralyzing feeling anywhere. On camping trips or sleepovers, nowhere was safe, which is why he made excuses to stay at home.

Michael felt like an idiot for not piecing it together sooner.

This wasn't how it went.

So he had to know. He had to. Maybe it wasn't Michael. Maybe it was the *room*.

When Bo and Andy first came over, he knew they felt it. The unsteadiness seeped through the floors. The creeping feeling of being watched followed them around the corner. How the house seemed more alive than Michael recently.

If they spent the night in his room and *saw* what he saw...

He couldn't tell them the truth. He knew what they were like.

Bo and Andy knew that ghosts weren't real.

Michael wasn't sure how they'd respond if they knew he had his doubts.

When Michael opened the door for the other boys, his eyebrows shot to his hairline.

They looked worse than he did, and Michael hadn't slept in thirty-two hours.

Andy was blank-faced and reserved, staring holes behind Michael. His hair, usually taken care of so intently, was disheveled and knotted. Michael noticed the wound on his lips as if he'd bitten down on it vigorously. Not only that, his sleepover bag was dragging him down. Michael was unsure if Andy was a heavy packer or if he was just weak at the moment.

Bo looked even more incapacitated but stood skittish compared to his friend. Michael noticed the way his hand gripped the strap of his backpack, his knuckles cherry red from the cold, and the skin cracking. His eyes were everywhere, bouncing between the house, Michael, and Andy before going back to the house again.

Michael had the flashing thought of slamming the door in their face.

He realized he had missed his chance when his parents came bouncing around the corner.

"You must be Mikey's new friends! Welcome in!" Bo and Andy flinched at Michael's mother's energetic demeanor. She pulled the boys inside and quickly got to chatting. "We apologize for the mess. We've been so busy redecorating the house, and we weren't expecting guests so soon."

"Not that we aren't glad to have you two over," Michael's dad interrupted.

"No, no, of course not. We're so happy Mikey managed to find such nice boys to hang out with." Bo and Andy exchanged a glance with each other, which made Michael's stomach twist.

"We're going to go upstairs, so don't worry about us getting in your way," Michael told his parents, giving Bo and Andy a curt nod to get them upstairs. Andy blinked, still clearly out of it, which caused Bo to step up and drag him by the collar upstairs.

"Do you guys want us to order pizza? Or would you all prefer something homemade instead?" Michael's mom asked.

"We'll let you know later!" Michael called as he followed his friends up the stairs.

His father stopped him. "Mikey." He turned to face his dad. He spoke in a low tone to Michael. "Are you going to be okay with them sleeping over? With the…" Nightmares, he didn't say.

"It's okay," Michael said. "I know what I'm doing, Dad." Even though he didn't.

Bo was waiting by Michael's bedroom door upstairs, his head against the wall and his eyes shut. When he heard Michael coming, he cleared his throat and stood straight. "Andy went to the bathroom. I don't think he's feeling his best right now," Bo informed.

"Oh." Oh. "Did he want to go home?"

"No, no. Honestly, I think he's kind of pissed about it. He's been wanting to check this place out for ages, and last time we were here, he was a little preoccupied with his whole exorcism roleplay." Bo rubbed his eyes with the back of his hand. "I think we're all a little out of it. Sorry that we won't be much fun."

"It's okay. I get that it was kind of last-minute."
Michael shrugged.

Bo huffed out a laugh. "Andy only does shit last
minute. I'm used to it."

Michael took the space next to Bo and leaned
against the wall with him, waiting for Andy. If he was
being honest, he was so anxious about organizing
this setup that he completely forgot that it had been
years since he last had someone over at his place.

Back home, he was constantly getting invited to
things. Either casual get-togethers or low-key parties.
He never hosted those kinds of things himself.

But he wasn't really close to people back in San
Francisco like he was close to Bo and Andy. He was
always swamped with school or track; his friends
were busy with their own lives, too, and he never
really had time to make a true connection. He had
people to compare notes with, to accompany him to
the mall, or even cover his meal for lunch, but never
people to sneak out with to a lake late at night or lean
against a wall silently with.

Michael didn't think there was a single person
back home that he'd stop to scrub a locker with his
sleeve for.

"Can I ask you something?" Bo said.

"Hm."

"Why do you let your parents call you Mikey?"

Michael paused and looked down at Bo. "They're my parents. They can call me whatever they want."

"But you don't like it."

He didn't think anybody actually noticed.

"It's not important," Michael said. Bo looked back up towards him and tilted his head to the side.

"Remember when we talked about... me? And that thing. Remember when you said it's important to talk about the things, even if they scare you?" Bo spoke quietly. Michael nodded. "What do you do if you *want* to talk about it but don't have the words?"

Michael thought of the Beckham girl and swallowed. "What do you mean?"

Bo's eyes scanned Michael's face as if looking for something. "Like, what if you don't even know how to explain it to yourself? How can you tell somebody else?"

Michael opened his mouth and then closed it. Bo didn't look like himself at that moment. He seemed fragile, like all Michael had to do was touch him and he'd break.

"Bo, are you okay?"

"I think there's something wrong with me."

The slamming of a door made them jump. Michael turned around to find Andy yawning in the hallway. He glanced back at Bo, but he had crouched down to begin to untie his shoelaces.

"Sorry, I'm such a hypocrite. I didn't even realize." Michael noticed how Bo's hands shook.

"Keep them on," Michael stopped him. "I keep finding glass in the floorboards."

Andy didn't say a word.

As the night drew on, they all fought to stay awake for some reason. Michael's mother had ordered pizza from the shop downtown, which was absolutely mutilated within ten minutes by Bo and Michael. Andy had insisted he had eaten before he left, barely glancing at the meal and instead staring off to somewhere Michael couldn't follow. Michael had put on some episodes of *Unsolved Mysteries* that he had recorded himself on VHS. At first, they thought about watching a horror movie, but when Bo pulled out *A Nightmare on Elm Street*, the mood died down for all of them.

Andy was practically swaying side by side. His head kept leaning forward, and Michael noticed him pinching himself awake every couple of minutes. Bo was no better, but he seemed too nervous to sleep. Michael wanted to ask about their previous conversation, but he knew there was no way Bo would talk about it with Andy right there. Even Michael worked to keep himself awake. He was far better at it than the others, which wasn't exactly something to brag about.

When he checked his clock radio, it was only ten o'clock.

"Andy, dude," Bo said, pushing the other boy off his shoulder. "I'm calling it. You need to go to bed already."

"Nuh uh," Andy said as he fell back onto Bo.

"He's right." Michael tried to bite down his nerves when he spoke up. "I think we should all get to bed." He felt such shame in his words, and he wondered if Bo and Andy could see the lie as clearly as day. When he called them over, he had convinced himself this was the only way. If they slept over and got through the night perfectly fine, Michael would know the truth—that he was completely out of his mind. However, if they went to bed and woke up like he did each night and saw...

Part of him was hesitant to push his friends into his nightmares, but he was so, so tired.

After a bit of back and forth, they finally came to an agreement. Michael helped them set out their sleeping bags on the floor, and they let a movie play on as they drifted off to sleep. Michael turned to his side to face the other boys and worked to keep himself up.

Andy was the first to drift off to sleep, the rise and fall of his chest steady, and his lips parted. In the glow of the TV, Michael watched his eyebrows furrow and ease in his fitful rest.

Bo was next to go. He must have been warm under the layers because his arms were out and stretched towards Andy's side by the time he was sleeping. Michael noticed the back of Bo's knuckles grazing Andy's spine. Even unconscious, they reached for each other.

He didn't understand why Bo had yet to tell Andy. If Michael had learned anything from being friends with them, it was that they *needed* to talk to each other more.

However, he understood that some things were understood even without words. If Michael was being honest, he was a bit embarrassed that he hadn't realized Bo was gay. He remembered when they first started hanging out. Michael was glad that the other boys hadn't brought up the topic of girls or dating. It's not that it bothered him. He just preferred to talk about other things.

Back home, all his friends were always dating each other. He'd tried it out himself, going out with a couple of girls here and there, but nothing ever stuck. In his experience, dating was more of a production than anything. The back of the movie theater was the scene, Michael playing his role as the sweetheart boyfriend, reciting lines he knew girls liked to hear, even if he didn't really mean them. At first, he felt bad about it. He felt like a fraud when he held the door open for his date. Then he realized that all the girls were doing the same thing right back to him, so it didn't hurt his feelings as much. Nothing was ever truly sincere in those cases.

When Bo never talked about the girls at school, Michael assumed they were on the same page. They had better, more productive things to do with their youth and didn't feel like wasting their time and energy on meaningless, short-lived flings.

Looking back, he should have realized it sooner.

He didn't think he was alone in his blindness, though. Michael was certain that Andy had no idea, either. It wasn't anything in particular about the way Andy acted around Bo, just a vibe Michael had picked up. There was a static disconnection between the two of them, thick enough to cut with a steak knife.

As he was thinking about it all, Michael's eyes had grown heavy. Before long, he was drifting out of consciousness. It was like when he lay on his back in the lake by the dock, light as air but surely sinking.

As he floated to sleep, he felt his body shut down. The weight of his arms on the mattress, the heftiness of his head, the pressure of the blankets wrapping around him. Sometimes when he slept, he could feel it all one way or another.

He wasn't sure how long he had been out for before the paralyzing sensation began. It was like his bones had turned to lead in seconds, or as if someone had severed the nerves that connected his brain to the rest of his body. He felt the hot breath from his nose, felt the sweat building on his forehead, felt the scrunch of his eyebrows, but nothing else.

His eyes were open, somehow, and Michael's eyes focused in the dark.

From the side, he could hear the television still on. His head was still angled towards the floor. He watched Bo and Andy rest from above, motionless. Andy had flipped over, and they now faced each other in their slumber. Michael wondered if they felt it too. The paralysis, the fear, the sense of reality slipping between their fingers.

Behind him, he heard the creak of the door. His father had promised to grease the hinges but had yet to get around to it.

Somebody stepped into the bedroom.

He heard the echo of their footsteps on the wood as they approached. There were long pauses before each step, as if it took immense effort to drag their feet. As they drew nearer, they seemed to become heavier, until it was like somebody was dropping a bowling ball each inch they grew closer. It rattled his bed.

He couldn't comprehend how Andy and Bo were still asleep. Surely they could feel it—the thing coming closer like an earthquake. Yet they slept blissfully unaware on the floor.

The footsteps finally stopped at the edge of his bed. Michael felt his breath shake his body, and even though he couldn't move from below the neck, he knew he was quivering. His eyes were trained on Bo and Andy as he felt a presence loom over him. He watched a shadow cast over the boys, at first so tall and menacing, before shrinking down. Michael swallowed a noise as he realized that whatever was behind him was leaning closer to him.

He couldn't turn from his side. He couldn't move a muscle at all.

He heard a groan right above his head, so close that Michael *felt* the vibrations that passed the lips of a stranger. Michael shut his eyes as they gasped in his ear, a sound like glass shattering on the tile floor.

Go away, he thought. If he could have, he would've screamed the words until his lungs were hoarse.

The creature must have heard him somehow, though, because they arched away.

Michael didn't have time to revel in the relief as he heard a wet slap like a soaked towel hitting the floor. He felt something push the mattress from below him, and he realized that the thing must have crawled under his bed. He listened to the rustling as the creature maneuvered underneath.

Then, so shrouded in the shadows that Michael thought it was a trick of his sight, he saw it.

An arm reaching out from under his bed.

It was elongated and unnaturally stretched, like one of those sticky hand toys Michael slapped around as a child. The skin was ghastly white and cracked like a crumpled sheet of paper. It was rigid and sharp, paired with the sound of bones snapping as it edged closer and closer to the boys on the floor.

Michael felt a scream build up in his chest as the arm was raised towards Bo.

The hand hovered above Bo's head, still and patient, as if relishing Michael's fearful suspense. His whole bed was shaking now, and Michael felt tears prickle in his eyes. As his vision grew blurry, Michael watched as a finger jutted out and aimed straight down at Bo's head.

Then, just like the arm, it began to extend. He watched as the dirty finger strained until it reached Bo's ear. Michael watched as it traced the helix, following the swirling line of his ear until finally slipping inside.

There was no way to describe it.

Michael watched as the finger dug deeper into Bo's ear canal until it seemed impossible. The ugly limb kept lengthening until it became too thin to make out. Michael watched, paralyzed for what felt like hours, as it violated Bo. The worst part was that Bo never woke, never so much as twitched, as this thing penetrated his ear.

Michael thought he knew what it felt like to be terrified. He was wrong.

Nothing compared to the moment of watching Michael's nightmare transgress his friend and being completely unable to do anything.

It felt like dying.

Michael jerked awake.

His body was his own again, and he felt his hands come up to cup his own ears. For a second, he was dazed and unable to recall where he was. The voice of Robert Stack reminded him of reality. Michael almost laughed when he realized it had just been another fucked-up nightmare.

Then he turned his head to the floor and realized that Bo was missing.

Ch. Twenty-Five

B o stalked down the hallway of the McKenzie's' house. He swept his hair out of his face as he made his way through the dark. In reality, he couldn't see a damn thing. Instead, he relied on the whispers urging him to seek them out.

Over here, Bo. Just a little closer. Over here.

He didn't know how they knew his name. Just like when the girl said it over the phone, it started strained and arduous. As if the words pained them, every syllable a stab to the gut. Each chant of his name made them more powerful.

They were too exigent when Bo rested on Michael's floor. He tried shutting his eyes, curling in on himself, and forcing himself to sleep like the others. The voices never stopped, though. Just like the ringing. Louder and louder until it deafened his thoughts.

Bo gave in and followed.

They ordered him out of Michael's bedroom. It was late enough that Michael's parents were finally asleep, and he quietly crept by their door. Further and further, twisting through the unfamiliar house blindly. He kept his hands wrapped around himself, seeking comfort in any way he could.

Stop

He stopped.

Look up

He raised his head.

Reach

He brought his hand up.

Pull

He tugged on the rope.

It took some effort to bring down the step ladder. Bo brought his hands to the sides of it to soothe the landing. He didn't want the loud noise to wake anybody up. Carefully bringing it to the ground, he gazed up the scuttle hole.

The opening was a grave, black as tar. Whatever resided above held a weight that was suffocating. Bo's knees shook under him as the dark sucked him in. He took a shaky breath.

The voice inside his head told him this was a horrible idea.

The voice outside his head told him to climb.

Climb, climb, climb

Bo made his way up.

Each step was painful. The creaking of the wood made him cringe. The call of the dark was beckoning him. Bo swept an arm over the edge to steady himself before pulling inside. He couldn't suppress the shiver that tore through him from the drastic drop in temperature inside the attic.

As he stood, a breeze threatened to knock him off his feet. He grasped at his short sleeves and attempted to pull them down to protect himself from the cold. There was a crack in the ceiling that let some moonlight in. Thin beams shed light, spotting the floor like footsteps leading to a chest pushed to the furthest wall.

Bo didn't need to listen to the voice to know what to do.

He crossed the attic one fretful step at a time.

He shouldn't be doing this. He shouldn't be doing this. He shouldn't be doing this. Bo knew that. He couldn't stop, though. Not when the last phone call had described this house. From the porch to the foyer, the winding steps to Michael's bedroom, to that arch of the ceiling. Even this, the attic Bo had never seen before, was already imagined in clear detail from the description he had been given earlier.

There was no reasonable explanation for any of this.

The only thing Bo was certain of was that a little girl needed him.

He pushed on.

Bo placed his hand on the top of the chest. He felt the aged wood, dusted and smooth. He couldn't imagine the history it held inside—ancient compared to his short life. He gave a weary tug to the lid, but nothing gave. It was locked.

He sighed and let his hand fall to trace the face of the chest. His shortened finger grazed the keyhole, cool against his flattened skin. Bo let it rest there, just for a moment. He let his eyes fall shut and focused on the surrounding whispers.

So many words all at once, he couldn't pinpoint a single sentence. Fragmented and expeditious. He wasn't sure if it was from the same voice or thousands of different strangers. Low and high pitches, the timbre of the calls slipping into his ears and squeezing his core, the nagging making him vibrate. He felt strapped between two speakers, the distortion melting his brain to nothing as the sound bounced up and down, back and forth through him.

He just wanted it to be quiet again.

The voices fell silent as a click echoed through the empty attic.

Bo opened his eyes to find the chest unlocked. He gently lifted the lid. A cloud of dust spilled out into the room, and Bo covered a cough with his arm. As he blinked earnestly, he reached into the chest and felt around for the contents.

His hand hit the bottom of the smooth wood. He patted around for a second before finally hitting something solid and cool. It took effort to carefully bring it out.

In his lap sat a telephone, antique and rusting. It looked like something from a haunted mansion, the color of charcoal paired with a hand crank at the side. Bo set it down on the floor. It seemed to glow in the dark, but other than that, it was nothing special.

He checked the chest for anything else, but it was completely empty now. Such a big cage for such a small thing.

Wind it

"What?"

The crank

"Oh."

He really didn't want to.

Bo began to twist the crank round and round. He could hear the machinery inside get to work, the cogs churning around as Bo forced each spin of the handle. When he thought he'd done enough, he pulled back into himself and brought his chin to his knees.

At first, nothing happened. It was painful in a quiet sense, like that brief moment when you watch the blood trickle down your finger after pricking it. Bo stared at the telephone, waiting, waiting, waiting.

The ringing echoed throughout the attic, making it seem louder than it was in reality. Bo grasped at the phone. He brought it to his ear, the metal chilling his skin as it made contact.

"Hello?" Bo called out.

"*Hello?*" She whispered back.

Bo swallowed. "I'm here, but I don't understand." He brought his free hand up to grip his hair. "This isn't— This is my friend's house. How can you be here?"

"*I was here first.*"

"I just," he said, covering his eyes with his arm. "I need to know if you're hurt. Are you hurt?"

"*It hurt before. Not anymore.*"

"Before? What does that mean?"

"*I don't know.*"

She was whimpering on the line, and Bo silently prayed she would just *shut up* already. The thought was mean, far meaner than Bo knew himself to be, and any anger he felt quickly dissipated on account of his guilt.

"*I'm scared.*"

"It's okay. It's going to be okay. I'm going to help you." Bo tried to convince himself that he wasn't lying through his teeth. "You're here?"

"*I didn't want to leave.*"

"But you're here, right now?"

"*Yes.*"

Bo snapped his head around. "I don't see you."

"*I don't want to scare you.*"

Bo suppressed a shiver.

"I won't be scared." He gripped the phone tighter. "I promise."

The phone disconnected. Bo was waiting to be met with the dial tone before he realized that there wouldn't be one. The phone was completely useless and isolated on the floor. It shouldn't have even been able to pick up on the call. Nothing worked as it should anymore.

Nightmares that plagued reality. Phone calls that shouldn't reach him. Pleas from voices that didn't exist.

Selene told him she didn't remember pulling the card. She had no recollection of *The Devil*.

He pushed himself to his feet. A wave of dizziness hit. After bringing a hand to the side of his head, he tried not to groan as his fingers came back bloodied. His ears bled more often than not. Only after picking up the phone, though.

He'd been gone too long. Bo never should have gotten out of bed. He should never have left Andy and Michael's side.

As he took a step forward, he winced as his foot met glass.

The crack startled him more than anything. He hadn't managed to cut himself. Bo bent down to see what he stepped on. A photograph framed in gold. He was surprised he hadn't noticed it earlier.

Bo brushed the glass away and examined the girl in the photo.

She was young and bright-eyed. Probably around eleven or twelve. Bo traced the outline of her curly blonde hair. Victorian photographs often caught him off guard due to their dead expressions. It was like the camera took more than a photo, but one's spirit too. The girl didn't seem to fall victim to this phenomenon. She looked childish and dynamic. She felt more real than anything in that moment. It seemed like such a punishment to keep her trapped in a photograph.

Bo's eyes trailed down to the rim of the frame. Engraved in the metal was the name of the girl.

He dropped the picture.

"*You promised.*"

"I—" Bo tripped over his own foot. "Fuck—"

The whispers came back in a furious rush. Vicious and all-consuming until he was grabbing at his ears, trying to quiet the noise. Bo cried out when it did nothing but worsen the severity of the calls. They didn't cease, pushing further inside of him until he was tasting their words on his tongue, blinking their sentences out of his eyes, and exhaling each letter through his nose.

He couldn't bring himself to beg or plead. His voice failed him, lost somewhere in the mess inside of himself.

Please. A voice of his own

"*Down.*" Came the response.

Ch. Twenty-Six

Here was what the lie had been:

Andy had been at it for weeks.

He'd sneak out through his bedroom window, trudge through the woods with a light jacket and a handheld flashlight, and make his way to the Beckham property. He'd go through the back door, where he had managed to pick the lock. It was less suspicious than the front door, just in case anyone came by.

Then, he'd take his EMF reader and dowsing rod around the layout of the house. It always led him the same way.

He followed the identical path Earnest Callaway took all those years ago, minus the shattered glass on the floor, before coming upon the bedroom where they found the corpse. It was on the second floor, occupying a corner of the house with windows on each wall, so there was a perfect view of the woods outside.

Andy would sit on the floor and take out his ghost box, a compact kind of radio that constantly scanned through AM and FM frequencies, before waiting hours for... something. Anything. He even stole his older brother's cassette recorder for observations.

The first couple of nights, he'd fall asleep on the job. But as he snuck out more and more, his venturing becoming more frequent, he learned to keep himself awake and alert. He would jump at any sound and snap his head over to where he noticed any movement. He knew it was only a matter of time before he found her.

The ghost of the lost Beckham child.

And then he did.

He hadn't gotten much sleep, practically a corpse himself.

The static of the ghost box was a lullaby threatening to pull him under. The sound of the cassette rolling did the same.

He tried to pinch his ankles as a way of keeping himself awake, but before he could help it, he felt himself slip away.

His father had always told him that the line between the living and the dead was slumber. It was a preview of what was to come. Everyone knew that sleep was death's brother—not the same, but close enough.

It was in that moment when he fell into the middle ground of life and death did she come to him.

He heard her voice on the spirit box. Quiet. Grainy. Pleading.

It

Cuts

Into

Me

What does?

It

Holds

Me

And

Cuts

The glass?

You do not belong here.

The freezing temperature of the room brought him back to his senses. He rubbed his eyes, the skin of his hands stung as he realized they were cracked and bleeding from the cold. Even though his eyes were open, he was still clouded in the dark. Andy reached around until his hands met the handle of his light, and he realized that the glass lens had been shattered.

He ran all the way home through the dark. Never faulting, never stopping, his heart never resting. But it wasn't fear that Alejandro Romero-Almada was feeling. The rush of adrenaline came from deep within him, his desires pumping the blood through his body. The grip of pure fascination refused to let him go.

My father, he thought. *My father.*

He had lain in bed all night listening to the cassette. He noticed the exact point he had nodded off because the static became unbearable, then he heard the hushed whispers of the ghost. Through the recording, he could faintly make out her words.

He was going to go back the next night. He had to. This was just the beginning.

But then the McKenzie's moved in, and it had ruined everything.

He hadn't even realized it at first. It wasn't until he went to sneak into the back door and found it locked that it dawned on him. There were people there. Someone had claimed what Andy thought was his.

He stumbled back from the door, planning to flee, before he looked up and saw the flashing lights of the bedroom above him.

A boy looked out, unaware of Andy's presence.

A boy was living in the room where a girl had died a hundred years ago, and he had no idea that she was there again.

So yes, Andy had been watching the Beckham place. He had no idea what was going to happen. If the spirit decided to plague, what would befall the new boy living there?

Andy knew it was up to him to prevent any damage that would come from there. It was his heritage. His potential. It was *his*.

Alejandro Romero-Almada believed in ghosts because they lived in his basement.

For generations, his family had conquered the spirits of the island that was now named Whalesborough. They had exorcized and cleansed the wretched. They had defeated and captured the evil. They had shielded the town from the damnation of the ghastly spirits and kept them from harm's way.

It was the Romeros' burden to bear, and their lineage bore it well.

In the cellar of their house, they held the spirits their ancestors had harbored over the years. Rows and rows of shelves with spell-cast jars that held the violent wraiths captive. He wasn't sure where the powerful glasses came from, nor did he know how to read the protective symbols and runes etched into them. What he did know was that a spirit couldn't escape unless purposely let out.

His father had shown him the basement when he was ten. He was never allowed in before. Who in their right mind would let a clumsy child in a room full of apprehended ghosts? But he remembers the day he was finally let in on the family secret.

His father took down a jar from the highest shelf and carefully placed it into Andy's hand. He had been shocked by its freezing temperature but held it tightly nonetheless. He watched the swirling clouds on the inside of the glass, like a storm brewing in his own two hands.

"We come from a long line of spirit hunters, Alejandro," his father said. "Our family spent their lives protecting our town from dangerous wandering souls. When I was your age, my father trained me to follow in his footsteps."

"Will you train me now?" Andy had asked.

"No, we don't do that kind of thing anymore. I captured the last ghost haunting this town years ago. There are no more." Andy was a bit disappointed when his father said this. "But you still have an important job to do. Your brothers and sisters would not understand like I know you will. They have their own duties, and you will have yours too."

His father bent down to his knees to reach Andy's height before clasping his hands over his son's. "You must watch over these jars and make sure they never break, or else the spirits will escape."

Andy had promised.

His father pursed his lips. "Aye, mijo. Nunca puedes decir a nadie lo que aquí pasa. Only our family, okay? Nobody else can ever know."

He thought of his new friend Bo. "I swear it."

The life of a ghost watcher was a solitary one.

His siblings did not share his interest in the paranormal; instead, they opted to live traditional lifestyles. Andy was grateful for that. His siblings would thrive in school and go on to become successful academics, something Andy was incapable of doing himself, and he would stay home and make his parents proud in other ways.

It had been enough, until it wasn't.

Even though they never said it, Andy knew his parents were growing weary of him. He was failing school miserably, and he lacked any other redeemable qualities, like a gift in the arts or excelling in a sport. He was falling behind his other siblings, whose accomplishments seemed to do nothing but squander any hope of making his parents proud in his own way.

But there was this.

His father had said ghost hunting was what gave him life, and Andy knew he was the same. His father was wrong when he claimed those days were behind him. The dead were never truly left to rest, after all.

Which led him back to the old Beckham place.

Andy just had to wait for his time.

He found it when Michael McKenzie finally invited him over to spend the night.

Andy was used to fighting off exhaustion in the Beckham house. When he was younger, he perfected the art of pretending to sleep. Either to avoid Jaime's nagging or getting out of chores, Andy taught himself how to lie like the dead. Letting his mouth fall open and soft snores escape his lips, splaying out his limbs in a manner that replicated ease, steadying his breath to seem as passive as possible.

He did just that on Michael's floor.

Until he actually fell asleep. In his defense, he was absolutely exhausted.

By the time he awoke, it was well past midnight; everyone else should've been out of it. He double-checked the clock on Michael's desk before sitting up as quietly as he could. He reached for his heavy duffel bag.

Bo had joked about it on their way over.

"Packing heavy tonight?" Bo commented.

"It's different when I'm over at your house. Half my stuff is already there," Andy replied. He was glad Bo didn't mention it again. Andy wasn't sure how he would explain his ghost-hunting gear if Bo had gone through his bag.

Andy spared a glance over to his best friend, who... wasn't there?

"Shit—" He smacked around the empty sleeping bag as if Bo were hiding inside, but no. He was truly gone. Sometime in the night, without

Andy noticing, Bo had managed to slip away right past him.

Which meant that Bo was stalking around the house with a dangerous ghost.

Which meant that Bo was probably going to get himself hurt.

Andy tore the sheets off and gripped his bag, slinging it over his shoulder as he raced out of Michael's room. Then he remembered that he had to do this right. He couldn't risk getting caught. Andy slowed down and forced himself to grow quiet.

In one hand, he gripped the EMF reader he stole from his father; in the other, he held one of the spare jars from the basement. He let his finger drag across the engraved glass, feeling a sense of comfort from the protective markings that would hold the spirit.

Once he closed the bedroom door behind him, he let his EMF reader lead him away. The soft beeping echoed through the hall as he slowly stepped through. The only light to accompany him was the red glow from the radar.

He began to push through tarps hanging from the ceiling that blocked off rooms under more serious construction than the other parts of the house. He stepped over hardware tools and planks of wood, following the spikes in the reader as he got closer and closer to the source it was detecting.

Andy bit back a yelp as he spun to meet the figure he noticed in the corner of his eye but let out a sigh when he realized it was just his reflection he had caught. He faced the long mirror covered in dirt and grime from the years left abandoned.

He took a step closer before setting down the EMF reader and laying his palm flat against the cool reflective glass.

Andy tried to ignore the dark bags under his eyes. He was glad Bo never asked about them. Bo never asked about anything, though.

He took his hand from the mirror and ran it over his face, a yawn threatening to escape him. He knew he couldn't go back until he caught the ghost, but each step felt heavier than the last, and he wasn't sure how much longer he could go on like this.

He felt a cool hand touch his chin.

Andy snapped his eyes open to see the girl reaching through the mirror. He fell backwards. The shock he felt was so sudden, he didn't even have time to let out a scream.

When he hit the ground, he heard a terrible crack. For a second, he thought the fall had cracked the jar he had brought, but he realized that he had instinctively clutched it close to his chest to shield it.

He looked back up to see the mirror shatter before shards of glass rained on top of him.

She's right here, he thought. *She's right—*

"What are you doing?"

Ch. Twenty-Seven

M ichael was frozen in place. He wasn't sure what he was expecting when he heard the shattering of glass, but it wasn't Andy looking guilt-ridden and petrified, lying on his back. For a second, they just blinked at each other. Then he carefully asked again, "What are you doing?"

"This, uh—" Andy quickly scrambled to his feet, brushing the glass away from his head and sweater. "This isn't what it looks like."

"What is it then?

Michael looked around the room and examined the damage. The mirror before Andy was shattered, just like the day he came over to do the séance. God, that felt like years ago. Had it truly only been a couple of weeks? Time had slipped Michael's mind to make room for the nightmares, he supposed. Andy looked worse for wear. In the dark, he seemed ghastly. His brown skin was pallid and slicked with sweat as if he'd run a marathon. His eyes were bloodshot and wild, glancing around the room in every direction except Michael's. Any ill feelings Michael had in the moment evaporated, immediately being replaced with concern for Andy's striking fear.

Michael reached out to Andy. The other boy almost fell off his feet trying to evade Michael's touch. Michael noticed the small box that Andy had to step over.

"Is that an EMF reader?" It was blinking spastically, the red light a beacon in the dark.

"You know what this is?" Andy's voice shook as he spoke.

"Yeah, I've seen it used in shows and..." When Michael brought his gaze back up to Andy, he went stark. In the dark of the room, the moonlight shining on his back and shadows concealing his face, Michael felt a wave of déjà vu. The atmosphere surrounding Andy, so unlike every other encounter Michael had shared with him before, was familiar in a different way. Realization set into his bones. "You lied."

It was so obvious, so undeniably reasonable.

He remembered that day on the trolley when they first met, when he asked Andy if he had been watching his house. The dismissive answer, the endearing smile that distracted Michael from his unease, the aversion of Andy's behavior. He remembered all those nights the paranoia ate at him, when his crippling self-doubt drove him crazy. The boy outside his window, grasping at the private school uniform through the woods, the constant feeling of eyes on him.

Michael waited for the denial. He waited for Andy to dispute his claim and make sense of it all.

"I didn't lie." In the dark, he couldn't see Andy's face, but the hollowness of his voice was enough to make his mouth go dry.

"No," Michael shook his head. "You did! You still are. You've been watching my house. You've been watching me! You lied and—"

Andy reached across swiftly to clasp his hands over Michael's mouth. He was so taken aback by the gesture that he didn't react. "Keep your voice down." Andy's voice was low, demanding, and vacant. It was like he wasn't even there with Michael. "You don't want to wake up your parents, do you?"

Michael pushed Andy off him. "You better start talking or I'll—"

"What? You'll do what?" Andy scoffed. "You still don't have a goddamn clue what's going on right now. When are you going to realize that the thing to be afraid of in this house isn't each other?"

A gust of wind ripped through the tarps, sending chills down both of their spines.

"Where's Bo?" Michael's voice broke.

The question seemed to finally bring Andy back to reality. His face contorted in a mix of emotions—conflict and hesitancy—before Michael saw Andy settle on pure dread.

"He's in on this, too, isn't he?" Suddenly, it was all Michael could think about. Bo befriended Michael, acting as a sort of lure while Andy did whatever he was planning on doing. "That's why I can't find him. He's off somewhere."

"Bo has nothing to do with this," Andy snapped. "He doesn't even know I've been watching this place."

"So I was right!"

Andy groaned. "Fine, yes! I've been watching this whole time. I know that it's—Whatever. I never meant to scare you."

"Can you cut the bullshit?" Michael said. He was shaking from the cold and his exasperation. He didn't think he could stand any more of Andy's abstruse reasoning. Every explanation he gave Michael only led to more winding roads of inquiry.

"You don't get it." Andy shook his head. "I've been here longer. I was here *first*."

"For God's sake, I get that. I get that you grew up here and that this town is yours, or whatever."

"No, the house. I've been watching the house for months, before your parents even signed the contract to own it."

"Why?" Michael asked.

"I—"

But Andy was cut off by the ring of a telephone. Michael hadn't noticed before, but beside the mirror rested a phone. They both exchanged a glance. Andy took to step towards it. Michael gripped Andy's shoulder and pulled him back away from the landline. Andy went to shove him off when he saw Michael pointing his finger at the floor. His eyes followed where Michael led, and then he saw it.

The cable of the landline had yet to be inserted into the ancient house.

The phone that was ringing was not connected.

Michael began to hyperventilate. Andy gripped his face and dragged his eyes away from the ringing phone, forcing Michael to meet his gaze. "I never meant to scare you," Andy said again, and for some reason, Michael believed him. He knew he shouldn't. Andy's earnestness had done nothing but prove to be a facade for his creeping activities. Yet, as Andy's eyes urged him to calm down, Michael couldn't find it in himself to doubt him.

"If you really want to know, I'll tell you," Andy said, slowly and carefully, like he was leading Michael into the icy water of the dock. "But I won't be able to take it back. You'll be stuck in it just like I am, and once you know the truth, it's impossible to ignore."

"Andy, where's Bo?" Michael croaked. The lacking presence of the other boy made Michael far more nervous than the anomalous ringing of the telephone. Especially after the nightmare. Michael had the feeling that something terrible was going to happen to one of them.

Andy shook his head as if he couldn't think about Bo at the moment. "Focus, Michael. Right here. You might not believe me. I know I seem crazy to you. I swear everything I am about to tell you is true." He grabbed Michael's wrist to pull him closer. The wind was strong enough to threaten to knock them off their feet. The ringing of the telephone was unbearable. Michael heard the sound of glass shattering. "I know it's the truth because it's been my entire life. All of it."

Andy's hands grazed the scabs of Michael's arm from the glass in his bed. He didn't think Andy even realized he was doing it. It brought Michael back to every time he stood in this house and felt utterly and invariably adrift from reality.

Andy placed something cool in Michael's hand. He looked down to find a glass jar in his palm. Smaller than a mason jar, the glass was thick with engravings of strange symbols Michael couldn't comprehend. The weight of it soothed him.

"But now you live here, so it's just as much of yours as it is mine," Andy said. "It's too real now. There's no point in denying it. But I can't tell you unless you answer me first. Have you seen her?"

"Who?"

"Michael."

Yes. *Yes.*

Always, since the beginning. Edith Beckham watched him over his bed. Screaming and crying, desperate to be heard, but her voice was lost on Michael. Her presence was so demanding that he couldn't even sleep. Even in the security of his consciousness, he felt her in his house. Through the creak of the stairs, the specks of dust caught on the light, the cobwebs in the corner of his ceiling, the stains along the wood floors. If he placed a hand on the wall, he could feel her in the pulse of the house.

But he couldn't admit it. He couldn't let it be true.

"She's not real."

"How do you know?" Andy urged.

"Because..." Because then Michael would have to come to terms with the fact that he wasn't crazy, and he wasn't ready for that. His mentality was something that he could fall back on; the diagnosis was always there to help him reason his way through the inexplicable. Even the uncertainty of his mind had rhythm and sensibility. If she were as real as Andy was, Michael would lose that.

"I know you feel it. This town, this house, this *room*. She's here with us now, Michael." He squeezed his eyes shut at Andy's words. The air felt thick, like the wind was trying to choke them out. "Do you get it now?"

Michael wanted to say no.

He gripped the jar in his hand.

"The girl, it's Edith Beckham." He swallowed. "She's dead."

"For years, Michael."

"This town... everyone was right." He shook. Andy gave a sympathetic nod. "How—Why are you here?"

"My family, they're entangled with it all. The ghost stories, the history of this town, all of it," Andy explained in a rushed voice. "It's complicated, and we're running out of time for me to explain it all, but ever since there were spirits here, it was my ancestors' job to capture them. For years, we worked to keep the people safe from things like this. We've kept them locked in my basement for decades to protect the town. Now, though, they're coming back. Nobody else seems to notice, but I felt it. That's why I've been coming back here, why I did everything I could to find the Beckham girl. It's my job to get her."

"But that... No. Come on, Andy. Don't play with me right now."

"I swear it. On whatever, my life or yours. I told you it's hard to believe, but it's the truth." Andy choked on his words. Michael watched his face twist. "I was never supposed to tell anyone. I've never—"

"Nobody?" Michael asked. "Not even Bo?'

Andy snapped his head up. "*Especially* Bo. This... It's dangerous. I tried to find a way to keep you guys out of it, but there was never a time I could get here and capture her without giving myself away. I shouldn't even be getting you involved. It's too risky." He was breathing hard. His grip on Michael's wrist was desperate. "But it's too late, and if I don't sort this out now, someone could get hurt. There's no other choice. I'm sorry I can't explain it better. I've never had to. But you need to understand, I *have* to do this. I have to—"

"Andy," Michael interrupted. "It's okay, I believe you."

He looked so full of remorse, like it was spilling out of him. "I don't want anything bad to happen to you."

Michael pursed his lips. "I know."

Andy let out a shaky breath. "It needs to be now. Before Bo finds us."

"What can I do to help?"

Andy glanced up at him. Michael was terrified of what he would ask of him.

"Can you punch my lights out?"

Ch. Twenty-Eight

"Erm," Michael began.

"Listen, okay." Andy took a step back. "It's like this. You ever wonder why you only see Beckhams' girl as a nightmare? It's because there's a very thin line between the world of the living and the world of the dead. Sometimes, if the dead get worked up enough, they can exert themselves in the mortal world. In other cases, it can be the opposite. Like that instance before you hit the ground and you see your life flash before your eyes? That's sneaking a foot between the lines. The most natural instance, though, is sleep. It is a sort of limbo that acts as a drawbridge. The subconscious is a neutral ground between the worlds. Are you following?"

"Um..."

"Okay, okay. Let's backtrack." Andy was trying not to lose his shit as the world fell apart around him. He was completely aware that he had to be patient with Michael, even though they were *literally out of time*, but it was fine. Never mind that this was quite possibly the worst-case scenario in every imagined situation Andy had spent the past months conjuring. Whatever, it was fine. "Ghosts are real."

"Ghosts are real," Michael repeated.

"Sometimes when people die, they leave behind parts of themselves. This can happen when the death is abrupt or traumatizing." It was better to start with the groundwork, he realized. Then he could lead Michael to the finer details.

"Like a grand piano falling from the sky and crushing you?" Michael asked.

"Sure. That works. But also, think more of being brutally murdered by someone close to you, and in your final moments, you waste your last breath cursing them and vowing to take vengeance any way you see fit. It's more like that."

The phone began to ring again, which caused Michael to let out a whimper.

"Stay with me, dude." Andy squeezed his shoulder. "Ghosts aren't real people. They're more like fragments of manifested emotions and memories. Like when you let glue dry on your hand and peel it off. It's a pretty good copy; you can even see your fingerprints and the fine lines of your palm, but it's not actually you. That's what spirits are like. A cast of the people they once were."

Andy remembered his father explaining it all to him. He had taken out journals and diaries from his ancestors, depicting their experiences and theories of the spirit world. While most of the Romeros put effort into cleansing the town of ghosts, some pursued their studies instead. Book after book dedicated to academic research, from sketches to theories to discoveries to experiments. Andy had spent hours poring over the ancient pages, soaking up everything he could about his family's history.

"Ghosts are fueled by dominant emotions, usually the final one they experienced before they passed over. It's all-consuming in a way that's painful to them, like when you're so hungry it hurts and you can't think of anything else. That's what it's like for spirits all the time. The only way they can suppress those emotions is by lashing out and spreading it to others," Andy told Michael. "Mostly it's anger or fear, but sometimes it's sadness. The Beckham girl, she must have been petrified. That's why you feel frozen when she's around."

Michael shook his head. "I've been dealing with paralysis since forever."

"But I feel it too. Not as severely as you, but it's an underlying sort of feeling." Andy rubbed his eyes. "It's way more complicated than that, but we can't get into all of it right now. What I'm trying to say is that we need to make contact with the ghost to capture it."

It's why Andy hadn't been able to do it thus far. The conditions were never right. He was never prepared, never tired enough. The spirit hadn't been able to break through fully yet, still trapped in its own emotions to push into the living world.

Andy's father explained his methods of defeating the ghosts of Whalesborough. He had perfected the art of losing consciousness at will. Through constant and strenuous meditation, he had been able to teach his body to enter the line between life and death. Then, his father had been able to draw the spirits' presence close enough to him to strike.

Either that, or provoke the ghost enough to cross over themselves through violent action.

Andy didn't want to put Michael in any more danger than he'd already been subjected to, so he went with the prior option. The only issue was that he wasn't tired anymore. If anything, he was wide awake.

Bo's disappearance had sent him reeling, the scouting for ghosts made him apprehensive and anticipating the next apparent threat, Michael's interruption forced him to focus and deliberate. All of it had exiled any past exhaustion, and he was too restless to go back to sleep.

"So, you're gonna knock me out or what?" Andy raised his hands up

Michael's eyebrows flew up to his hairline.

"Come on, man. This is the only way. I need to get close enough to the crosspoint to actually do anything to the ghost. Otherwise, we're just sitting ducks waiting for it to make the first move." Then more quietly, he added, "Plus, I kind of deserve it."

"What?"

"You don't have to pretend. I know how pissed you are at me. I totally fucked everything up, with the stalking and the lying and—"

"Andy, I'm not going to hit you." Michael seemed almost offended.

"You *have* to," Andy argued.

He reached for Michael's hand and brought it up to the side of his face. He'd been punched before by his brothers (and sisters) when they'd get into wrestling matches, despite their mother's wishes. He'd been knocked unconscious before. Andy wasn't nervous about the idea; it's what he needed to do.

"Just, um, don't give me a concussion or anything. Just enough to get me dazed," he added. "But, yeah. Go crazy. Get it all out of your system. I can take it."

Michael pulled his hand back.

"No."

"No?" Andy echoed back.

Michael shook his head sternly. "You think this is a problem to fix on your own. That this is your fault, but it's not. I'm not angry at you, Andy. You did the best you could."

"Dude, I'm a total fucking creep."

"Well…" Michael cringed. "A little, but it's fine. I mean, yeah, I was really mad before." He faltered and raked a hand through his hair. "God, Andy, I've spent the past couple of weeks out of my mind. It was like I couldn't trust anything I was seeing or feeling."

Andy curled in on himself. "I'm sorry."

"I know," Michael said. "I know you're just trying to help. I'm not going to punish you for doing what you thought was right, especially when you've been trying to protect me this entire time. Not just me, Bo too."

Andy paused.

The mention of Bo halted his train of thought. He still had no idea where his best friend was, and clearly neither did Michael. It worried him not knowing where Bo was, but more than that, it worried him that Bo might stumble upon them at that moment.

The hardest thing about the job his father had given him was keeping it from Bo. When he was younger, it was easier for some reason. They had never kept secrets from each other at that age. He felt a sort of rush from it, not used to having something to hide from his best friend.

When he got older, it became harder. He thought it would be the opposite, like the longer he sat with it, the more in place it would feel. Yet it was always a sort of burden, especially when he had to hold onto it quietly at Bo's side.

Then Bo started keeping secrets too, and suddenly the thrill of it was gone, leaving only a sludgy guilt inside of Andy.

He tried to convince himself that it was better this way. Even though keeping it a secret ached, Andy couldn't imagine sharing the weight of it with Bo. It would have been like clinging onto his best friend as they both drowned.

Bo already had his own ghosts. The empty space his mother left behind, the neglect of his father, the isolation of the town, and something else. Andy couldn't place his finger on what it was, but he could sense it. It pulled on Bo's shoulders, tying him in chains, unrelenting and heavy. Whatever it was, Bo carried it like Andy carried his family's history—all on his own.

Andy wouldn't even know how to bring it up. They had gotten so used to not talking to each other, so used to not talking about the superstitions of the town. If Andy tried to seriously discuss it, he was certain Bo would take it as a joke and dismiss it. It was better, *easier*, to shrug it off entirely.

"Hey, thanks, man." Andy shrugged. "I'm gonna need you to completely disregard that train of thought, though, because I really do need you to hit me. I promise I won't take it personally."

Michael frowned. "Seriously?"

"Do you want to die?" He had meant it as a joke. Kind of. Not really. Andy wasn't actually sure. "Just do it. Quick."

He took a step back to give Michael some room. Michael glanced between Andy and his fist, which he had finally clenched. He seemed uncertain, like he wasn't sure he could bring himself to do it.

"Um, I get that we're kind of in a hurry, but…"

"But?"

Michael seemed sheepish in his confession. "I've never actually hit someone before."

Andy blinked at him before bringing his hands over his face and groaning.

"I'm sorry! I just want to make sure I don't really hurt you, you know? Like, what if I completely knock you out and you're just lying defenseless on the floor and Edith comes back and—"

"Chill, chill, chill. It's not something you can screw up, okay? You just need to do it. Take a step back and swing with your whole body. Try to aim for the side of my head, preferably. I'd rather my nose stay unbroken. Pretty please."

"Just do it?" Michael clarified.

"Don't overthink it."

"You're sure?"

"Oh my God. Yes."

Michael took a deep breath before bringing his arm back. Just as he was taking a step towards Andy, ready for Michael's fist to collide with his face, Andy noticed his stance and brought his hands up to protect himself.

"Wait, wait, wait!" Andy cried out.

Michael stopped so abruptly that he stumbled. "What? What?"

Andy regained his composure. "Make sure your thumb is *outside* of your fist, otherwise you'll fuck up your thumb." Michael stared. Andy shrugged. He untucked his thumb and tried again.

There was a short moment right before Michael hit Andy where he thought, *I'm about to get hit*, which wasn't exactly the revelation of the century. He realized that he'd forgotten what it was like to be punched. A thrust so quick it sent him spinning. Michael got him right in the cheekbone, blood bursting into Andy's mouth as his cheek scraped against his teeth. It was a blaze, like the light of flint and steel scuffing.

The landing was far more effective in leaving him dazed than the punch itself. Andy's head hit the ground first. He could've sworn he felt his brain knock against his skull. The rest of his body came crashing down soon after, leaving his left shoulder severely bruised.

He heard the faint muffle of Michael's apologies as he groaned into the floor. His vision blurred as he turned his head over.

For a second, all he could see was a shaking Michael. Then, while taking steady blinks to keep himself conscious, Andy lifted himself off the ground. His arms were shaking from under him as he brought his pounding head up.

From behind Michael, Andy watched as a figure rose.

At first, he didn't understand what he was seeing. Her contorted limbs. Her hunched back. Her screaming mouth. Her streaming tears. Her pained expression.

Then she dove from above Michael and crashed right into Andy.

He felt the contact immediately. Her touch was frigid ice cubes penetrating his skin. The air was knocked out of him, and he found himself choking on his breath. She had her hands on his neck, her mouth opened for cries that never came out, as she lashed out her anger at Andy.

He had no idea what it must have looked like to Michael. His brain was having trouble processing the encounter on its own. The way the Beckham girl flickered through reality—one moment she was there, killing him, the next she was gone. Each second made her more solid. Before long, Andy found himself shaking himself out of shock and fighting back.

He brought his hands up to swat her away, but his grip slipped through her like he was grasping at the wind. The look on her face was enough to finish him. So resentful, so repugnant, like the sight of him was worse than death itself.

But then Andy saw something flicker in her expression. So brisk he thought it was the consequences of a bending mind, but there once more. When he gazed upon her, Andy couldn't see the vengeful spirit he had been conditioned to fight against. Instead, he saw a scared little girl.

Her hands on her throat didn't feel like a deadly grasp, but a desperate reaching of sorts.

And he faltered. He *hesitated*. Because she looked alive? No, because she looked human.

He couldn't hear a word she said, but he could read her lips.

You don't belong here.

The same words Andy had heard unsaid at the dining table. The thought that plagued him when it was late and he could hear everyone else in his house talking about him. Familiar enough to find a home inside of him.

Her grip was back, and he felt it all at once.

"Neither—" Andy choked out, "do you."

He reached out for a glass beside him. It must have fallen sometime during the night. The sight of the glistening jar sent the spirit into a frenzy. She fought him harder, clawing at his face and reaching to scratch out his eyes.

Andy unscrewed the lid as quickly as he could before thrusting the open container into the Beckham girl's chest. The effect was immediate. Andy watched as she began to drain away from reality. It was like she was being pulled into a vacuum as she gripped onto Andy for support. He felt her fingernails drag across his skin as she collapsed into the jar.

The lights of the house flickered blindingly. Andy thought the sheer amount of energy would blow a fuse throughout the entire town. So bright, he had to shut his eyes to escape the burning sensation, and even then it reached him.

The turbulence of the breeze was so great that it pinned him to the ground. His hair blew wildly, and his clothes felt as if they'd tear off his body, the freezing air leaving a coating on him in a frosted sensation. He felt himself dragged by the power of the jar, so ancient in enchantment it defied all he knew to be possible.

He squinted against the burning light to catch the final glance of the Beckham girl.

Andy blinked.

She blinked back. A tear trickled down the corner of her eye.

Andy clasped the jar shut, and she dissipated completely. The world went silent once more.

Everything went back to the way it should be.

Andy felt arms come to his side and lift him off the ground. Too exhausted to move or fight back, he groaned in protest but did nothing more. His head was killing him to the point where it hurt to breathe. Even furrowing his eyebrows brought waves of pain.

He opened his eyes to see Michael looming over him. He was speaking to Andy, though it was hard to make out the words. A pulsing in his skull made it impossible to think straight. He felt Michael bring a hand up to graze a wound on Andy's face, but he shifted his face away to evade the touch.

When his gaze drifted across the room, everything seemed to stop.

He became aware of Michael's hushed warnings.

Bo stood in the doorway, dripping in his blood and his expression stark. They didn't have to exchange words to understand each other. They never did.

He knew that Bo had seen all of it.

Andy brought a hand to reach for him just as Bo turned and fled.

Ch. Twenty-Nine

H elp me up," Andy called from the floor.

Michael watched Bo race out the door. He hadn't even realized Bo was there in the first place.

"Michael, please. Just— Shit, man. Get me off the floor."

Michael snapped his head back over to Andy and offered him a hand, pulling him up. It wasn't impossible to do since Andy probably only weighed about a hundred and fifteen pounds. Andy's feet swung under him as Michael pulled him into the air. He leaned on Michael to steady himself.

"Where'd he go? Is he gone?" His words were slurring, and Michael suddenly realized that it was probably his fault. His hand still ached from punching Andy, but the guilt was harder to sit with. Michael had never hurt anybody on purpose before. The feeling was oil in his gut.

"Andy, calm down. You need to lie down before we do anything else." Michael tried to ease him, but Andy wouldn't relent.

He shoved himself off Michael and tried to chase after Bo, only able to take a few steps before crumbling to the floor once again. Even on the ground, he crawled. The sight was demeaning as much as it was commendable. How desperate Andy was to get to Bo, how trivial the challenge.

Then again, Michael realized that was their entire dynamic on some level.

He sighed and walked over to Andy, crouching on the ground next to him. Andy was pressed facedown against the wooden floorboards, mumbling to himself. Michael rolled him over on his back to get a good look at his face.

"I'm getting you out of here."

"To Bo?"

"No, Andy. Jeez." Michael huffed. "*Home.* You need to go home and rest. You're a mess."

Andy gave Michael a dirty look. "It's fine. I'm fine."

Michael poked the forming bruise on Andy's face, causing him to bite back a groan. "Right, sure. Because this entire night has been fine." Andy swatted at his hand. "What are you even going to say to him?"

Michael watched as Andy's face fell. He stared off at the ceiling as if doing some calculation in his head, but he couldn't get the numbers right. Suddenly, he was sniffing and blinking rapidly, bringing up his arms to cover his eyes with the heel of his hands. It took Michael an embarrassing moment to realize what he was witnessing.

"Are you crying?" Michael asked, not judging but genuinely confused.

"Fuck off, Michael," Andy said, hoarsely.

"Hey," Michael reached over, but Andy turned to his side. "It's gonna be okay."

"Nobody was supposed to know."

"What?"

Andy sat up abruptly. "Don't you get it? The truth? It screws with your head. This reality of spirits and hauntings—it's too much. That's why it's been shrouded in horror stories and gossip by the town. So it doesn't break their minds. Right now, you feel okay because you've got adrenaline pumping through your veins, but when you lie down in your bed and actually think about it, you're never going to be able to sleep again."

The way he was speaking was so unlike the Andy he had known. This wasn't the carefree boy who dragged Michael and Bo around town and led them to mischief. He was weary and judicious, an aged player in a world Michael had just set foot in. This, Michael realized, was Andy who stalked outside his house in the night.

Even more than that, this Andy reminded Michael so much of Bo.

For so long, Michael had watched the two with novelty. The way they interacted was seamless, magnets snapping together like they couldn't resist.

Their pairing was natural, like it was all they knew to do. On paper, though, it seemed impossible for them to exist on the same plane.

Just then, Andy was a striking and uncanny thing. Peculiar in motion, curious in speech, and conspicuous in his knowledge.

Michael was frightened by his friend's gaze.

"You've been prepared for it, in some ways, I suppose. The nightmares eased you into it, but I can tell you're already feeling it. It's like tension building up behind your eyes, pushing and pushing until it cracks. You can feel it, right?" Andy spoke surely.

Michael clenched his sides, scratching the fraying pajama pants in an effort to exude Andy's words.

When he closed his eyes, he saw Andy wrestling on the ground. Grasping at nothing, fighting with everything, dying at hands Michael couldn't even comprehend. It was mind-bending and exhausting to watch, to the point where he had turned away.

He had felt the scene grow more powerful as the physical world around him began to respond. The lights, the breeze, the temperature, the jagged feeling inside of him. Michael had hunched over, grasping at his head and pushing his hands into his eyes as pain seared throughout him.

But when a vexing gasp echoed throughout the room, Michael felt peace come back to him. He brought a hand to his pounding heart, beating so hard it felt as if it would break out of his ribcage, and turned back to Andy. There he was on the ground, clutching a cloudy jar, looking as if he'd return from war.

Even thinking back to it made Michael's head hurt all over again.

"Nobody was supposed to know," Andy repeated. "For you, it might be easier. But, Bo..."

Michael hadn't even realized Bo was there until too late. He still didn't know where Bo had wandered off to before he found Andy. For all he knew, Bo had been lurking since the beginning. When Michael finally brought himself to fight through the pain, he saw him.

Bo was austere and still. Michael had the thought that he was seeing a second spirit.

That look on Bo's face... It was the same look he had when he told Michael he thought there was something wrong with him. The same face he had when Michael watched him pick up the phone on the first day of school. The exact same expression he held when his ears bled for the first time at the séance.

Michael couldn't place what it was, but he knew Andy felt it too in that static moment.

Bo had seen Andy capture the Beckham girl, but not the way Michael had.

"Andy..." Michael began, but his mind was racing faster than he could keep up with, and his words failed him.

"He's not like you," Andy sighed. "He's not like me, either. I'm not talking about the way the town sees him. It's something else that I don't even know."

Michael heard Bo's words echo through his mind.

There's something wrong with me.

Over and over. The way he had said it, not as a question but an affirmation.

"Not just that, but with Selene and his mom—"

"What about his mom?" Michael interjected.

"I don't know, it's just," Andy was panting and had to slow himself down. "I think something happened to her."

"Like, something supernatural?"

Andy shrugged. "I just have this feeling like something is missing. Like, watching a movie and knowing that a scene was cut? That's what it feels like whenever he talks about it." Andy scoffed. "Or, you know, from when he alluded to it. It's not like he's actually ever brought it up."

Michael felt defensive on Bo's behalf. "You know what it's like for him."

A stark chill glossed over Andy's gaze as he turned on Michael then. "Don't." His tone was the pressing of a blade against skin. "Don't act like you know him better than I do."

There was a pause in the atmosphere as they regarded each other. Michael, attempting to hold his ground, versus Andy beckoning him to yield. Eventually, Michael gave in first and averted his eyes. Andy didn't seem to revel in the victory.

"All I'm saying is that I think it's hard for him to remember," Andy murmured. "It's the same thing with some stuff from when we were younger, too."

"What do you mean?"

"Just strange things. Strange, like your nightmares and the shattering mirrors and..." Andy trailed off. "Fuck."

Andy quickly shot to his feet.

"What?" Michael asked, but Andy wasn't paying attention.

He watched Andy stumble over to the wall and grasp at the landline. His fingers pulled at the cord until he drew up the unconnected end and gripped it between his fingers. "The phone calls," Andy said. "He said he was getting phone calls.

Michael remembered Bo mentioning the prank calls during the night before school. He hadn't given much thought to it. Now he felt like kicking himself.

"He got one at school. It made him scared or something." Michael swallowed. "His ears were bleeding."

"*Fuck*."

"Andy, what's wrong with him?"

He snapped his head towards Michael. "Nothing. There's nothing wrong with Bo."

Michael quickly raised his hands in surrender. He was realizing how taxing it could be to deal with Andy. Especially when Bo was involved, apparently.

"I just meant what's going on with him," Michael said cautiously.

Michael could tell Andy was trying to use his anger to mask his deteriorating fear.

He watched as Andy bit his lip and shut his eyes, his hand coming up to feel his wound.

Michael was about to ask Andy again when he shook his head. He didn't have an answer.

"Let me take you home."

"I need—"

"You can't help him now. You need to take care of yourself first," Michael argued.

Andy slid his gaze to him. Michael watched as his fingers grazed a key tied to his neck.

Michael didn't realize how often he would catch Andy doing that until then.

Always, Michael finally understood.

Always.

Ch. Thirty

In his freshman year, Bo started doing track.

He was never much of a sportsman growing up, preferring quiet and less straining activities instead. He didn't feel the need to exert himself among a rowdy team, those groups so motile and complicated. It was too demanding of a hobby, and Bo found himself dreading Little League practices after school. He only signed up because Andy wanted to. Selene had encouraged him further. "Exercise is good for you," she'd argue. "Besides, you need to get out of the house more. You must be going crazy, cooped up in here all day long."

Andy had agreed with her on some levels. He thought Bo needed to socialize with other kids so they didn't think he was such a freak. Andy never said those words, of course, but Bo heard them regardless. Something that confused Andy was that solitude was never a burden to Bo but rather a comfort.

Besides, Bo didn't need a sports team to excite his day. Andy did more than enough all on his own.

Then they went to separate high schools, and suddenly, Bo was lonely.

It was a strange feeling, unacquainted with his body. Even in his sequestered childhood home, he wasn't isolated. His mother had taken him to parks on weekends; he'd gotten along with his classmates; he'd busy himself with housework or activities. He was alone, but not lonely. The difference was distinct.

Being surrounded by people to the point of feeling claustrophobic in the tight hallways did nothing to soothe his desolation, only furthering the disconnection he felt with the rest of the world. And wasn't that *embarrassing*? To be completely encompassed by others and still so forlorn.

So he had joined the track team in hopes it would help.

He wasn't expecting to be welcomed with open arms by his peers—Bo wasn't delusional—but he had hoped there'd be one instance when he wouldn't be completely turned away by others.

He remembered double-knotting his shoelaces as the other kids stretched around him. Bo felt someone tap his shoulder, and he looked up to see a boy, Camden Abbott, regarding him. He asked Bo if he was trying out. Bo shrugged. Then he asked Bo if he was any good. Bo shrugged. Finally, he asked if it was true that his mom chopped his finger off before killing herself.

If there was one thing Bo Cassidy could do, it was run.

He ran past Camden, past the other kids who were still warming up, past the coach coming down with a water jug, and past the track over and over. Never breaking for a breath, because if he kept his legs moving and his chest burning, he couldn't think too hard about anything.

That's what it was like now.

Bo didn't think about Andy or Michael or Edith Beckham or whatever he had seen just a moment ago. He didn't think about his mother, father, or Selene. He didn't even think about the blood pouring from his ears, flowing down his neck, and into his cotton shirt.

What he did think about was that he'd forgotten his shoes.

As rocks and twigs punctured his feet, his pursuit never ceased. He wasn't going anywhere, just like that day on the track field, going round and round in circles for the sole purpose of moving. Running away, he realized, and though he thought he should feel a sort of shame in that, he couldn't bring himself to. Why should he feel remorseful in protecting himself?

Then again, Bo was always running in a sense.

His brain worked overtime as it evaded the constant grasping of his inner turmoil. His mind was both offensive and aggressive, the defender and the attacker. It was like constantly playing a game of ping-pong against himself, racing back and forth between the opposite sides of the table just in time to hit the ball back.

To think about Andy or not. To think about his hand or not. To think about his mother or not.

He used to think all he had to do was be able to run. In a way, he was right. He could leave behind his classmates and Warren. Leave behind his father and the empty house he'd grown up in. He could even leave Andy if he tried hard enough, though he always found his way back somehow.

Cliché as it was, though, the only thing Bo couldn't run from was himself.

He'd come to realize that the only person he'd always certainly had was his own. Anyone else could leave him on a whim. He wanted to think of it as an assurance. He'd wanted to be unbothered by who he was. Instead, whenever he thought of that fact, it was always *what a waste* that came to his mind.

What a waste it was to be stuck with himself.

Bo wondered if he ran fast enough, he'd break out of his own body and finally find some peace.

His insides felt mobbed, like stuffing hundreds of cotton balls into a compact jar. There wasn't even room for his lungs anymore. His breath was a torn and burdensome thing.

A root snagged his foot, and he tumbled to the ground. He managed to fling away from the tough forest floor, instead landing in soft mud. His outstretched arms were sucked in by the thickness. He attempted to pull his arms loose, but he was too fatigued to make any progress.

Bo heaved as he kneeled to the earth. He was shaking the blood and sweat off his forehead, and as he worked to catch his breath, the throbbing pain of his head and the burning sensation of his legs began to filter through his mind. As the pulsing of his heart faded from his ears, the whispers drew him back.

Loud and invasive, crawling into his ears as termites into wood. He could feel the breath of the voices slithering inside of him like threads of string. It stirred his entire body to a vibration. He felt like a hum was building up right inside of him.

Bo couldn't even pinpoint the words being spoken to him. All he could understand were the *emotions* behind the murmurs.

Desperate and callous, splenetic and harrowing, apprehensive and disconsolate. Bo felt it all in their pleading and warning and insults and *noise*. That's all it was at that point—just noise, noise, noise.

Then, from deep within the mud, he felt something else grab his hand.

The voices in his head yielded for that second, a short pause as he felt another hand slip between his fingers and tug at him. His body was pulled forward as he felt another pair of hands come to grip at his wrist, then another and another until it was as if hundreds of fingers lodged into his skin from under the earth, rushing to pull him down with them.

Bo found himself crying out as he jerked away. They held tight to his arms, but he was far more determined than the things keeping him down. As he finally broke away from the mud, he stumbled back.

A screaming burst inside his head as he returned to his stance. He backed away steadily, his hands coated in mud. There were cuts on his arm from the fingernails digging into his skin, and blood had begun to drip from his new wounds.

Bo turned on his heel and ran.

Always running, always running, always running.

Ch. Thirty-One

Bo was gone. Andy had forgotten he was planning on leaving from Michael's early to meet Selene at the ferry slip. By now, he would have already made it to the mainland.

Earlier, Andy had thought about calling Bo, but then advised against it, considering a ringing phone was the last thing his friend would want to hear. Also, Andy didn't have a damn clue what he would say. Maybe he could act like nothing had happened, like there weren't bruises forming on his neck from the hands of a dead girl. He was good at that.

Lying right through his teeth like a fucking coward.

Each time Andy closed his eyes, he felt her above him. Her hands were on his throat. His eyes bulged out of his head from the straining. Tighter, tighter, tighter. The cold never wavering, never faltering.

Andy didn't know what to do now.

Ever since he had become aware of the Beckham girl hauntings, he kept telling himself that all he had to do was catch her. School didn't matter. Getting older didn't matter. *Nothing* else mattered. He just needed to get her in that jar to have proof that he could do something right for a change. That he could be good at something, like Jaime and Mila and the twins were good at something. Like his father had been good at something.

Now he had her, and he couldn't even think about taking another step forward.

The thought of bringing her to his father terrified him, which felt like such a squander. Wasn't this the point? To do something to make his father proud in the way that mattered? Yes, it was. Yet Andy couldn't bring himself to do it.

Because if he told his father about the ghost, then he'd have to tell his father about the days he'd spent chasing it. He'd have to tell him about the struggle—how it was like he was fighting against death itself instead of just a shell of it. He'd have to tell his father about Bo and Michael and how they knew the truth now.

Andy shut his eyes. His hand came up to touch his neck, then trailed down along each bruise carefully. He pressed into the one forming on his Adam's apple, where her thumbs had been. He found his breath hitching at the pain. Andy let his hand drop to the key hanging between his collarbones.

He had done everything right and yet failed completely in his tasks. The jar, his winning trophy, felt heavy in his hands.

Andy kept seeing it. That look on Bo's face as he stood in the doorway. It wasn't confusion or hesitancy at the scene. He wasn't shocked by the impossibility of Andy wrestling against a thing that slipped through reality. It was a discerning gaze. One that Andy recognized from that first day Bo had set foot in the Beckham house.

Bo had somehow seen it as Andy had seen it.

For some reason, the spirit in his hand was more feasible than that fact.

Michael stopped by early in the morning, the sun rising behind him as he stood in Andy's doorway. For a moment, they just stared. That's all Andy had done the night before, too. He just stood in his bedroom. Still as a statue, every inch of him shaking, his vision tunneling as he stared a hole into the wall. Andy just stood in the middle of his bedroom and stared.

"I slept," Michael said. "I fell right asleep, and I didn't wake up at all."

Andy squinted. Partly due to the blazing sun, partly from the dizziness of his exhaustion.

Michael shrugged and turned away. "I just thought I'd let you know."

As Andy looked at him, he realized that his perception of Michael had changed throughout the hours of the night. He was no longer a stranger, a new kid to dissect and discover. He wasn't the thing

Andy had to protect from evil spirits. He wasn't just a recurring character in his life anymore.

Michael was his friend.

Of course, Andy had been aware of this. They hung out, they got along, and they fit together. But the weight of the term, the word *friend*, hadn't registered in Andy's head until then.

For some reason, Andy didn't consider himself to have many friends.

There were people he was friendly with but not friends with. People he talked to, but not people he walked with. He had acquaintances, and then he had Bo.

He thought, perhaps, that Bo was the reason he couldn't give a second glance to others. Not Bo as a person specifically, but what he meant to Andy. After all, Andy had struck gold right at the start, hadn't he? What would be the point in wasting time to keep going?

But being friends with Michael wasn't like being friends with Bo at all. At first, that seemed like a shortcoming. Now, Andy was aware that his friendship with Michael was just as valuable, despite it sitting differently in his chest. Just because it felt different didn't make it a bad thing.

"Do you want to come in?" Andy offered.

Michael regarded him. He stepped inside.

Andy brought him straight to his room. Mila and his great-grandmother were still in bed. The rest of his family was out at church during the early Sunday morning. Andy tried to shake off any self-consciousness he might feel about his home. Small and crowded, with belongings scattered across every surface, and portraits hung along each wall. The Romero-Almadas weren't messy. There was an order in the cramped living space. He'd just wondered if Michael would see it that way, too.

"Where are you?" Michael said from behind him.

Andy paused as he spun around. "Right here?" He was suddenly uneasy. *Shit*. Did last night really scramble Michael's mind that much? He didn't seem too affected by it, both during the hours before to now. Maybe Andy had misjudged, though. Maybe he'd broken Michael without realizing.

"No, no," Michael pointed to the wall. "In the pictures."

Andy followed his gaze and scanned the framed photos. Old family portraits of them all lined like porcelain dolls on a shelf; candid shots of Andy's siblings when they were all younger; yearbook and graduation photos; old black-and-white shots of his parents' wedding. There was even a photo of his great-grandmother posed with her flapper girl friends from the '20s. His family was in every crevice of the house.

"These are all your siblings, right?" Michael said. He began pointing at each solo picture of his brothers and sisters. "I mean, you're in the family portraits. But where are the photos of you alone? Are they somewhere else?"

His gaze was so earnest. Andy couldn't bring himself to say it out loud. Couldn't even... find the words.

Andy cleared his throat. "My room is this way."

He didn't turn to see if Michael was following him as he pushed open his door.

Once he had snapped out of his stunned daze, Andy had made a mess of his room. Walking in on it now, it was a visual representation of Andy's thoughts. Torn pages of old report cards, sheets strewn around in a fit of rage, Jaime's side completely in disarray from Andy's offense. Nothing had been spared.

Andy kicked at a pile of laundry by the door. He averted his eyes from his schoolboy uniform sitting on the top of the mountain.

"Sorry about the..." Andy trailed off. There wasn't anything he could say that Michael wouldn't notice on his own.

Michael didn't seem bothered by the mess. He carefully stepped over any stray items on the floor and headed to what was obviously Andy's side of the room. "Is it okay if I sit on your bed?" His politeness pissed Andy off, which he quickly felt guilty over. There must have been something seriously defective in him that even kindness had a sting to it.

He shrugged, and Michael took a seat, leaning forward and resting his elbows on his thighs. "Has Bo—"

"No," Andy answered. "Or, well, I don't know. He's gone."

"Gone?" Michael snapped his head up.

"Off the island with Selene. Shit, dude. You sure you got some sleep last night?" He didn't want to come off as defensive, but he was certain Michael had picked up the tension of his words. "It doesn't matter. It's not like he'd want to talk to me anyway."

"That's not true."

Andy scoffed. He opened his mouth to snap, but bit back. He wasn't going to argue about Bo with Michael. There was no point in calling attention to the fact that Andy had known Bo longer and that *they* were best friends first and foremost. Despite their efforts, the dynamics between the three of them were clear.

Andy had felt guilty over it before. Then, it felt like a sort of victory, something to brag over. Right in that moment, though, he just felt disdain toward everything.

Because there was this: even though none of them had mentioned it, Andy knew that Michael was aware of the thing that had been silently plaguing Bo for the past couple of years. Andy didn't know *what* it was—what had been weighing on Bo and pulling him further away—but he knew how it was affecting Bo.

He'd spent years trying to carefully pry his friend open. Attempting to gain just a glance behind all the walls Bo had put up. It was unfair of him to want Bo to be honest without offering his truth right back. Andy knew this, and yet.

Alejandro Romero-Almada was as much of a hypocrite as he was a liar. This was the way his life was ordered. This is how the world kept spinning.

"You just need to talk to him," Michael suggested.

Andy shrugged dismissively. "We do talk. We talk all the fucking time."

"You know what I mean, Andy." But he didn't. He didn't know anything anymore.

Andy bit his lip.

"What did he tell you?" He had to know. More than he needed a passing grade, more than he needed to find the Beckham girl, more than he needed air in his lungs.

Michael's eyes drew away.

"It's not my place to say," he said softly.

"It's about me, isn't it?" Andy spoke. It squeezed him on the inside, twisting and tugging at his chest and making his eyes sting. He kept thinking about each time Bo had yanked his hand away, embarrassment and aversion tracing his expression.

Growing up was more than just pain in his legs and a weariness in his bones.

"It's not," Michael said quickly.

Andy shook his head away so Michael wouldn't see his gulp.

"Andy, seriously." He crossed the room and rested a hand on his shoulder. "It's not about anything you did. It's..."

"Just give it to me straight."

"I *can't*," Michael said before immediately shrinking. "I mean— Ugh. *He* has to be the one to tell you. Not just for your sake, but his too. We're not hiding things from you."

"Like how I hid stuff." Andy flinched. "That's what this is about? Some kind of payback for everything I've done?"

"What? No, of course not! Andy, no one is punishing you, okay? Bo is just dealing with a lot right now. He had been for a while."

"You don't think I know that?" Andy snapped. "You don't think I notice how people treat him? How they just *spit* on him like he's shit on the side of the road. How they—" He brought an arm over his face to cover his sniffle. He quickly cleared his throat and regained composure.

He couldn't admit it. It was against their rules.

Andy and Bo were never to talk about it, never to acknowledge it. It was how they lived off each other. They were the breaks in each other's days, the short pause that allowed them to catch their breath. It had been that way since the beginning. Andy couldn't give in now.

He didn't even register as Michael let his hand reach past Andy's shoulder and fall around his shoulders. He pulled Andy in and held him tight. For a second, Andy was right back in that house, his body planted to the floor as the pressure of hands suffocated him. He blinked furiously as Michael hugged him. He stood completely limp as Michael held him.

It was such a strange thing to be on the opposite end of touch. It was always Andy reaching out, offering an arm, or extending a hand. He was never the one being pulled into an embrace. Never the one to be caught off guard by contact.

In an embarrassing moment, he was unsure of what to do. Then he carefully brought his arms up to Michael and hugged him back. It was an awkward hold. Michael was bulky and tall, causing him to lean over Andy, practically engulfing him. It didn't seem to matter, though. The solidity of him was enough to ground Andy.

He pushed back and rolled Michael's hands off his shoulders before drawing his arms towards his core.

"I think you need to sleep," Michael said.

Andy let out a huff. "You know, usually this is supposed to be the other way around."

"Funny how things turn out." Michael spared a tight smile. "Listen, Andy..."

Andy knew where this would be going. He didn't know how he was to prepare for it.

"The thing between you and Bo," Andy felt a pang in his chest at that for reasons beyond him. "You need to cut it out. The... not talking or whatever you guys do. It might have worked before, but it's not anymore, and it's *hurting* both of you."

"You're not my shrink, McKenzie." Andy bit back. Michael blinked at him, and Andy shrank. "Sorry. I'm sorry, Michael." He'd remembered that Michael didn't like to be called anything but his name.

Andy was a total asshole. But then again, what else was new?

Michael tucked his hands into his pockets. "You know how I got Bo to talk to me?"

Desperately.

Andy shrugged.

"I told him something about myself first. Something honest."

The impossible.

"Then, I asked."

The obvious.

"And after, I listened."

Andy brought his gaze up to Michael. His brows were furrowed softly, and his mouth crooked into a thoughtful frown. Michael was, decidedly, a good friend. Too good a friend for Andy.

"Just think about it."

Andy always did.

Ch. Thirty-Two

Bo stepped foot on the mainland, and suddenly he was eight years old with his bag slung over his shoulder, Selene's grip on his hand desperate, and the weight of his mother's death yet to settle on his shoulders.

Those days, the ones leading up to her passing and the ones that followed, were such a blur. It felt as if Bo was looking through thick-rimmed glasses, heavy on his nose and hurting his eyes no matter what angle he shifted to. He thought that maybe it was better that way. The not remembering, that is.

Besides, he suspected that it wouldn't matter how much or how clearly he could recall that month. He'd never let himself think about it anyway.

It felt like a betrayal, no matter how he dealt with it. Refusing to think about his mother was a disloyalty to her, but a savior to himself. If he did the opposite, if he let his mind wander and linger on the ghost of her touch and the soft smile on her lips, the betrayal was angled at himself. He was a Judas in whatever way he went about it.

Selene placed a hand on his shoulder. "It's a bit of a walk."

"I don't mind." He wasn't ready to face it anyway.

As they walked to where she was buried, Bo felt a growing sense of shame fill his lungs. Each step was more straining. He wondered if the people he passed on the streets knew from his guilty expression,

Do you know? Bo thought. *Do you know it's been almost a decade, and I've never gone to see her?*

The remorse fit right beside the humiliation of his leaning desire.

Bo Cassidy was a queer little thing, in every sense. Unorthodox and sporadic in the world around him. Growing up beside Andy was a constant reminder of that fact.

Whenever they'd walk around, pretending to smoke the candy cigarettes they'd snagged from the convenience store down the block, pacing themselves so their steps lined up identically, Bo felt it. Every few paces, someone stopped them in their tracks to greet Andy. A handshake Bo couldn't follow along with, a conversation he managed to lose halfway, and smiles that never made Bo's direction.

It served as a reminder that Andy had always been a boy while Bo had always been a creature of obscurity.

But Andy never let him feel that way. Dragging Bo around by the hand through town, nudging him into mischief, the grip he'd hold on Bo ensured he didn't drift too far away. Always keen, always dedicated, always waiting with an earnest smile on his face.

Bo suspected that he had only grown to become a person because of Andy.

He shivered against the breeze, and Selene leaned over to tighten the scarf around his neck. He pointed towards a florist, with poppies and mums lined in rows at the window. Selene nodded and took him inside. They spent a moment browsing. Selene picked up some roses and sunflowers.

"She liked peonies," Bo interjected.

He remembered the days his mother would spend gazing upon the paintings she'd done long before. Pieces of her favorite flowers were powerful acrylics, those watercolors of nature had been done in one sitting, and the charcoal sketches of their family made even those deep shadows feel warm. For some reason, after Bo had started school, she had stopped painting. While he waited for his father to come home late one night, he asked her why. She softly shook her head and disappeared into her room.

Selene gazed at him. "I forgot." She gave a short smile, but Bo noticed it was forced. She gently set down the other flowers before reaching for Bo's suggestion.

"And—" He began, but Selene cut him off.

"Dahlias. I remember now." She nodded. "I'm surprised you remembered. It's been so long ago now, and you were so young."

Bo tried to conceal his disappointment. Selene always seemed shocked whenever he remembered something about his mother, as if he'd have no recollection from being eight years old. So dismissive, too. Often, it felt like his aunt thought she was the only one to remember his mother. Bo didn't have it in him to argue, though. He kept his mouth shut as they paid for the flowers and continued on their walk.

When they approached the cemetery, Bo found himself surprised. He'd imagined it barren, cracking graves and brittle trees arching out as if grasping at the sky. Instead, it was clean and serene. Fresh flowers were laid among many graves, each of them polished to pristine condition. Bo's eyes read along the names as they walked through, scouring for his mother.

His foot slipped off the stone path and slid into some fresh mud. The feeling of his shoe being dragged into the ground brought him right back to the night before. Bo urgently yanked his leg away and clenched his fists to steady himself.

Don't think about that, he ordered himself. *Think about mom.*

One thing at a time. One thing at a time.

But he couldn't. His mind was in disarray. Even with the miles of distance from Whalesborough, his head refused to quiet. The whispers were muffled, as if shouting through a pillow, but the presence of their voices still shook him.

Even more than that, he couldn't shake away his thoughts. He kept seeing Andy on the ground, face growing pale and lips turning blue as veins popped out of his forehead from straining. He couldn't stop hearing the gasping sound he made, choked and desperate. It was louder in his head than anything else.

At first, he couldn't comprehend what he was looking at. It didn't register in his brain—Andy fighting against nothing but a cool breeze. He blinked furiously, trying to make sense of it, and then he saw her as clear as day. The girl from the photo in Michael's attic.

Bo brought his knuckles to his eyes and used the pressure to snap himself out of it.

It didn't matter. His thoughts could linger on Andy on any other day. Today, Bo would have to get his shit together and think about his mother. It had been long overdue.

By the time he removed his hands from his face, Selene had ventured off without him, leaving Bo to catch up. She stood solemnly, gripping the flowers close to her chest as she stared down. Bo came to her side and followed her eyes.

Here Lies Lori Cassidy, Beloved by All

Bo stilled.

For so long, he had known his mother was dead. It was an objective fact, something he couldn't argue against. He'd spent years missing her, grieving for her, and dealing with her empty presence. It was one thing to know somebody was dead. It was another thing to see the proof.

He found it a bit ridiculous.

Obviously, he'd *seen* it. He had the finger to prove it. But to see the grave, to see where she was buried, was something different altogether.

Bo just looked and took long, shallow breaths.

Selene knelt and placed her hand on the smooth stone, tenderly tracing each letter of his mother's name. Through a glimpse, Bo caught glistening tears rolling down her face, and he remembered that it had been a long time since Selene had seen his mother, too.

"Did you know," Selene began, "that we all grew up together?"

Bo shook his head.

"Your father and I were born here, but your mother came later. The three of us were tight, but she was my friend first. Not at the beginning, though. When we first met, I couldn't stand her."

Selene laughed a bit. "I don't know why. I just didn't like her all that much. It wasn't mutual. She thought I was..."

Selene bit her lip and removed her hand from the grave before setting the flowers down. "She thought I was special. Not just because I could see things, though she liked that bit too. Most people, if they believed me, thought I was extraordinary because of my ability. She thought I was extraordinary because I was... myself."

Bo could imagine it. He didn't remember much before his school years, but he remembered a smile of his mother's reserved just for Selene. The way they interacted reminded Bo of how Selene made her tea. Easy and mindlessly, just like the way she spun her spoon in the teacup to infuse the herbs with the water.

"When we got older, your father came and swept her off her feet. Obviously." She spared a playful glance at Bo, the walking proof of their romance. "The three of us, it was... a dream. There's a reason why the number three carries significance across cultures." She let her finger dig into the dirt and draw patterns without meaning.

"And then I came along, right?" That's what she must be getting at. A disturbance in their solar system. Selene shrugged and patted the spot next to her. He hesitated before taking a step next to her. She stared ahead, past the gravestones, and out towards the sun in the sky.

"I love you, Bo," Selene said first and foremost. "But, yes. It was hard for me. Hard for your parents, too. Your father wasn't sure— Ah, nevermind." She quickly cut herself off.

"He wasn't sure about me?" Bo finished.

Selene flicked the dirt off her hand before resting it on the back of his head. "In a sense. But your mother convinced him."

Bo nodded. He had already known that, though. He was something his mother wanted more than his father. He thought that if the roles were reversed, that if it had been his father who had died, his life would look very different. He quickly shook the thought away, though. It felt cruel inside of him.

"And you? Did she need to convince you?" Bo asked, mostly as a joke, but he was anxious for her answer.

Selene smiled and shook her head. "I already knew. If Lori was happy, I was happy. And if Lori was happy, your father was happy too. That's the thing we share most of all, I think. Growing up, we got along well enough, but it was Lori who kept us together."

Bo swallowed. "Until the falling out, you mean."

He remembered it all so quickly.

Creeping out of his bedroom at six years old, his father was screaming in the middle of the night. One hand gripping the telephone, the other hand gripping a warm beer. His mother was nowhere to be found.

You want to see Lori? Go fucking see Lori.

In those days, his father spent all day on the telephone, arguing with Selene about his mother, who seemingly disappeared. After a couple of weeks, the phone rang without an answer. Bo had picked it up once to be greeted with profanities from Selene, vicious and cruel, clearly aimed at his mother and father. He let her ramble, silent as he let her blow off steam, before she hung up without letting him utter a single word.

When his mother finally came home from wherever she was, it was too late. Everything was different then. Selene never came by anymore, his father barely looked her way, and his mother didn't bother trying to fix anything. The air was thick with the things they never said.

He tried to ask his mother about what had happened, but she would kneel to cover his mouth with her delicate hands and kiss his forehead to quiet him. He remembered the chill of her hands. It was always a shock when she touched him then. Growing up, he had always known her to be so much warmer.

He'd pieced it together as he'd gotten older. An argument that left the family shattered. His mother fled the wrath of his aunt and his father, letting the siblings deal with whatever fuse his mother had lit. Bo suspected that it was a selfish act from his mother that set it off.

The leaving, he thought, was the nail in the coffin. She had left the two of them to deal with it, and when she came back, the only thing they could compromise on was a punishment. Ignoring his mother for two years seemed to be the only thing Bo's father and Selene could agree upon. His mother must have felt she deserved it in some way, because she accepted the ignorance and moved on with Bo.

Bo couldn't help feeling that it was unfair to him, though. He'd never done anything wrong, just collateral damage. Still, he felt every second of silence like a small needle piercing his skin.

Selene was silent at his side, but he didn't want to look at her. He didn't want to admit how unforgivable his aunt had been those two years leading up to his mother's death. He didn't want to think about how much he hated Selene for it.

"Do you regret it?" He asked. She must have, he thought, but he wanted to hear her say it.

It was a mistake. Or maybe even, *Every day*. Anything to hint at the remorse Selene must have felt would be enough to satisfy him.

But she didn't. She did what the Cassidy's were good at. She ignored it. "I don't know what you mean."

Bo stuffed his hands in his pockets so she wouldn't see his clenched fists. "Come on, Selene. It's over. She's dead. Just cut the bullshit with me," his voice shook. For so long, he'd been afraid to speak about his mother. Now it was all he wanted to do. "Why'd you do it? What did she do that was so terrible?"

"Nothing. She never did anything horrible," Selene said softly.

"Then why'd you ignore her those last two years?" Bo choked out. "Did you just not care? That's what it is, isn't it? You and Dad, you just didn't give a shit towards the end of it. Even after she passed, you still didn't care."

"Bo—"

What about Mom?

Take him.

His shoulder arched up to his ears. He let his head fall, his chin tucked into his chest, his bangs falling to hide his gaze. He couldn't even close his eyes. Every time he did, he saw his mother falling to the floor. Or worse, he saw the Beckham girl and Andy.

Selene's hand came up to reach him, but Bo shrugged her off.

"I just want to know why," he finally said. "Why did everything fall apart back then?"

"She was gone..."

"*Before* that. Before she died. What did she do?"

He brought his head up to look at Selene, but she was scrunched in confusion. All he wanted to do was wipe that stupid look off her face. One she wore each time Bo had brought up his mother after moving in with her. As if Bo was the only one to truly remember her. As if Bo was the only one who actually cared that she was gone.

He snapped his head away and turned back to the grave, his mother's name burning in his gaze. As he read the rest of the tombstone, he wasn't sure if he should laugh or cry. "You didn't even care enough to get the date right." It hurts to get the words out.

Here Lies Lori Cassidy, Beloved by All
January 1957 - August 1986

His nails dug into his palm so hard, he felt the burst of blood in his pocket.

"How could you get the date wrong?"

"I didn't."

He cut his eyes towards Selene, furious and dismal all at once, but any loathsome feelings he felt towards her dissipated as he met her gaze. Something about her quivering lip, about the tears welling in her eyes, about how she worked to keep her breath steady made him realize that there was something wrong. Something very, very, wrong.

A static in the air made him feel electric, like he'd crack with a single touch.

"I didn't get it wrong," Selene repeated.

But that couldn't be true. Bo *knew* that wasn't true. The date on the gravestone... the math didn't add up.

"When did she die?" Selene asked him.

"When I was," he doesn't know why, but he hesitated. He brought his hand out of his pocket and looked down at his finger. Selene followed his gaze, and he heard a sharp intake, as if something were clicking into place. "Eight."

Selene brought her hands over her face quickly and started shaking her head. Bo watched as his aunt crumpled in on herself. He wanted to reach out to comfort her, but he couldn't. He was too fixated on the date of the tombstone.

"She died when I was eight."

"No." Selene was crying now in the same way she was when she picked Bo up from the emergency room after his mother had died. "No..."

"But..." *1986, 1988, 1986, 1988.* Two years off. It wasn't right. It wasn't what Bo knew to be true. "She was *there*."

Walking him to the bus stop each morning for school. Directing him when he made himself dinner.

Tucking him into bed and tying his shoes when he couldn't. Gently caressing his face and kissing him softly. Playing with him. Watching him. Touching him. *Loving* him when there was nobody else to.

Selene was gone. His father as well, in a sense.

The only reason Bo had managed to survive those years was because of his mother.

"She was right there," Bo said quietly. Right there, when no one else was.

Selene threw her arms around him and dragged him close to her chest. She shook as she held him, her tears dampening his hair and her sobs echoing in his ear. Her words were broken by her cries, but she held him tighter and tighter as she tried to make out hushed apologies.

He didn't hug her back—he couldn't bring himself to move at all. He just lay in her arms as he stared at the date on the stone.

He gently pushed out of Selene's grip and reached a hand for the grave.

The voices in his head grew louder.

As his fingers brushed against his mother's name, he felt it.

A trail of blood trickled out of his ears.

Then Bo knew.

Ch. Thirty-Three

Michael lay flat in his bed.

It was a surreal feeling to find peace in his room. It was how most people lived, he supposed. Then again, Michael didn't think he belonged to "most people" anymore. There had always been an unnamed trait that he'd grown up with, but only when he was beside Bo (and now, Andy, too) did it become apparent.

He'd thought that if someone pulled away all the layers, like peeling away the skin of an apple until they reached the seed, they'd find an abnormal core that was of himself. Michael was finally realizing how hard he had worked to cover it up with obedience and silence. Everyone liked a follower, and they'd never question his true intentions, as they were too wrapped up in the good feeling of being listened to.

It wasn't a calculated manipulation. It was just an instinct. Listen to his parents without question or go along with the other kids to make them like him because what else was there to do? It was just easier.

Despite this, he knew they noticed his curious character. How his eyes would linger on shadows, how he'd become infatuated with the uncanny of the everyday world, how he'd been drawn to macabre.

Soft aspects that could be ignored, but once pinpointed, were strange in themselves.

Bo was similar, though he couldn't hide it as Michael did. There was just something about Bo Cassidy, a peculiarity that tainted him. Something about the cut of his eyes, the arch of his hands, or the stance that he took. It gave the same feeling as a crow residing in the distance. As if his presence was an omen of some sort on its own.

Andy could conceal it better, Michael finally realized. Though, he suspected Andy clearly spent a long time learning how to. But it was like that night at Michael's had been a breaking point—a crack in the dam before releasing a flood. Now, Michael couldn't view Andy in any other light. Watching Andy maneuver throughout the world was like flipping through channels on a radio, different voices and tones to capture attention and distract you from the underlying static.

Michael supposed he was just like them. Andy was beginning to see that now, too. It wasn't his obsession with *The X-Files* or his nightmares. It was the fact that his head wasn't hurting anymore.

The way Andy had described it, the aftermath of a haunting could be brutal on one's psyche. But Michael had already managed to find his footing. The concept of it slotted into his mind as seamlessly as slipping his foot into his tennis shoes. Spirits and the Beyond? Sure, why not?

Though Andy hadn't yet gone into the finer details of the supernatural world like he'd promised, Michael didn't mind. From what he knew, it seemed rather simple. He didn't feel any more dismay or timidity; it just *was*.

If anything, it was savored.

Lying in bed, he wondered how many times he'd stared at his ceiling and worked to convince himself he wasn't crazy. Now he knew the truth, and it was *marvelous*.

Ghosts were real, and Michael McKenzie had aided in defeating one.

His skin was buzzing, like he was plugged into an electrical outlet. In the quiet of the house, he could hear the wind howling outside. How many nights had he lain awake like this? Before the questions were anxiety-induced. Now, they pumped adrenaline throughout his body.

Were the prior nights terrifying? Undeniably so. Yet Michael had never felt so present in his life before. It was like running track for the first time all over. Desperate to prove himself, a beast in him worked to claw its way out of him as he powered through with each step, the burning sensation doing nothing except fueling him to go further.

When he first tried out for track, he'd stumbled across the finish line and crashed so hard into the ground that he'd slit his forehead open. The scar across his eyebrow was proof of it. Evidence of not only his blunder but of the feeling that came with it. It wasn't a bad thing to live with forever, he decided.

That's what it was like at that moment. Watching Andy struggle on the floor against an inexplicable force, Michael's heart had been pounding in his ears while he stood frozen. Andy, who was small enough to be tossed over Michael's shoulder, had been fighting like a ruthless and unmovable thing. Andy, who was all smiles and sweet-talking, was spitting and baring his teeth. If he was being honest, Bo had always seemed to be the more interesting one of the pair. But Andy had flipped Michael's entire world upside down in mere minutes. Not just with the newfound knowledge of the dead, but with Andy's true nature coming out. He was menacing and frightening then, and Michael had never been more fascinated.

But more importantly, Michael felt a hint of jealousy curling in his stomach. With Andy's family and heritage, with his autonomy and assurance in himself, with the ability to *snap*.

What was that like? How did it feel to crackle and break out against all past reservations?

Michael wanted to know. He wanted that kind of life.

He wanted the all-consuming tenacity and the vigor that came with the life of a ghost hunter. Andy had described it as a burden, but Michael could only see it as anything but. The consternation was nothing less than familiar—Michael knew how to handle being scared. It was a way of life by now. He could get past the fear of the dead and persist in the thrill of the chase.

He wanted in.

Michael knew Andy viewed it as a solitary thing, or at the very least, a familial one. As if being a ghost hunter was a thing to be inherited through genetics and not through ambition. But Michael could be diligent when he needed to. He could find a way to convince Andy. He could become a part of something larger than himself.

But now wasn't the time to ask. Andy was a nervous wreck, twitching and fidgeting over Bo. Michael shared some strain, but he knew Bo could handle himself. Andy wasn't there to witness the weary school days. He wasn't aware of Bo's durability the way Michael was.

Of course, Michael was concerned. A small part of him related to Andy's struggle with Bo, the nagging that there was something else Bo refused to acknowledge that dragged him down. Michael suspected it ran deeper than the town's rumors about him and the real truths behind the gossip. There was something else that none of them had yet to figure out that made Bo more *other*. Michael wasn't sure what it was, though.

He brought the sheets closer to his chin.

Michael wasn't sure when he'd get used to it. The house, the town, his classmates and his neighbors, the chilly air of the East Coast, and the raging ocean outside his window. He wasn't sure when he would start feeling like he belonged with his friends or if he was always meant to be the odd man out. Too quiet, too strange, too late. Michael had never been somebody's best friend.

He thought about that a lot.

Michael tossed his blankets off and scurried out of bed. He didn't bother slipping his shoes on. He wasn't finding shattered glass in the floorboards anymore.

He crept down to the kitchen, careful not to wake his parents, and quietly punched in the Romero-Almada household phone number. Andy picked up on the second ring.

"Is your mind fucked?"

"No," Michael answered. "Not anymore, anyway."

"That's good to know, I guess."

Andy must have still been up. Michael could imagine the other boy leaning against the wall, his head pressed beside the phone as he held the receiver close to his face. He could imagine Andy's worn expression, slack-faced and defeated.

"How'd you know it was me?" Michael asked.

Andy sighed. "Only Bo calls at this hour."

Michael pursed his lips and recognized the words Andy had yet to say. *But he's not calling*.

"I don't think it's because of you," Michael said. "He's had a lot going on. Besides, maybe he hasn't been able to access a phone from the mainland."

"Do you know why he went?" Andy's voice crackled through the phone.

Michael began to shake his head, but then remembered that Andy couldn't see him. "No, no. Do you?"

"It's his mom. It's the anniversary of her death."

"Oh," Michael hushed. "*Oh.*"

"Usually I try to distract him, you know? Selene kind of goes away. Not actually, but in her head. So there's never anyone there to keep him company," Andy told him. "When we were younger, we'd just watch a lot of MTV or whatever else was on and stuff our faces with candy. As we got older, we started sneaking out. Not doing anything, but just taking long walks around town and shit."

"Did he ever... You know? Talk about it?" Michael wasn't sure if Bo had also been reserved or if it was something he'd learn as he got older in Whalesborough.

"Sometimes. Never directly. He would sometimes slip her into the conversation or briefly mention her. I never pressured him to talk about it, though." Andy paused, and Michael knew he was twisting the wire of the phone with his pointer finger. He hadn't even realized he had made note of that habit, but he could picture it so clearly.

"I know you want us to talk. I know it's mind-blowing to you that we don't, but you don't get it," Andy said softly. "Everyone wanted him to talk about it. The town, I mean. It was like he couldn't catch a fucking break. Then there was Selene, who didn't even acknowledge it in the first place and pretended like nothing had even happened."

"Isn't that what you guys do?"

"Not like that. When we... ugh." Andy brought the phone closer to him. "It's just different, okay? Selene doesn't talk about it because she wants to act like it doesn't hurt. *We* know it hurts. And by not talking about it, it's a way to make it sting less."

Michael shut his eyes. "But it's not working anymore."

"How do you know?" Andy argued.

"Because I've seen it. He's talked to me—"

"Do you want a fucking medal?"

"Stop," Michael spoke sternly. "Andy, come on. Why are you doing this? Really."

The other line was silent, and for a moment, Michael thought Andy might have hung up on him. Then he heard a shaky breath like it hurt.

"I don't know how to."

That's all he said. Michael waited for him to elaborate, for him to clarify or give at least *something* more, but that was it. Just that small confession.

Michael bit his lip and let his back hit the wall. "Well, tough shit, Andy." He could practically hear Andy straighten up through the telephone, but Michael wasn't going to back down. "You're gonna have to figure it out one way or another, because I can't be the one to talk to him. It has to be you this time."

"Michael—"

"You're right," Michael said. "I don't know him like you do. I wasn't there to share your history. So you're going to have to step up and talk to him. *Actually* talk to him because he can't deal with this on his own anymore. I don't think either of you can."

He listened to Andy's quiet breathing over the phone.

"I'm not his best friend, Andy. It has to be you."

Andy was quiet. Michael squeezed his eyes shut.

"Sometimes I wonder if he's friends with me because I'm myself or because I'm the only one who's stuck by him," Andy whispered. "And now you're the walking proof of it."

"Of what?"

But he ignored this question. "Someone else is trying to call the line."

"Bo?" Michael questioned. He hoped it was him so Andy could find some peace and finally get some sleep. "You can hang up. It's okay."

"Yeah, okay," Andy said in a fretting tone. "I'll call you later. Or no, you'll probably be asleep. I'll see you tomorrow."

"I'll stop by Selene's after work," Michael offered.

Andy gave a hum of approval. "Thanks, Michael. For... just thanks."

He hung up before Michael could give a response, and he was greeted by the silence of the house once more. Michael held the phone to his ear for just a moment longer, listening to the comfort of the dial tone as he fought against the lull of sleep.

He wasn't sure if he'd ever get used to it. Not just the newfound ease of rest, the lack of nightmares waiting at his doorstep, or the harmony of being in control of his body. No, he wondered if he'd get used to being the spare in every pairing he came across.

Though it didn't matter much now.

Michael returned to his room and rested flat on his back. He stared at the dark ceiling, not ready to fall asleep just yet.

The world was changing around him at every angle, shifting and bending in unfamiliar ways, and all he could do was sit shotgun and feel every sharp turn with his entire body.

Ghosts were real, and Michael McKenzie was not crazy.

He reached for his Walkman and let the cassette play. The words of W. Flick echoed in his ear as he closed his eyes.

Then, Michael finally slept.

Ch. Thirty-Four

Andy biked as fast as he could to the Cassidy's household. Selene was waiting at the shop register, her face resting in her hands as she leaned against the counter just as Bo always did. She didn't look up right away as the bell above the door chimed at Andy's entrance. She almost seemed like a posed figure in her stature. Passive and quiet, like she wasn't really there.

Andy approached her side, and she brought one hand away from her eyes and rested it on his cheek. The gesture was familiar to him. It brought him back to when he was still light enough to fit in his mother's arms. His father would meet them in the middle and lend a hand to each of their faces.

When Selene finally met his gaze, Andy felt himself take in a sharp breath. She looked dire. Andy tried to neutralize his expression as he leaned in closer beside her and offered an arm for her to lean on.

They never called her Aunt Selene or Ms. Selene. Always Selene. A friend, before anything else.

Selene rested on his side and squeezed his hand slightly before pulling back and bringing his hands to her. "I should've realized," she murmured.

Andy didn't know what she was talking about, but it didn't matter. "It's not your fault."

Selene shook her head. "It is. It *is*." She wiped a tear from the corner of her eye. "Alejandro..."

Alejandro was never the name they used for him. Some kid at the playground, at some point in time when he was younger, had called him Andy, and so it had stuck. He supposed they took it from the "Andro" part of his name, which never made much sense to him, but the thing about nicknames was that they were hard to shake off even when they lacked reason. Selene and Bo had called him Andy for as long as they knew him. Alejo was for his family, his brothers and sisters, his aunts and uncles, and his many cousins. Alejandro, though, had places of distinction. It was unspokenly reserved for his mother and father, who had rarely called him anything else. Or, more recently, it was a signifier of heavy situations, whether he was an accomplice to trouble or a bystander to tragedy.

He was unsure of the role he would be taking in this particular scene.

"If I talked about her, we would've realized it sooner," Selene broke off. "But I never did. I couldn't."

Andy understood the feeling.

"He doesn't want to see me, but he can't be alone. I'm sorry to call you this late," she apologized.

"I don't—" His voice cracked and he quickly cleared his throat to conceal the stumble of speech. "I don't think he wants to talk to me right now. We... fought." It wasn't the truth; it never was. But it would have to do.

"That doesn't matter." Selene pressed her lips together.

"I just don't want..." Andy paused. "To hurt him more."

She regarded him. Then, let her head fall to the side as she looked upon him. "You won't. You're always so gentle with him, Andy." She brushed loose strands of his hair away from his eyes and turned towards the door.

Andy couldn't dwell on her words or argue against them. He let her hold of him drop as he made his way to the staircase. As he stood at the bottom step, the same feeling washed over him as when he stood before the cellar door. It felt like a haunt.

Andy quickly kicked off his shoes and persisted.

Part of him was terrified of seeing Bo. Some of it was due to whatever had happened on the mainland to leave Selene so shell-shocked, but a more selfish part was that Andy dreaded finally facing Bo after the night at Michael's. He'd spent the last couple of hours turning it over in his head, walking through each possible conversation that he might find himself in. In each one, Bo had the same spit and bite in his words, the same resentment towards Andy. He wasn't sure if he was ready for it.

Andy hesitated at the door. He wondered if he should knock.

He never had before.

He pushed through.

Bo lay on his bed with his back towards Andy, his arms wrapped around himself tightly, with his knees brought to his chest in a fetal position.

He was wearing his shoes.

For a moment, that's all Andy could stare at.

Bo, desolate, with his shoes on his bed.

He was wearing his shoes.

Andy gripped the door handle before gently pushing it shut and making his way over to Bo's side. He stood before him, unable to see his face, while he contemplated what to do.

Then he took a deep breath and made his way to Bo's shelves of cassettes.

He began digging through the tapes before landing on *Grace* by Jeff Buckley. Andy remembered when they first listened to it together. It was almost two years to the date. They had bought it after the anniversary.

Andy inserted it in the cassette player, letting the tape roll for a minute. He watched it wind through the machine. Jeff Buckley's voice filled the melancholic room, his torment bleeding alongside Bo's.

Andy would often poke fun at Bo's taste in music, always so gloomy and dejected. Bo would let him, acting like a good sport and rolling his eyes at Andy's own taste in Sublime and Blur, which was fair, he supposed. When it was late one night, though, Bo admitted that he felt less lonely when he listened to sad music. Like happiness, misery was something better when shared between two.

Andy made his way over and softly sat on the edge of the bed. He was careful when reaching for Bo's shoes, mindful not to touch his legs when going to untie the laces. Andy pulled at the knot, and once the shoes were loosened, he slipped off the Converse as gently as he could manage.

He carried them to the closet, setting them down on the shoe rack so as not to track any more dirt onto Bo's carpet. Then he came back over to the bed. There was just enough room for him to squeeze himself on.

Andy slid beside Bo but gave enough room to not touch him. Bo still lay motionless. The only reason Andy knew he was awake was the faint shaking of his shoulders. Andy noticed flecks of dried blood trailing around his ear.

He brought his gaze away from Bo and looked right above. He strained his eyes as he focused through the skylight, making out the thick outlines of growing clouds in the storming sky. He hummed along to "Lilac Wine," the melody of the song soothing the tension he felt.

It took him a second to realize that Bo had begun to hum along beside him.

The two of them lay side by side. *Talk to him*, he told himself. Or maybe it was Michael's words, or perhaps even Selene's.

What people didn't seem to understand was that just because Andy talked didn't mean he had a way with words. He could run his mouth till the end of time, going around in circles without saying one true, meaningful thing. It was Bo who said the worthwhile things when he spoke.

Andy realized that many people were wrong about the two of them. They weren't opposites. They weren't the same, either. They were compliments to each other. Two sides of a scale that balanced each other out.

He spared a glance over to Bo.

The unrelenting part of him, the ache he carried with him throughout the years, wanted to reach out to him to lend some comfort with a touch. It was easier than talking. Better, too. Andy didn't know how to formulate his thoughts in coherent sentences. Translation in speech was always so faulty, and touch was uncomplicated.

But he restrained himself. Because Bo didn't like to be touched anymore. Because they weren't supposed to need that now. Because being held was a token of boyhood, and they had outgrown that long ago.

When they were younger, all they would do was touch. Hands intertwined, arms slung around shoulders and drawing each other close, limbs tangled in playful combat or when overcome by exhaustion, heads on shoulders and legs hooked around ankles. Andy's hands were never empty—he always had a grip on Bo in one way or another.

It was how he was raised. A family of contact. Kisses and hugs, gentle brushes and tight squeezes— another person always less than an arm's length away. Andy couldn't imagine a world without it.

It was fine when they were younger. It was still seen as endearing back then. Adults would fondle their closeness and comment on how charming it was to always be entwined. He remembered his aunt joking about how they could have been mistaken as conjoined twins, if not for the obvious differences.

Then they got to middle school, and suddenly, such tenderness was a thing against being a boy. He watched as his sisters held their friends and kissed their cheeks, but his brothers avoided the touch of their friends like the plague.

It wasn't just that, though. As they got older, they could finally understand the whispers tossed around town. Andy remembered the first time Bo flinched when he heard his name among the hushed conversations they passed by when running around town.

Andy had reached for his hand because that's what he always did back then. Bo snatched his away so quickly that Andy had gotten whiplash, as if Andy's touch was painful to him.

They just stared at each other for a moment, their eyes lingering on the space between them.

Bo stuffed his hands in his pockets and walked ahead, leaving Andy behind, frozen and impaired. It was like he could feel a bruise forming on his inside.

He knew it wasn't about him. Bo needed to protect himself. Rumors in Whalesborough grew like wildfires, and Andy's touchiness did nothing to smother the flames.

And there was this, too: nobody ever said a word about Andy. Only Bo. He didn't think that was fair, but a more insensitive part of himself was grateful for being left out of it. Nobody ever thought Andy was queer.

It shouldn't have mattered. It *didn't* matter. Because that's not what it was like.

Andy wasn't gay, and neither was Bo. There wasn't anything ulterior about their touching. It wasn't like those perverted stories he'd hear among the streets or as indictable as his classmates made it out to be. It was just a graze of the hands, a sweep of contact, and a brush of fingers against necks.

Even if Bo were queer, it wouldn't have changed anything. *They* weren't like that.

But that didn't matter back then, and so it wouldn't matter now.

Andy had learned to be careful when leaning against Bo. Small doses were best—a shoulder check here, a punch to the side there. Nothing that lingered, nothing that demanded attention. Barely noticeable except to the two of them. That's what Andy learned to live off of—those minuscule exchanges.

It felt like such a sacrifice, like letting himself starve, as he pulled away and tucked in on himself, clasping his hands in his lap so as not to try to reach out to Bo. But he made it in his head that when Bo needed him, Andy would be there, and until then, he would be patient and faint. Waiting for him, first. Waiting for him, still.

Maybe that's what growing up was.

Learning how to love somebody quietly.

Bo reached across the bed and brought Andy's arm around him, rolling Andy over to his side through the movement.

It was a swift and calculated action. Bo didn't turn over, didn't shift too much, but he dragged Andy's arm over himself until Andy's hand met the shoulder, digging into the mattress. Bo let his hand grip Andy's wrist for a moment longer before pulling back and letting Andy's arm stay there, pressed against his chest.

Neither of them moved. Jeff Buckley sang on.

"Hey, Cowboy," Andy tried, his voice something ragged. "Talk to me."

He heard Bo breathe for a moment. Then, so softly Andy almost missed it, Bo said, "They were all right about me."

Andy drew closer, turning further onto his side. His forehead was a breath away from the back of Bo's neck. "What?" Andy whispered back. He felt Bo shake his head and fall silent once more.

Andy let his thumb swipe at his shoulder blade before Bo turned to lie on his back. As his hair fell away, Andy could finally get a good look at him. For some reason, he had made it in his head that Bo was crying, but he wasn't. He was stone-faced, an absent look behind his eyes, but no tears. He had forgotten that Bo never cried. Andy couldn't even imagine what it would look like if he did.

"None of it was real," Bo said. Andy looked up at him. Bo blinked before looking down. "It was all in my head."

He swallowed.

"She had an aneurysm and cracked her head open on the counter edge. My dad was at work, and I was at school. Nobody was there to notice. She bled out all over the kitchen. She died." Bo took a deep breath through his nose. "Back in '86."

Andy furrowed his brows. He found himself shaking his head, but stopped quickly. He wasn't the strongest in math, but he could do a simple calculation in his head. In '86, they would have only been—

"I was six."

"But you—"

"She *died* when I was six," Bo said. "But I didn't stop seeing her until I was eight."

Andy turned this over in his head. It didn't make any sense. Nothing about... it just wasn't adding up.

Then it was like something clicked.

He thought of their first Halloween. He thought of the calls. He thought of the séance. He thought of the bleeding ears and the far-off gaze. He thought of Bo standing before him at the Beckham house and that knowing look on his face.

But most importantly, he thought of Selene.

He thought of when they were young, his mother having dropped him off at the shop, and Andy had convinced Selene to let them sit in on a reading. He watched her take her client's hands in her palm and read their past, present, and future. Andy listened to her insight and advice. Then he listened to her polite explanation when the client asked about her late husband.

I'm a psychic, Selene had said, *not a medium.*

Andy sat up, his hand still resting on Bo's chest, as he stared dead ahead of him.

Bo carefully took Andy's hand and pushed it off of him before sitting up as well.

Shoulder to shoulder, not saying a single word, sitting with the truth together as their minds wrapped around it. It was like that first time Andy's father had taken him down to the basement.

"Did you know?" Bo asked.

Andy turned to him. "How could I?"

"I heard you when you were talking to Michael," Bo said. "This is your... This is *yours.*"

Andy was too distracted to focus on Bo mentioning the night at the McKenzie's household. He gripped Bo's wrist urgently. "I didn't know."

Bo finally met his gaze. His eyes were empty basalt. For the first time, Andy felt the coldness of his stare. Then, Bo's eyes crinkled in the corner, and he averted his eyes. "I thought... I don't know."

"What?"

"With your family," he said softly, "I guess I got it in my head that that's the reason you picked to be my friend. Because you somehow knew that I... and that—"

"That's not it at all." Andy gripped his shoulders and brought Bo back to look at him. How could he think that? "At *all*." Bo had to know. He had to.

Bo brought his hands to hold Andy's wrist, but he didn't push him off. "I know, I was just saying I lost myself over it for a minute." Andy let out a breath. Bo pursed his lips. "I was just... worried."

Andy knew Bo could feel his heart beating through the pulse of his wrists. They slowly drew back in on themselves before leaning back onto the mattress. Andy tried to come to terms with it all while looking through the window above.

"Why didn't you tell me?" Bo asked.

Andy shut his eyes. "I didn't tell anyone."

"But—" He cut himself off. Andy knew what he was going to say. *I'm not anyone.*

"I wanted to," Andy said. "I didn't know how. My dad told me that telling people was dangerous. I never wanted anything bad to happen to you, or us, or... Fuck, I don't know. I just didn't know how to even bring it up. Besides, you hate this kind of shit. Would you have even believed me?"

"Yes." He didn't even hesitate. "If it were you, I would have believed you."

Andy didn't know how to respond to that. He would have preferred having the wind knocked out of him by a punch. It would have stung less.

Bo let his fingers splay out on the sheets as he whispered, "I used to hate Selene for how she talked about my mom. No, sorry, that's not right. I used to hate her for how *I* talked about my mom. She always responds like I was out of my mind, like I didn't know what I was talking about. Guess she was right."

"That's not—"

"I heard you, Andy." Bo tilted his head. "You told Michael they weren't real people, just shells of themselves."

"Bo..."

"All those days she was looking out for me when no one else was. All the times she walked me to school and made sure I ate something. Whenever she loved me—" He swallowed. "It was all just some fucked-up projection. None of it was real."

"No," Andy said. "That's— I wasn't explaining it right. It's more complicated than that."

"It doesn't matter. She's gone. She's *been* gone." Bo blinked rapidly before squeezing his eyes shut tight. "I don't remember a single true thing about my mother."

"You remembered that you loved her."

He wasn't even sure why he said it, but Bo opened his eyes and turned back to Andy.

Andy's eyes scoured Bo's face for a give. "That was real. And the love she had for you? That too." Andy spoke carefully. "What I said to Michael was simplified. The nuisances—they're harder to explain. But one thing is true: that when a person dies, their most prominent emotion sticks with them in the afterlife."

He thought about everything Bo had ever said about his mother. He thought about his friend's soft gaze and gentleness, the blush on his cheeks, and the shy expressions. Andy thought of how Bo had truly been alone all those years in that house back on the mainland.

"Her's must have been love," Andy offered. "That's the thing that kept her with you."

Bo looked at him earnestly. "Do you really believe that?"

The only thing that came easily to Andy Romero-Almada was lying. But he didn't have to just then.

"Yes."

They sat with that. Lying on their backs, Jeff Buckley in their ears, and the realization that the truth didn't leave a sour taste on their lips. Andy thought that Bo could ask him anything and he'd tell nothing but the truth.

Bo reached for his hand.
"Will you show me the basement?"

Ch. Thirty-Five

Bo had spent years watching Andy paw at the key slung around his neck and never once questioned it. He assumed it was a house key to the front door, held by a chain so Andy wouldn't lose track of it easily. Bo had never known Andy to be especially careless, but maybe his mother took extra precautions with him.

Now he followed as Andy led him to the back of the Romero-Almada house. In the years of their friendship, Bo had been over to Andy's house far less than Andy had been to Bo's. It was easier for Andy to come over to the shop. They preferred fewer people and more space. That wasn't to say that Bo had rarely been there; he knew the layout of the home as well as his own. If he were blindfolded, Bo would have been able to maneuver past each end table and around every corner effortlessly. It was a sudden surprise that he realized he had never been in the basement. Andy had never offered to show him.

Andy hesitated at the cellar door. They stood shivering as they stared at the ground. Bo thought that he should reach out to Andy again, but he had lost the familiarity of touch, and it was all becoming too much for him. Small exchanges, he decided, would work best in the meantime. He wondered if Andy felt the same way.

His friend took a shaky breath before kneeling on the ground and taking off the chain. He slid the key into the lock and lingered for a moment. Then, with a swift churn, Andy snapped the padlock off and tossed it to the side. He gripped the door handle, veins bulging from his forearms, as he pulled the doors open.

Andy stood up beside Bo as they gazed down the tunnel staircase. The cool breeze coming from the basement drew him in, the whispers in his head growing impatient. They urged him to come closer, to follow their voices and greet them. Bo held himself back.

"I've never..." Andy started before trailing off. Bo looked over. It was such a strange thing to see Andy Romero-Almada completely uncertain. Bo thought it would be unfamiliar, but it wasn't. He recognized the squinted eyes, the lightly chewed bottom lip, and the angled eyebrows. Looking at Andy, Bo realized that his friend was always in a state of pending of sorts, a constant calculating effort. He didn't know why it shocked him. He supposed he assumed that Andy was always beyond doubt in what he did. "No one else really comes down here."

"Not even your siblings? Or your parents?" Bo asked.

Andy shook his head. "It's always kind of been mine. You know?"

Bo watched Andy's shoulder rise and fall with each breath he took. He wondered how Andy managed to stay warm in nothing but his worn jean shorts and baseball tee. The bruise on Andy's face was appalling. "That sounds lonely," Bo said.

Andy shrugged but didn't meet Bo's gaze. "It's a bit creepy down there, if I'm being honest. I don't have a flashlight or anything to lead us. I just want you to know so you're not too freaked out when we finally..."

"I think I'll manage." Bo humorously nudged Andy's shoulder, but the playful gesture didn't do much to improve their moods. They remained at the foot of the cellar. Bo spared another glance at Andy before he took a steady step forward. Bo was quick to follow behind.

They descended further and further. The darkness made Bo second-guess each step, nervous that his foot would miss the ledge and cause him to stumble into Andy. He heard the echo of water dripping. He was careful not to listen too closely to the furious whispers in his head. He wondered if one of the strained voices was his mother's and quickly shook the thought away.

Andy paused when they reached the bottom. Bo bumped into him, his chest hitting Andy's back.

Andy reached out to balance him. In the miserable shadows, Bo could barely make out the faint outline of Andy's stare.

"Just... don't freak," Andy murmured.

"I won't."

There was a click and then a blinding light as Andy tugged at the light above them. Bo blinked, his eyes adjusting, and when he finally gazed upon the basement, he was glad Andy's hand was on him to ground him.

The basement was lined with shelves stretching from the floor to the ceiling. Crooked and aged, giving Bo the impression they were built a long time ago. Along each shelf was a misshapen glass jar, like the one he had seen Andy holding that night at Michael's house.

There was a storm in each jar. Violent swirling of clouds, flashing like lightning, shaking the containers like they were working to claw their way out. But worse, each one was screaming at Bo. It was worse in the light than in the dark.

Bo cupped his hands over his ears and stumbled back. Andy reached out to pull him away from the stairs, ensuring that Bo's back hit against the stone wall instead. His vision blurred as he glanced between each jar. How many were there? Hundreds. There had to be hundreds of them. Each one holding a different person.

No, that's not right. They weren't real people anymore.

He could hear Andy's muffled voice breaking through the ceaseless noise. Gentle and hushed. Bo slowly brought his hands down from his head and took another look around.

Some shelves held books and journals, appearing just as worn as the shelves themselves. There were tapestries of ancient markings that mimicked the ones Andy had sketched on Michael's bedframe. Here and there were tools, both modern and obsolete. Radios taken apart, flashlights that had been altered, old clocks and watches scattered around, each one stripped to its core.

Bo took a step forward. He heard the sound of crumpled paper under his foot. Bending over to pick it up, Bo found a report card. Andy snatched it from his hands and stuffed it into his pocket.

"How many times do you come down here?" Bo asked Andy.

Andy looked away. "Does it matter?" Which Bo knew meant more often than not.

Bo's face twisted.

"Why?"

Andy walked past Bo and placed a hand on one of the shelves. Bo noticed that Andy grazed each jar just as his hands grazed Bo. "I guess it makes me feel more important, in a way," Andy said softly. "Does that make sense?"

Bo watched his fingers gently trace the markings etched into the glass. It seemed like an absent-minded gesture, like Andy had spent hours doing it to the point where it became reflexive.

"Your parents make you come down here every day?" Bo asked.

"Yeah... No. I don't know. I mostly come down on my own," Andy said. He turned back to Bo. "Does this scare you?"

Bo looked between Andy and the rest of the room. How easily the two fit together. Bo could feel Andy's connection to this other world, like lingering fingerprints on a chilled glass. Not just by the time Andy devoted to it, but all other aspects. He understood what Andy had meant when he was talking to Michael.

It's been my entire life, Andy had said.

Bo saw it. He saw how deep this ran through Andy. It was thicker than the blood of his ancestors.

It's just as much of yours as it is mine.

"You don't scare me," Bo answered honestly.

"That's not what I asked."

Bo shifted. "Yeah, it scares me. No shit, Andy. This is..."

"Terrifying?" Andy finished. Bo nodded.

"Is that why you never told me?" Bo didn't know why, but he felt defensive at that. He didn't need Andy looking out for him like he was something fragile.

"At first," Andy admitted. "But then I guess it was more for me instead."

He took a shaky breath. Bo took a step towards him.

And suddenly, he was thinking of a night so long ago, back when Bo still let Andy grip his hand under their covers. Blinking sleep out of their eyes, voices so low it was hard to make each other out, Andy's lips brushing against Bo's cheek. In that faint, fleeting moment, he had heard Andy whisper softly enough that it came out as a breath. "Have you ever had something that hurts to carry, but you do it on your own anyway because you feel like you deserve it?" And he had to take a moment to turn it over in his head, to make sure he truly heard it right, but by the time Bo had lifted his head to look upon him, Andy had already drifted to sleep, and it hung in the air like a haunting.

He supposed that's what it really was, in the end.

"I didn't do it to hurt you, Bo," Andy said.

"I know."

"Yeah?"

Bo thought of each time Andy had bitten his tongue when they talked about the spirits of the town.

He thought of each time Andy reached for him and Bo pulled away.

Bo knew it pained Andy. The other boy lived off of physical contact like it was the groundwork for his hierarchy of needs. Bo watched as Andy interacted with other people, always leaning in and offering himself to them. It was a way of life for him, and Bo deprived him of it.

He did it to defend himself. That's what Bo always tried to convince himself of. He yanked himself away from Andy to make it easier on both of them. To deflect against the rumors of the town.

But then it became something else. Stepping away from Andy's touch wasn't just to diffuse the speculations anymore. Both of them had changed from the boys they were years ago. Things weren't allowed to be simple now.

Pulling away, Bo knew, was never supposed to be an attack on Andy. It was aimed towards himself more than anything else.

"Yeah," Bo promised. Andy's shoulder eased. He watched as Andy raised his arms before hesitating. Bo reached forward and pulled Andy into a hug.

He felt Andy tense. He couldn't remember the last time they actually held each other like that. It could have been years. Long enough that they couldn't figure out the newfound height difference. They had always grown taller together rather equally back then, often barely off by centimeters. Now, their bodies were crooked things trying to remember how to fit beside each other. It worked to remind Bo of how much time had truly passed.

As Andy wrapped his arms around Bo's back, it came as a sudden shock to realize how much he had missed this. The clarity that could be shared through contact, how grounding it felt, all of it was waking back up. A small part of his brain ate at him, more persistent than the voices of the dead.

He squeezed Andy tighter and tried to convince himself that he was allowed to want this. That he was allowed to *have* this.

Bo was tired of punishing himself when it came to Alejandro Romero-Almada.

They were all right about him.

"I don't know if I want to do this on my own anymore." Andy's face was buried in the crook of Bo's neck. When he spoke, Bo could feel the vibration from his lips on his skin. Bo shut his eyes. "Will you help me?"

Bo pulled away. Andy was looking at the ground. Shoes pointed out, ever so slightly angled inward before he shuffled forward until the toe of his sneakers met Bo's. For a moment, the two of them just stared down.

Then, Bo stuck out a hand cautiously, his pinky extended.

He didn't even have to think about it.

Andy hooked his pinky around Bo's, and their fingers matched up before pressing their thumbs together and leaning down to seal the promise.

So long ago that Bo could barely remember how it came to be, they had done it.

"Yes."

Absolute and without doubt.

Andy closed his eyes. Bo couldn't tell if he was suppressing a smile or a cry.

Epilogue

To be a Romero was to be a liar.

His father was waiting in the kitchen, a glass of rum gripped in his hand. His face was concealed by the shadows of the overhanging light, but Andy could see the disdain in his eyes. It was a familiar expression. One Andy had grown used to seeing.

Andy stopped in the doorway. His father raised his head.

It was a complicated thing to grow into his father. When he was younger, he never saw the similarities. Even in photos from decades ago, Andy had never looked much like his father. Now, though, at sixteen, he could see the similarities he had come into. The arch of their nose, the outline of their eyebrows, the angle of their eyes, and the cut of their jaw. To stare at a person and see your future, Andy found, was an uncanny occurrence.

His father took a timid sip of his glass. "What happened to your face?"

Andy had to stop himself from reaching out to touch the bruise on his cheek.

"Just, messing around with the guys."

"Guys?" Plural.

Andy shuffled. "Bo," he said. "And this new kid, Michael McKenzie."

His father tilted his head. "Beckham?"

Andy looked away from his father as he nodded.

His father chuckled into his glass as he took another swing. "I remember that one." He said. "That spirit was... dull. The ones that looked like kids were always more difficult, I found. Still, I got it in the end."

He always spoke about those days with such endearment. Like it was the best years of his life.

"Your mother and I talked."

Andy tried to maintain eye contact with his father. There was this game they used to play when they were younger, all of them. Holding a gaze as long as they could without breaking away was all that was needed to win. Andy always wanted to claim victory, but he always shrank away from their stares.

He looked to the ground, away from his father.

"We've agreed. We're locking up the basement." His father set his glass down and rose to his feet.

"What?" Andy shot up. "No, wait. What about—"

"It's been long overdue. There's no need for ghost hunters anymore. There haven't been spirits for decades now." His father finished his drink and set the empty glass on the table. "The days when

Romeros captured spirits are over. It's time for us to move on... to greater things."

Greater things. Things like academic excellence and making strides in promising careers. Things like what his siblings were doing that he couldn't seem to follow along with. Greater things that Andy couldn't be a part of.

Andy crossed over to his father's side. "But— What if more come?" Andy argued.

His father shrugged dismissively. "Then I will deal with it. The rest of you have other things to focus on. I shouldn't have distracted you with our family's task."

His father rested a hand on his shoulder. Andy's eyes darted around his father's face, looking for proof to call his bluff. It couldn't be done. The basement was too dangerous, too paramount. Locking it up would mean finally cutting ties with their history, not just of the Romero family but of Whalesborough.

Locking the basement would mean shutting the door on Andy.

"Dad," Andy stepped back, letting his father's hand fall off of him. "I know what this is really about. I know the school called."

He recognized the number on the receiver.

"I'm *trying*. I know I'm not good like Mila or... but I'm getting there. I'm doing better. Don't—"

Don't take this from me. He couldn't bring himself to say it. *Not when I finally found something to be good at.* "You don't need to throw this away just because of me. I can manage it."

"That's not what this is about," his father said.

Liar, liar, liar.

His father offered a hand. Andy stared at it.

"Darme la lleva, Alejandro." Give me the key.

Andy's hand shot to his neck, where the chain was. It was still freezing from being exposed to the autumn night. "You gave it to me." It was pathetic; he knew this. But he didn't know what else to say. "If I were any of them, you wouldn't do this."

His father took his hand down his face and sighed. "I don't know what you mean, Alejandro."

"If I were Jaime, you wouldn't ask me to give it back," Andy fought. "Would you?"

His father let his shoulders slump. "What do you want me to say here?"

"I know he's your favorite."

His father spared a sympathetic glance that Andy couldn't stand. It did nothing but make him feel smaller. "He's not my favorite," his father said.

"Louis, then."

"Your mother and I don't have favorites."

"But you have *least* favorites," Andy said hoarsely. His entire body was shaking. Pressure built up behind his eyes, and he felt the urge to crumble weigh down on him. His throat felt tight as he spoke. Like the hands of the Beckham girl were still gripping him. "And I know it's me."

Andy sniffed as he brought his gaze level to his father's. He didn't meet Andy's eyes right away. His father pointedly stared at the key slung around his neck before raising his head. They looked at each other for a moment, and as his father heaved a heavy breath, Andy could smell the alcohol on his lips. From the long work days, Andy only ever saw his father at night. He only ever spoke with his father when he was drunk. Andy wondered if that was intentional or not.

This was the part where Andy's father was supposed to dismiss that train of thought, the part where he disputed Andy's claim and told him that nothing was further from the truth. It was the part where his father convinced him that nothing Andy did could make them love him less—that Andy was wrong in thinking they could ever grow tired of him. He was a Romero through and through.

But his father didn't do any of that. Instead, he softly said, "Maybe if you tried harder—"

Andy reached for the bottle of rum at the table and flung it at the wall.

The glass shattered in an instant, the alcohol splattering across the kitchen like plastering rain. It was a gunshot in the silence. Both Andy and his father stared at the mess he had made, but neither of them had yet to move.

He waited for his father's wrath, for heavy hands to come gripping at his shoulder and shake the spitefulness out of him. He expected the screaming, the curses, and the questions. *What the hell is the matter with you*? Andy didn't know. He didn't know.

As it drew on, he realized he wanted it. He wanted to be reprimanded. Because at that point, it didn't even matter if his father was furious with him, so long as he was looking him in the eye. Attention. That's what it was. He wanted the attention. He was so fucking pathetic.

His father said nothing. Andy didn't even realize he had started crying until he was licking the salt of his tears off his own lips. "I'm sorry."

"Just go to your room."

"Let me clean it up."

"Alejandro."

He left.

Andy didn't go to his room, though. He stumbled out the front door and into the night. For a moment, he thought of running to Bo's house.

He stalked to the back of the house. He hadn't locked the cellar door again. It was still open from when he had taken Bo down. At the time, it had felt glorious getting it all off his chest. Now he knew he had betrayed his family. He couldn't even do the simple job his father had given him.

Andy walked down the staircase, the cool stone sending shivers up his legs. He reached for the light. The spirits of the dead welcomed him as they always did. It was a pitiful thing, Andy knew, that the ghosts greeted him more often than his own family.

He came to the furthest wall and stood before the shelves.

The spirits in the jars beckoned him.

Andy reached out and gripped the glass tenderly. So many nights, so many years.

He wiped his face with his sleeve.

How did it ever come to this?

It didn't matter anymore. It was happening.

After all, Alejandro Romero-Almada was his father's son.

But more than anything, he was desperate.

He picked up the jar and let it shatter on the floor.

END OF BOOK ONE

The Line is Dead

ACKNOWLEDGEMENTS

First, thank you to the horror that is eight-grade mandatory state testing. It would be dismissive to say you gave me nothing but a superiority complex due to scoring above my grade-level in English (and an inferiority complex due to my mediocre Math scores), as you gave me something precious in those minutes between the two sections of testing, with nothing offered but a blank piece of scratch paper and the droning of my school's unfortunate HVAC system. You gave me *The Line is Dead*. I just wish I could have had the scratch paper of the original cover sketch back.

In all seriousness, I would like to my family, who may not have always been able to offer a quiet house to write in but more than made up for it in their endless support. Regarding the drive that strove me to finish my third novel before eighteen, thanks Mom. Regarding my music taste I shamelessly plugged into this novel, thanks Dad. For my love for reading and writing, thanks to Jojo, always. To Lucy, who will always be funnier than me, though I try not to admit it. To E.B., who makes me less nervous about how our boys will turn out.

Thanks to Madison, for all those years I spent boring you. Thanks for sticking by me. And thanks for reminding me why I write when the pen feels heavy.

Thank you to Ms. Tragas, who doesn't mind when I let my guts spill out on her fancy classroom chairs. I always forget why I do this, and then I remember while sitting in your classroom.

To the wonderful staff at Stevenson, especially Jordan and Nic. My time at the writing workshop made me certain of all of this.

Of course, to Ms. Sutherin, Ms. Klimes, and Ms. Reed. Thanks for letting me nap on the IB couch, and thanks for reminding me that I'm good enough without three novels to my name, but it is pretty cool, right?

And of course, again, thanks to Ms. Courtney. One day, I'll be a good enough writer to articulate my gratitude for all you've done for me. In the meantime, *thank you* will have to do. So, thank you.

ABOUT THE AUTHOR

M.J. Garcia is the author of works like *Vivipary* and *Hue (You)*. When she isn't listening to Mitski and re-reading her favorite books, she is participating in an assortment of hobbies due to her constant need to stay busy. She lives in Maryland with her family, and *The Line is Dead* is her second independent novel.

You can find her on Instagram @m.j.g_writes

www.ingramcontent.com/pod-product-compliance
Lightning Source LLC
Chambersburg PA
CBHW020015120726
47903CB00004B/1299